KENDRA TUTHILL

STITCHES

Copyright © 2021 by Kendra Tuthill

All rights reserved. No part of this publication may be reproduced, stored or transmitted in any form or by any means, electronic, mechanical, photocopying, recording, scanning, or otherwise without written permission from the publisher. It is illegal to copy this book, post it to a website, or distribute it by any other means without permission.

This novel is entirely a work of fiction. The names, characters and incidents portrayed in it are the work of the author's imagination. Any resemblance to actual persons, living or dead, events or localities is entirely coincidental.

First edition

ISBN: 978-1-7353043-0-4

For my best friend,
Harry Huynh Miller
1980-2017

Acknowledgement

A special thanks to Dawn Sperber, my friend and editor, who remained patient through every last revision. I would also like to thank Xavier Comas for stitching this cover by hand in some far away undisclosed country while working through his holidays for a much longer time than either of us anticipated. Navid Harmsen, my pandemic roommate and longtime friend, gave this a read, gave me his feedback, and thought there should be an oak tree in the backyard. Corina Sugarman, Renee Brooks Lofaso, Kara Grant and Erika Kluthe cheered me on every time I believed -if even for a moment- that I shouldn't dirty the world with my imagination. Although I love all of you, my biggest thanks goes to my mom, Patricia, who once mistakenly dared to call me "a good little writer." This is all your fault.

Dearest Reader,

By the end of this story, several people whom you've come to know and love will be dead.

This is your last chance to back out.

Thoughtfully Yours,
On behalf of the Porter and the Olsen Families,
The Unluckiest Families in the World

On a sweaty day in September of 2004, a tornado licked its way up a river and ripped a Baltimore neighborhood clear out of the ground. Children and dogs hung from trees. A kitchen sink slid half-way across a parking garage into an elevator door. Maudlin Avenue was leveled to nothing but splinters and guardrails. The storm sprang out of nothing and left as fast as a freight train. For the next ten years, adventurers discovered the strangest objects in the strangest of places – framed paintings in caves, box fans in the sewers, steak knives poked into electrical posts. One kid found a parrot living in her fireplace and her parents let her keep it. But, on the day of the Great Tornado, the most extraordinary mystery stood to be (and all the survivors agreed as they gazed into the new skyline with picks and trash bags in hand), not one of them could figure out who the hell started it.

Six months earlier, Mark Porter tried to use a hundred-dollar bill to buy $2.16 worth of gas at his local convenience store.

"Have anything smaller?"

"All I got," he said, "topping it off," he had said, pointing out toward the pumps and the white church van. Across the side, it read *The Second Great Awakening Protestant Church.* Ever since Mark lost his job at the auto parts place, he'd been delivering lukewarm meals to neighborhood seniors for six hours a week at five bucks and twenty-five cents an hour. Under the name, a vinyl photo of turkey, mashed potatoes and over-exposed carrots peeled away from the sliding door.

The cashier looked behind herself at the cameras or at the back room and then back at the bill. She leaned over the register. "Todd!"

"What!" he said. "I'm doing inventory."

Todd said he couldn't unlock the safe, but he had enough change in his wallet, so Mark walked out with his $97.84 and Todd ended up with that hundred-dollar bill.

The following morning, as Mark rolled out the yellow mop bucket from the downstairs church closet, Brother Joseph stopped by the kitchen for a muffin. His hair was brown, straight and short and his eyes always seemed about ready to pop.

"How's the wife?" he said.

"Oh, you know, she's good."

"And your son? You have one or two sons?"

"One. Or, I have two. One's here, one's in California."

"And your son's—" He grimaced.

"Yeah, he is."

"Sorry to hear about that. Church helping?"

"What? Oh, yeah. Yeah," Mark said. "Oh, definitely."

"Glad to hear it. Say," Brother Joseph put his white fist on his hip and sort of looked up toward the ceiling tiles. "You hear about—"

"No."

CHAPTER 1

"Yeah, well – stays between you and me, but—"
"Sure. Yeah."
"You know Margaret."
"Um, yeah?"
"The one with the hair?" he said, and motioned out a bob with the palms of his hands.
"Margaret, sure, yeah."
"She and Pastor Mike – now this is what Nancy told me – they think someone's pilfering from the collection tray."
"No," Mark said. "That's awful."
"Sure is. It's awful. The way they found out is Margaret wrote a little kind of note of some kind, an inside joke between her and Pastor Mike and when he didn't bring it up to her, she got a bit concerned."
"I imagine," Mark said.
"So, she decides she's going to say something even if it ruins the joke and turns out he never even got it. Hundred dollars. Who knows how much more they stole?"
"That's awful," Mark said. "That's a lot of money."
"Sure is."
Mark pointed his chin toward the industrial sink where he could fill the mop bucket. Brother Joseph got out of the way and apologized. Mark hooked up the hose to the faucet and leaned over the bucket with it running.
"She's sure she put it in there?"

"Oh, yeah."
"Only God knows, then."
Brother Joseph folded his arms and stepped back.
"All right, then," he said finally.
"Yeah, yeah," Mark said.

Moments later, Mark was parked in his blue-gray Volvo station wagon out front of that gas station. He pulled out another hundred-dollar bill he found laying around in the church office and headed in.

"Todd around?" he asked.

"Not until five," the little cashier said.

Mark went back to his Volvo. Todd showed up ten minutes after five and Mark rushed to get at him before he started his shift.

"Hey, hey. I came in the other day. And you broke that bill for me?"

"Yeah," he said, but he seemed a little stiff.

"I need it back."

"You got your change."

"I know. I know. And look, I have another bill – right here," Mark pulled it out. "I'll trade you." He pushed the bill into the guy's hand. "See, you have a hundred and I get my hundred and everything's okay. Everything will be okay."

"I don't think so."

"I need it back."

Todd pulled the bill from his wallet. "I need to know—"

"Oh, good!" Mark said at the sight of it.

"You scamming me right now?"

Next to Benjamin Franklin, there was a red-markered *Simpsons'* character.

"One second," Todd said, and picked up the phone. Mark stuffed his hands into his pockets, waiting patiently, staring at the rows of cigarette packs. The stress zoned him out, made him feel as though he were floating behind his body. His heart had vibrated all day. The packs of smokes seemed to be pulsing,

CHAPTER 1

red, blue, red, blue. He was just relieved the guy still had the bill. The man hung the phone up. Mark snapped back into place. He reached across the register, grabbed the bill from Todd's fingers and just as he pivoted out with money in hand, two police officers caught him by the elbows.

The next day, without a single hundred-dollar bill to his name, he flagged down a taxi from the jailhouse steps.

*

Twenty-three years before this, Mark and Freya met in California.

She took a cab from an airport to meet her pen pal Jack at a coastal café, which turned out to be more like a fish and wine stand, with round tables and big white umbrellas. Jack wore his winter blues—a nice clean outfit with a square bib on the back and a loose flap over the crotch. In all those amorous letters, he never mentioned being a redhead. He had a weak, white body, as hollow-looking as a paper cup and, instead of getting up when he saw her, he raised his delicate hand in the air and motioned her over. He'd already started eating his clams.

Jack bought a bottle of red wine. The wind ruffled the tablecloth. She couldn't think of anything to say. She held the glass over her white dress, pouring from the bottle, hoping the alcohol would help. She drank it, not speaking, and started on another glass, lighting up one of Jack's Pall Mall cigarettes.

"This guy," Jack said, after everyone was acquainted and a little drunk, "you should hear what he did last night." He pointed with his thumb, then pulled out a flimsy black comb to part his short line of red bangs so they made two rainbows reflecting each other. "Friday night, night duty."

Mark went stiff, unable to turn his head.

"We work in four-hour shifts, sleep in four-hour shifts. Mark's out there—it's fucking two in the morning—standing on top of the sub doing night duty. He starts fooling around with his gun, pulling it out and—"

"Come on," Mark probably said.

"—and he shoots it off!"

Freya tried to laugh when Jack tried to be funny.

"All those subs are right out there, you see?" Jack pointed out toward the ocean, but she never saw anything. "And they're lined up right next to each other, and then there's the big sub guarding all the little subs." She finished another glass and held the empty thing by its stem, teetering it like a metronome. "And our sub happens to be the farthest away, baby. And so, this stupidhead here fools around with his gun, spinning it, and *shoots the fucker off!*" He slapped his hands on the table. The clam shells jumped. "See what I'm saying?" He lifted his eyebrows and grinned, which he did after *everything* he said, as if the whole world ought to applaud because he ate two potatoes for lunch or lost the screw to his glasses under his bunk. "See what I'm saying? This lucky sonuvabitch shot if off into the water. If there had been another sub on the side—the sound it would've made!"

Mark giggled into his chin.

"And Mark, what did you do? Tell her what you did."

Mark caught his breath and said rather softly, "The guy doing night duty on the sub next to me whispered out, 'You hear that?' he says, 'I think it was a gun.'"

"And so, Mark looks around and he says—what does he say? He says, 'Who would shoot a gun off out *here?*'"

Mark and Jack had the same manner of speaking, but Jack

had wide eyes and a booming, jumpy voice, while Mark had shy eyes set sleepily into his face, and his voice, somewhat monotone, somewhat skittish, appealed to her.

"And then, he slowly went like this." Jack stood up. "With his thumb hardly moving at all, his heart beating hard, he puts the safety on and slides it away." Jack sat down. "But, ah man. You would've been out."

"I was bored," Mark said, and downed his drink.

"You had a death wish is what you had!" And the two laughed together and went on in a show like this for a long time, forgetting about her. When the sun set, Jack got up, took her hand in his, and said he wanted her to go around with Mark; he had things to do.

"Okay," she said, shakily. She had just been on a plane for a day—an entire day—to see him after all these years.

Turned out Jack had to head back to the submarine for the night, but Mark had liberty for the entire weekend.

She snuck him into her hotel for ladies— this coral and gold striped place— hiding him behind drapes and in maintenance closets down the long pink hall to her room. She pressed him into the velvet lounger and, using a sewing kit her mother gave her, patched the armpits of his sailor suit. After a little while— if she remembered it right— she leaned into him and, looking between his lips and his eyes and his lips, kissed his mouth, his forehead, and everywhere else.

When she thought of that time, for no certain reason, she thought of blue cornflowers.

Six months later, freshly discharged from the Navy, Mark proposed to her by mail.

With rosy cheeks and naturally pink lips, she didn't need makeup and wouldn't start wearing it for another decade.

When she laughed, she threw her hands over her mouth. Back then, he said, her optimism could've unflipped a boat.

Now, she had thicker skin, a baggy chin, and a frank way of speaking that made strangers apologize. She knew this. Life happened at the kitchen table during lunch, eating hotdogs or cold cuts with mustard or relish or whatever. It wasn't something she could pause with a remote and come back to when she felt like it.

Sometimes, the days were so long all she could feel was the weight of so many more to come and she couldn't imagine any way out of it all—out of life— except to do it herself. It wasn't that she hated being alive or breathing inside this human suit. Life just took too damned long. Once everything was decided—she would have this husband, these two sons, and live permanently in a place called Baltimore City—there was nothing left to live for but getting old and waiting it out. She counted the consequences and, as a result, knew exactly what would happen if she ended it, so she held out and hoped (but not too strongly) that something would happen to her (so it wouldn't be her fault).She could barely wait to not have to wait any longer.

It was, probably, a matter of impatience.

*

In the dark blue afternoon, Aleksia Olsen crunched together a ball of snow and threw it back at the door. On the bridge last night, she lost her necklace. Some things disappear when you lose them, the way dreams disintegrate upon touch, she figured, but might as well look, anyway. She reached the bridge, not far from her grandparents' house, and stood where she stood last night. Water rushed beneath, cars rushed past her, and she froze there next to a cold, broken, and runny

CHAPTER 1

sun spilling around the trees below. She pushed snow away with the rubber heel of her boot, then thrust herself into a hurry on knees and mittens. Bags were packed for Baltimore. Her grandparents waited in the living room, gripping their armrests. But there was all this snow, glowing and shiny, frosting every edge of Oslo.

When it fell, it hadn't made a sound. Her friends leaned their bikes against the fat ledge, drinking vodka from paper cups. Forget about it, they said. Without a flashlight, it was no use and going on about a necklace on her last night was a waste of a good time. Nate wanted her to get in his bicycle cart and go back to the park. She dusted herself off and took a long glance down below until she heard someone singing from behind her, "*Waillllll*," and she turned around. Ray Charles played "I Got A Woman."

Aleksia was the only one in the group who spoke English. Nate pulled her by the hand, swung her away, twirled her back to him. Spoke it her entire life. She shook her feet. Shook her mittens. One friend they picked up along the way smacked his chest to the music. She imagined what it was like to hear the words without understanding them. The tape player was strapped to Nate's bicycle seat. He pedaled like he was running through air. They rumbled through brick alleyways. Aleksia vibrated in the back, looking up, spreading her arms to either side. Streetlights streaked and jumped above her. Buildings jittered.Her teeth and eyes shivered. The cart flung to one side and the other around turns and down curbs. This was the best feeling vodka had to offer. She liked Nate. She had always liked Nate. They stopped at Vigeland Park, the one with the tower of concrete bodies crawling all over each other. Snowflakes floated like feathers from outer space. The cart and bike tilted when she got out and, lying in the snow with Nate, she forgot all about the necklace.

Her sense of stability slid off the kitchen wall last year. It just slid right down and crashed when it met its fate with the floor, splayed out, splintered, springs and wires and coils across the lime green and peach linoleum. At the time, she couldn't have called it by its name but, looking back as the melted snow bled through her coat to her shoulder blades, she could no longer believe anything stayed, that anything was certain, so she sought the thrill of the simple careless pleasures of stealing tiny things, breaking big things, and pranking her peers. But, in the snow in those moments with Nate, she didn't crave destruction. She longed to know that her mother would always be at her grandparents' house— like the front door or its key hidden in the flowerpot. But she already left. It was too much. It was all too much. As the events unfolded, each was revealed to Aleksia in the kitchen of her grandparents' house. There was *Tante* Kirstin's suicide that her mother told her about over breakfast; she'd jumped into Anne River, weighted by chains crossed and locked in an X across her chest. She followed her son, Levon, who'd done the same thing three weeks earlier and Aleksia heard about it as she pulled milk from the icebox. Before this, Alex's father built himself a coffin, sawed off his arm, got in the coffin, wrapped himself in cling-wrap and stayed there. This conversation also happened in the kitchen when she caught her mother under the green light stuffing the hem of her dress into her mouth. And then it goes on—just days before this—her grandfather, making a reindeer cutout for the rooftop, lopped off the tip of his index finger with the electric saw. The doctors reattached it and, ever since the surgery, his finger pointed crookedly.

CHAPTER 1

Aleksia's mother, Sophie Olsen, upset about the state of things, rented a one-room cabin up north in Bodø and told everybody to just leave her the fuck alone.

Most of the Olsens lived in Oslo. Some lived in Bigdøy, but all, except one, lived in Norway. The one who made it off this cold, overcast peninsula, Freya Porter, lived in a port town, Baltimore, an industrial gray slab of a city pushed deep inside the Chesapeake Bay on the right side of the States. When she remembered the postcards with all those mean stamps covering the picture, she thought of ships and streets and everything connected to everything else by cables as if you could snip one line and the whole place would fall down. It was a town caught in a series of cat's cradles. A town held in place by wires. A town with its mouth wired shut.

After the recent deaths and dismemberments, Aleksia couldn't keep herself out of trouble.As a result, her grandparents schemed to send her off to live with the only Olsen left who would take her: the one with thick skin and a sick child dying of a gross, rare disorder in Baltimore.

She first heard of the scheme from the kitchen. The voices carried from the living room -the argument, the word Baltimore, the word delinquent- and, finally, the sound of her mother stomping up the stairs. A week later, her grandparents gave her a plane ticket like a birthday present.She didn't fight it; if there was one thing she knew about herself at the age of seventeen-and-364-days-old, it was that she didn't like being where she wasn't wanted and, as far as she could tell, that meant she didn't like being anywhere in the country of Norway.

A few weeks before, she and Tante Kirstin stood in the kitchen wearing itchy black dresses. Her aunt said she wanted her to have something, this necklace with the yellow pendant.

The pendant had a real baby crab inside. It used to be an earring, but her aunt glued a metal loop to the back and made it into a necklace.

"Sometimes," she said, "I feel like a crab without a shell." She clasped it around Aleksia's neck. "Everything hurts me."

The Olsen Family was falling apart and no one knew when the falling-apart started or how it started or who was to blame, although this was a conversational topic as common as the snow on a Sunday afternoon. The family simply pulled rotten luck toward them, reeled it in like an unknowable creature plucked from the deep sea. For this reason, the surviving members walked around as gloomily as drenched school children. They stayed still for hours at a time. Every sentence started abruptly but lost direction by the end. And for that reason, friends stopped coming around.

Aleksia gripped a flashlight with her teeth and dug, crumbling chunks of white in her fuzzy blue mittens. She pushed her hair behind her ears and started again. Out of breath, she got up, and there she discovered, under her boot, a tiny crunch of a sound.

She held the smashed pendant. The crab crawled out.

When she got home, her grandfather asked if everything was good now.

"Ja."

"Your mother stopped by," her grandmother said in a hurry.

"She didn't tell me she was coming."

Her grandmother shrugged.

In solidarity, Aleksia shrugged back.

"She wants you to read this," she said, then stared off into the middle distance. Aleksia released the green and gray book from her fingers. There was an envelope with a debit card inside. She would take this book, this little piece of her mother. She would hold it close to her chest as she flew over the ocean.

Aleksia's least favorite places to be on the planet were airports and hospitals, places where a person waited impatiently for something they didn't even want in the first place—a surgery or a long, stale ride watching a little animated plane on a screen touch down in London and inch its breathless way over the Atlantic Ocean. But she thought of America: land of sunshine and drive-in theaters, rock bands and teenage road trips, neon art, billboards on skyscrapers, sidewalk hotdog stands, and delicate ladies leaving department stores carrying shopping bags as fresh as cream-filled birthday cakes; and America, big enough for highways to stretch three thousand miles, wide enough to spread deserts with rows of silver mountains spiking across them where the cowboys and Indians, the bull-riders and snowboarders lived, and where people said things like "salt of the earth," "under the weather," and "piece of cake." Watching that white plane wore her down, but maybe she was always this way and, once she got into Baltimore and realized she'd left her entire life behind, she could look beyond the middle distance to a new one.

*

216 Cabbal Drive was the last rowhouse on the block. In one room, Reddy stood with naked feet on the gray-blue carpet looking in the long mirror on the back of his hollow-core bedroom door. He couldn't punch it because the door went to the hallway and the hallway went to the living room and his dad sat there watching TV. He had to keep quiet. Music played through his headphones. He tilted his head to the side to examine the lumps grown under his hair.

He punched himself in the face.

His head knocked into the dresser. He scrambled to get up.

He would paper the mirror, he thought. He punched himself, again. His cousin was coming from Norway. His young, cool, popular, pretty cousin was coming from Norway, and she was going to be here before his surgery. When he blinked his eyes open, he pinched the blood under his nose. What fucking bad timing. He calmed down. Maybe everything would work out. He lifted himself onto his side. He looked into his eyes, breathing with his shoulders.

Last night, with the mp3 player stuffed into his jeans pocket and dizzy as hell, Reddy ripped pages from a Tolstoy book, and then Chekhov, then Plath, Woolf, and Morrison; from Céline, Nin, Eyre and both Millers, dropping the tan pages onto the bedspread until the bed flaked like the top of a croissant. Next, he grabbed *The Death of Ivan Ilyich*. The music stopped. He paused. He couldn't tear up *The Death of Ivan Ilyich*. Mazzy Star started up, again. Gently, he set the book back in a crate of composition notebooks. He gathered the pages and, with spray glue, began the wallpapering. The truth was –he couldn't hear the music, just the languid taps of the tambourine. Lately, he'd been collecting green things, anything green- a plastic green lunchbox, beer bottles, a thrift store T-shirt advertising a lawn care company. He was preparing for his eighth surgery and, because there was no way to prepare for such a thing, he collected apples, pears and garden hoses; he wallpapered his childhood bedroom with the pages of his favorite books and sometimes took hits at himself in front of the mirror.

He wiped his nose bleed with a loose page he found from the night before. He crumpled the bloody paper and got up, pushing his fist into the floor. Yes, he would paper the mirror, and anything else he didn't want to look at for the next six months, but maybe after a nap.

*

In the living room of the Porter rowhouse, a roundish mushroom floated silently across the TV screen toward the dials but never quite getting there. It could have been a chin in water. The way the cameramen lit up the thing, the mushroom ghosted through the dark, drifting weightlessly away in space with eight tentacles towing along behind it, flaccid and useless.

"A dumbo octopus effortlessly flaps its angelic wings. Energy must be conserved in the deep sea."

Mark heard the front door open and Freya come in. A commercial started, one of those kinds for antidepressants or diapers for elderly people or boxsets of CDs sent to you monthly at a low cost of $19.99. He'd seen a lot of these advertisements since he'd lost his job at the auto parts store and he liked to sing along with the jingles as he shelled the peanuts in his lap. She came in, setting her grocery bags on the floor. His son lay on the couch asleep with a blanket over him, the pages of his *Popular Science* magazine under his hand.

"He rescheduled the surgery. To tomorrow," she said. "We'll have to take him tonight." Then, she asked how the kid was doing.

"Look at him," Mark said. "He's fine." But then he remembered Reddy crawling across the carpet and leveraging his body onto that couch with his elbows.

"How long's he been there? I told you he hit his head."

Mark couldn't figure out what she wanted from him, and now his show had come back on. He couldn't do anything about Reddy. No one could. All there was to do was watch TV and wait it out like you did for anything.

"That's good," he said, and he meant it, increasing the volume to the TV with his remote. "They can take him early."

*

Raindrops scattered on the pavement like a handful of thrown dimes. A cabbie slid to a stop before her. For a moment, pulling away from the airport and into America, New York City, Miami, and Hollywood all uncorked before her. The cab went through a tunnel and everything turned black, and then, slipping out onto the open highway, the city appeared—far off, and then expanded from the ground up, getting taller and wider. It had been a long time since she'd seen daylight, like *full-on* daylight. In town, a line of police officers blocked off an intersection; a parade of papery floats limped by.

She gripped her suitcase. To keep the baby crab safe, she put it under her tongue. She had a dangerous imagination and she knew it. Her mother called it "the space," and said all the Olsens had it.

"Cabbal Drive?" The cabbie rubbed his hand along the curly lick of black hairs he had crawling up the back of his neck. She leaned forward. She lisped.

"Yes."

They drove under boxy shadows of featureless buildings, pallid and pockmarked buildings shifting their weight, standing tiredly between parking lots. He slowed around a bend and stopped at the corner of Maudlin Avenue and Cabbal Drive, an empty gray corner but for the tilted street sign and the powerlines swooping low and linking one house to the next.

"Are we here?" she said.

"That's it."

"I don't think that's the place," she said.

"Two-sixteen Cabbal. That's the place." He pointed toward

a door at the end of a strip of rowhouses, the only place inside ten thousand miles housing people she knew, this dark clapboard house where, with the slam of her cab door, a murder of crows jumped from one line and glided across the street to another. They held on as tightly as droplets of blood on a string.

Despite the foreboding imagery, her heart wiggled into her throat and the crab nestled beneath her tongue. The cab driver drove off. The Porters lived in a different part of the country (she didn't know where, could have been anywhere) the last time she saw her cousins, that time the youngest pulled her into his seven-year-old lap and read her a book about beetles. She may have been a toddler but remembered eating eggs and bread for breakfast and boiled peanuts for a snack in a big house with a long front porch surrounded by trees. Across the past year, she only spoke with her aunt six times and only because her grandparents forced the phone into her hands. And nothing remarkable stood out about her uncle except his excellent height. He was so tall as to be laughable. He ducked through doorways. He crouched in the driver's seat of his two-door car— his knees to his shoulders and the steering wheel the size of a teacup saucer. Her mother never liked him. Aleksia decided she did not like him either and couldn't imagine looking that man in the eye.

But she would be good. This was a new country. She could be anybody. One thing she knew for certain, and was likely the reason her pulse pushed against her clavicle now –on her cousin, Reddy, she endured a deathless crush with the kind of reckless devotion and wild abandon that could only be born of a four-year-old girl and kept alive by the loose occupation of her adolescence.

She took one last look at her loneliness and rang the doorbell.

*

"She's here," his dad yelled out, easing back into his chair. He wore a blue and black flannel buttoned to his chin. His legs were long, thin, and when he spread them apart to either side of the recliner, his tan corduroys zipped against the upholstery.

His mom pushed him out of the way as she rushed into the hallway. "I told you, if you're not going to stay in bed, then *something, something, something,*" she said to him. Reddy knocked his hand against the composition notebook. If she wanted to talk to him, she was supposed to write in it. When he got holes in his hearing, they started the notebooks.

She pulled Aleksia through the door like a prize and, for a moment, all stood there in shock. Then, with a clap of her hands, his mother ruptured into the highest pitch of joy.

"Come in! Come in!" she probably said.

The cousins stole furtive looks. Aleksia contemplated her green shoes. Reddy pinched his ear. With the quickest glance, the two became north-seeking magnets on opposite sides of the foyer. He wanted to hug her, but he had these cauliflower-shaped lumps on his head, and sensed that, by stepping closer, by scientific law, one small movement in her direction would cause violent repulsion. She lifted her free hand and politely wiped away the displeasure settling across her brow. She said something to his mom but, in the corner of her eye, he felt held.

He waited for a mention. His mom turned to him.

"Late! Sleep!" Then, right in front of his cousin, he was shoved into the living room.

"Stop touching me. Stop it," he said, falling into the arm of the couch.

CHAPTER 1

"He doesn't want to miss anything, but he truly is sick," he heard her say. He swatted at her. She never listened to him anymore. "We're bringing him to the hospital tonight, a week early for his surgery to remove the . . ." his mom whispered as she left him there, "the, you know, things on his head."

*

"Come on into the kitchen," her aunt said from behind her. "I've just burned another batch of gingerbread cookies, and you can nibble on the legs." In the kitchen, her Aunt Freya, a slightly heavier version of Aleksia's mother, pulled out an oven tray and told her where to sit. Settling into the commotion, she watched the flab of her aunt's arms swing and twitch. She moved her white hair away from her face with the back of her hand. "Some of these body parts are still good, I think." Her aunt set the broken cookie pieces on a plate in front of her. *I'm related to these people*, she thought. *These people look like me.* "I took off the burnt pieces. They're not so bad. Taste them." She paused. "So, your flight was good?"

Alex said it was long, and then, taking in Freya's frenetic movements across the kitchen, she said, "I should probably call my grandmother."

"In the morning," her aunt said. "You'll have to tell me everything about everything when we get a chance. Just, right now is crazy."

"How long am I staying? Did they tell you?"

Her aunt broke off a gingerbread hand. "Indefinitely." She popped the hand in her mouth. "I'm trying to finish these by tonight so they cool before I frost them," she said, and as she worked on her cookies, she explained how she felt bad about pushing Reddy around that way but someone had to take control. And then, at some point she said, "Maybe you two could become friends." Thunder rumbled outside and her aunt's flip-flops clapped as she got up and circled the kitchen island to the sink. She licked her fingers, then put them under the faucet.

Aleksia said, "And how's Uncle Mark?"

"Oh, you know, he lost his job." She rubbed her apron. "He's all right. Go on in and say hi. I have to finish these for Thursday's church meeting."

"That's nice," Alex said, getting up.

"They're supposed to be little disciples. Someone else is making a cake of Jesus." She pushed her hands into the silver bowl. "God knows I'd be the one to burn them all."

*

Alex paused before she crossed the television screen. She sat on the couch opposite her cousin.

"This is what we do a lot," her uncle said. "Watch a lot of TV." He flipped through stations until he landed on *Baywatch*. Reddy put his notebook next to him. He sat up straight. The sound from the little box TV rattled against the dinner stand it sat on.

Aleksia craned her neck to see around a treadmill placed in the center of the room and finally said, "I'm going to get some sleep."

The bedroom had a lamp, a digital clock, and a dresser. The window overlooked a backyard which had an enormous tree taking up most of the space. She picked up a hand-held mirror off the dresser.

The Olsens had passed down this blonde-white hair, this dangerous imagination, and this crooked affliction—a dangling chromosome. Reddy was the only Olsen in a hundred years who had it. Aleksia couldn't help but feel a little sick, placing the mirror face-down, considering the unlucky reality of it.

The sun dropped beneath the clouds, making another egg yolk of her view. She was far away from home, as far as all that space that passed under the plane. This is what the sun looked like on the other side of the world.

She sat down on her new bed. The embroidered pillows with the red and blue diamonds and the green vines spiraling upward through them must have been a wedding gift. Her mom had the same ones. She flipped one over revealing a gray stain the size of her hand. Everything smelled gray— if gray had a smell. She flipped it right-side up. She thought about what she might do tomorrow when she heard an ogling from outside, a sound roughly human.

In the yard next to theirs, a long-necked animal with tan and white matted hair knocked its head into the yard fence. It stepped back, dazed.

She took pictures with her Lomo camera and crawled back into the bed, pressing her thumbs to her eyes. She liked to see the phosphenes, but instead it was simply the plane. Sinking into the darkness, an impending disappointment descended in her chest, the fear that some part of her old self stowed itself away inside her, and now fell asleep in the same bed and, like a heartache, would wake with her in the morning.

In the TV room, Uncle Mark dissolved into his chair with his jaw dropped and his neck cocked back—a rough corrugated snore sawing out from the back of his throat. She thought of her mom and her eyes turned cold. She had the urge to drop a penny down his throat to see what would happen. On the couch, Reddy, with his head wrapped now in a black scarf, lie on his side, his cheek pushed against his closed eye and his hands wound tightly under him. On the floor, a white dish dirtied with food and utensils had not been put away.

She found her aunt in the kitchen at the table listening to the radio news, tapping at an electronic calculator, writing notes into a book. Noticing Alex, she said, "You missed it. I just shaved Reddy's hair off. You also missed dinner, so you'll have to fend for yourself," and she pointed behind her at the fridge. "I wish Mark had let us move to Norway."

"Why?"

"Medical bills, honey."

Aleksia retreated to her room.

The book her mother left her had a picture on the back of the author, this shaman with antlers and dressed in furs with a dreamcatcher nailed to the wall behind him. She pulled out her fashion magazine with its four-hundred pages of pictures and perfume samples and thumbed through it from back to front. It had started to rain again. She lifted the window frame. The seal of paint along the ledge split. The window sucked the drapes to the screen.

*

Reddy rubbed his hands over his shaved head where his mother had nicked him. He didn't want to nap before they left for the hospital at nine tonight. By tomorrow afternoon, the lump under his eye and the tumors above his ears would be gone.

Once, at JC Penny's, a woman in line asked him to talk to her toddler. "Just please show him you're not a monster." He didn't know what to do. "Hey," he said. That's all and, stunned, the kid stopped crying. Then, the kid scrunched up his nose, opened his mouth—and *screamed.* Reddy set his polo shirt on the gum rack and left.

He started to wear black, started to wear sunglasses, and fingerless gloves. He wanted to disappear. When he walked past storefront windows, he covered his face on the side to block out the reflection. He bought shit-kicker boots off the internet.

"You're up," he said, opening Aleksia's door. His thoughts had circled back to his cousin, this fresh new thing in their house. He had smelled her—a sort of powdery, baby scent. He went to her room. He watched her lips. He could hear the rain pouring down but couldn't hear her voice. He said, "hold on," and got his notebook. When he came back, she had dressed herself in a blanket.

She wrote in the book, "jetlag." He liked the way she pulled her hair away from her neck and tied it back with a band she had around her wrist.

"Are you deaf," she wrote without a question mark.

"Kind of. Not permanently," he said, and launched into the explanation he prepared for her. "Nothing's wrong with my ears." She furrowed her brows. "Nothing's wrong with my brain, either. It's just the cord between them. The nerves. That's what's fucked up."

She nodded.

"They're fixing it tomorrow morning. The doctors."

"How?" she wrote.

"They have to cut out the tumors."

"Are you scared?"

"Nah," he said.

"What if they mess up?"

"Nah," he said, again. "It'll be okay."

She nodded and wrote, "Today was my birthday."

"Really?"

She wrote, "18."

They were three years apart. He left for the kitchen. The twelve disciples frosted in togas were spread out evenly on wax paper. In the utensil drawer, he found a packet of multicolored candles. He opened the sun-yellow cardboard box, stuck three into one of the cookie bodies, and edged it from the sheet. She stood next to her bed when he went in with the candles lit, humming Happy Birthday. But she was pointing out the window at the next-door neighbor's llama. He set the paper plate down on the bed.

"Yeah, I know," he said. "When we first moved in, that thing tried to neck-wrestle my dad."

She lifted an eyebrow.

"Neck-wrestle," he said, again. He handed her the notebook.

She wrote, "I suppose I'm going to learn to speak with my face."

Reddy laughed.

"Happy Birthday," he said. "The candles are burning."

"Thanks," she wrote, and then, "I don't know why people only take pictures of pretty things. Pretty things are boring." She took the notebook back into her lap and drew out a caricature of Reddy with his scarf on. He looked closer in the candlelight. He didn't have eyeballs.

"I only draw sleeping people and I only photograph ugly things," she wrote. "I act like it's an eccentricity but, the truth is, I can't draw eyes."

The candles got shorter.

"You should really blow these out before something catches fire," he said, but she didn't do anything. Then he said, "if you have a camera, I could show you something ugly." He touched the fringe of his scarf. "I sort of wanted to take a picture of them anyway, for the record or something." He looked for a micro reaction in her face as he unwound the material. She retrieved a small black plastic thing from her bag and motioned for him to move toward the Birthday Disciple. His hands pushed into the carpet and he scooted over. "Here?" he said. His head was naked now.

She kneeled on one knee, snapped a shot, snapped several from different angles. The rain lightened to a mizzle. She whipped out another camera, this one with a fat short lens she screwed on. She got closer, taking pictures of the tumors on either side of his head. It wasn't normal to grow tumors on the outside, but his had grown on the inside *and* the outside—on his brain sheath, on his nerves, and under his skin—and for this reason, doctors photographed him and sent pictures off to medical journals around the world (he was famous!), but no one ever gave *him* any of those pictures or sent *him* any articles.

She stepped over his legs, bending over his head and, at one point, pushed her sharp knee into his thigh. When she was done, the cameras were tossed unceremoniously to the bed, jumping the candles.

"Whoa." He steadied the plate.

He wrapped his head again.

They sat before each other with the dripped wax dried to the plate in flat rivers and the last flame-flickers lighting their faces. She took up the notebook. "Do you think you'll miss them?"

"What?"

She motioned toward his head, tapped one of his tumors. It made him laugh, and the laugh bent the candle flames until they snuffed out.

*

He wrapped his shaved, malformed head with his scarf. Then, he left the door partway open to let light in for the patient on the other side of the sheet.

On the way to the hospital, he tried to tell his parents his worries.

"What if I don't wake up? What if they cut my auditory nerve?"

His dad waved a hand, a hand that said, *Oh, come on.*

"Who cares," he said to himself. "Who cares." And he looked out the window.

Sometimes he wished the whole world would worry with him for four seconds. Two seconds. Even one second. Could everyone just stop and say, *Holy fuck, Reddy, you're going to die!?*

But no one wanted to talk about it.

His pre-op thoughts repeated surgery after surgery. He thought, *you get your entire afterlife to be a ghost, and only this short period to be human* -which is why he left the hospital.

He convinced himself into a state of amazement. As he walked, he started with a generic love for basic things—the woods, the city, human animal activity— and moved on to a focused love for the specifics, the weight of a quarter in the palm of his hand, the color of the gibbous moon hanging between buildings, the unexplainable feeling of pain moving through the body.

When he came out through the front hospital doors, he bumped into a girl with dark hair and freckles, and when she apologized, he stopped.

He didn't make the decision fast enough to follow her and,

CHAPTER 1

as he left, walking into the wind and holding his trench coat against his frame, he thought of her and of this new life he would have without these tumors. He might not be able to hear after the surgery, he was aware of that, but he would look better, and he could learn sign language, and certainly there were cute *deaf* girls. He noticed them years ago, but especially lately. He hoped he would run into her again. He liked hospitals and very quickly imagined the story they would tell people, how they met at the hospital. He wanted to know why she was there, where she lived, who she visited.

He made his way toward a silver closed-up hotdog stand on Carolina and sensed that familiar imbalance he'd been experiencing lately, a sort of swishing that moved like water, like osmosis really, from one side of his brain to the other. The wind emphasized this, pushing against his legs. He aimed for the hotdog stand with one hand leading him, his feet walking on a slant. He reached it, knelt, and after resting a moment, lit a cigarette. He felt like calling someone to get rid of his loneliness, but he could no longer use his cellphone. With one hand in his pocket, he flipped open and closed the lid to his Zippo, enjoying the clicks it made.

This was Baltimore, and he was in the center of it.

His family moved out of the backwoods of Alabama when he was seven years old. He'd only left Maryland three times since then –with his best friend, Emma, and didn't really have any plans on leaving, again. They caught a bus or hopped in a car, going wherever she wanted to go. They filled themselves full of coffee and smoked a bunch of cigarettes until she got it all out of her system. He never understood what it did for her, but he was needed, and that's what mattered to him. Her foster parents, her social workers, and later her girlfriends said she was *too much drama*. It might have been true, but he never felt that way about her. Sometimes they talked. Sometimes he read a newspaper or the classics while she stared down the road away from her problems. Never crying, always thinking.

Now she had a girlfriend.

He didn't like being away from home, but she convinced him to run away with her, hand in hand and literally running, for the first time when they were in the fourth grade and going to separate schools. That night, they stayed in a treehouse one block from the rowhouse. She twisted in her sleeping bag, kicking at the bottom of it, whining in her sleep, so he balanced on a branch pretending to keep an eye out, pretending to protect her. When he passed out from exhaustion, he toppled from the tree and broke his ankle. It took his mother a decade to get over it. Emma and Reddy kept their friendship secret. Later, they ran away to real houses several cities away. When she got what she needed, they sprang back to Baltimore. That's when he felt ashamed -when he realized he'd lived most of his life in a bad-smelling city, and he had never even known it.

First, there was the ever-present gray pillow of industrial haze, then the black imported smells disembarking from the docks at the shipyard. But driving in deeper, there were other smells, indecipherable smells, running and oozing together like foods in a trashcan. Even the cement gave off a smell, along with the cars ramming potholes. He smelled the dinnertime windows wafting greasy, spicy, and sweet diets; Black, Indian, Chinese. But smelling deeper, working harder, there was the earthy brick of the buildings; the fuzzy, flaking, cat-haired carpets of the apartments within them; the toilet cleaners; the rotten-egg faucet rims; the toxic hairspray itching at his lungs; the chalky scent of lipstick; the fibers of fabric; and then, he

CHAPTER 1

always thought he could smell the tiny salty smells inside the tiny wet armpits of every fleshed human being living and dying there in Baltimore City.

It only took twenty minutes to adapt. His mind looked for the relevant smells—fire, food, and sex—unable to smell the smell he lived in. Reddy put his nose into the collar of his trench coat and, for no reason he could think of, thought of his eighteen-year-old cousin, Aleksia. She arrived and took pictures of him. They talked and ate a gingerbread cookie. He wanted to know her, to watch her slip her straight blonde hair behind her ear. She had these dimples. She had soft baby fingernails and long thin hands.

His father used to tack butterflies to a board under plexiglass, a weird idea to Reddy now, but Reddy liked the magnifying glasses. He was like that. He enjoyed tools and gadgets more than their use. His father bought him an assortment of magnifying glasses with wooden handles. Then later, guiltily, Reddy enlarged the lingerie models from his mother's catalogues. The hint of a nipple, the bellybutton dimple, the V from the hips pointing exactly where he wanted to go. And then, even his own thick hand with opened pores and hairs erect, holding the page down one minute, unlatching his belt the next.

He thought again of the girl walking into the hospital lobby, and this image merged with the face of his cousin. The combination of these memories—the magnifying glasses, the butterflies under glass, and the thoughts of these women—awoke in him an energy that straightened him out. He stood up, flicked the cigarette into the curb, and strutted back to the hospital. The doctors told him to be asleep by this time, but he wanted to stay up through the night to see the world for the last time with these ugly things on the sides of his head. In the hospital, he walked around the first-floor hallways. Not seeing the girl, he checked the cafeteria and gift shop. He took the elevator to the second floor and third, which was his floor, when he was too tired to search any longer.

*

Freya woke every hour on the hour. Once the sun came up, she prepared herself with a cup of coffee, but wrapping her hands around her mug, she grew aware of her age, her failing mind and found it difficult to organize her thoughts. Details grounded her, she reminded herself. She ought to make breakfast for her guest.

Her niece stepped in -as if on cue. She wore a light-green, one-piece pajama suit, the kind children wear with the vinyl feet, but that somehow looked lascivious on a teenager. Freya dropped a pat of butter into the hot skillet, seeing herself at that age, brimming with potential, face and arms and legs wide open to it all, at the start line poised to pounce, to have her way with the world, to swim it, to squeeze and exploit it. The butter sizzled, and when she lifted the skillet, tilting it to the side, it skated across.

Not that she had any control over any of it, but if it still made sense to say: she didn't regret it (how could she -with regret by a mother being banned in all countries around the globe? And if it weren't banned around the globe, then it was certainly banned, if not outright illegal, throughout the universe). There was nothing to do but accept it— except in a moment like this, when confronted with a charmed girl *blossoming* into womanhood while Freya felt kind of like a wet rat scratching at the bottom of a trash can. She silently regretted it, hiding her regret like contraband in her 18-hour bra. She didn't feel like a fucking flower. She was more like one of those plastic toys with the rubber bands running through them—if you pushed the left button, she swung right; if you pushed the right button, she swung left and, if you pushed them both, she stretched and fell over.

"I have to get Reddy his socks," she said absently, breaking an egg on the faucet. "After we get home, I have to take a shower." She pulled out a plate for Alex.

"I don't eat breakfast," her niece said. "Not in the morning anyway."

Freya lifted the skillet from the burner.

"No, no, it's okay." Aleksia danced her hands up. "Really."

She served the breakfast, poured more coffee and handed Aleksia a napkin. They picked up their mugs and sipped.

"I was reading this book." Aleksia said. "It's one Mamma gave me." She closed her eyes for a second. "By this Native American shaman guy. He says if you want to be lucky, you just have to feel lucky, so I'm trying that today."

"Well, I don't feel lucky," Aunt Freya said. She scratched the side of her face and looked back at her niece. "We're an unlucky family, if you look at us right." Aleksia didn't say anything. "I'm glad you saw your mother. I was thinking about what you said last night, about calling your grandparents."

"Yeah."

"Honestly, I don't think it's a good idea."

Aleksia pressed the back of her fork into the eggs.

Freya said she was sorry.

"This book, it's written by a guy on a reservation. It's pretty good." She dropped her fork to her plate and put her head in her hands. Freya walked out; she couldn't help it. She had everything to manage—her niece in one room, and then her son in the hospital—while all her husband had to do was feed himself and put on his slippers or something. She separated the heavy drapes in their room. As usual, his covers had fallen between their beds, and as usual he would leave them there for her to pick up. As if she didn't have enough to pick up.

Leaving the alarm going, she left the room and found herself at the door, a lightness lifting from her center, making her insides spin. She fed Aleksia but forgot to feed herself. An intrusive thought came to her, a memory sudden and harsh: the church decided not to help with the medical costs this year and those gingerbread men cookies weren't going to make a bit of a difference.

This thought alone jolted her. She packed a duffle bag of Reddy's clothes, blank notebooks, and pens. She added a fruity trail mix, a canned soda. Her niece looked as if she grew up farming the fields with those firm feet and strong tanned hands but then her blushed face, surrounded by straight blond-white hair, made her look as if she'd never been exposed to daylight. Her beauty spooked her, made her want to look away, made her want to avoid the kitchen.

*

Mark hadn't run on his treadmill for six months, but he had a strong urge now because an electrifying anxiety buzzed through his insides. When he got up to a good pace, his elbows bent, running in place toward the TV, Aleksia came in. She crossed her arms and looked toward the television.

"Do you need me to do anything?" she said.

"We have to hurry," Freya yelled from the other room.

"Not that I can think of," he said, gripping the handrails. He adjusted the difficulty. Now, he ran uphill. "You going?"

On the TV, a young, brown-haired evangelist with his wife

shouted out to a cheering audience. It was the only thing on this time of morning. The evangelist said, "If you don't take control, somebody else *weel.*" The wife guided her lemon-yellow hair out of her face by scooping it away with the curled fingernail of her pinky finger. She was careful not to touch her mustard foundation, where a stripe of orange fanned out from her cheekbone. Why couldn't Mark wake up to a woman like that? The wife wore slippery lipstick. Mark got the impression that if this woman turned sideways, he'd see that, behind her bangs, her head just ended. A cliff. A quick drop-off. Like a convenience store cardboard cutout. Looking over at Aleksia, he had that same impression.

"I'll just wait here," she said, dropping her arms to her side.

"You can." He hoped she would pass off this invitation to come along and agree to see it as an invitation to stay home. She could see it either way. *You can.* She flicked a piece of the paint off the doorframe and left it curled on the carpet.

With that little flick of the paint, it was evident that she'd rather stay home alone in the house, which is what Mark wanted because she made him uncomfortable, but then a series of terrible images came to mind—knowing her history of delinquency—and so he found himself saying, "Maybe you ought to come along. He is your cousin."

"No," she said, "I'll hold down the fort."

"Do they say those kinds of things in Norway?" he asked.

"No," she said.

He was slightly out of breath. As soon as she left the living room, he could get off the treadmill, but not in front of her. The situation had become delicate. If he lifted a finger, or dipped his posture, it could mean something he didn't mean it to mean. The dryness in his mouth spread down his throat.

"It's okay," she said.

He smiled at her, just moving his lips, lifting his eyebrows.

"It's okay," she said, again. She pushed her hands into the pockets of her pajamas.

She walked out. Others let words slip here and there all over their lips like it didn't matter where they landed. For him, a single sentence strung out a system of obstacles and back-stepping. Freya collected odds and ends around him. She said Reddy would want his ankle socks and asked Mark two times where he thought Reddy's new hat might be. When he said he didn't know, she accused him of not caring. He ran with his hand on his heart, a sudden burst of hot energy thrusting through his veins. On the wall behind the TV, Freya's shadowbox collection of porcelain angels shook.

"What are you doing?" she said from behind him.

"Running."

She watched him get off the treadmill, folding his arms across his chest. Standing there, he felt extra tall and as if he were gliding along on a moving sidewalk. He took her hand in his.

"You feel comfortable leaving Aleksia in the house?" he asked, whispering across his heartbeat.

"She's an adult."

He looked for something important to do down the hall.

On the way to see Reddy, Freya fiddled with the strap of her purse, reaching for her wrist, a habit he noticed she was into recently, of checking her pulse.

"I swear, there's a bee thumping against my skin." She let go. "I feel bad for Aleksia. I think it's good to show a little trust. What do we expect? I mean, really. This family does seem doomed. Everything else in the world is guided along but us.

Don't you think so? All this death. And I hear she was the last one to see Kirstin. Did I tell you that? And then, of course, there's Robert—which was even worse. Just truly terrible. I told you. Remember? She saw Kirstin acting funny. I wish I'd been there. I wish I could've been there and done something about it."

"I think Aleksia's like us," Mark said to her.

"Like how?" she said.

"You know. Secretive."

"You think we're secretive?" Freya pulled her wool hat down, tucking her hair into it as they rolled into the lot. "Interesting," she said. "I'd like to know more about that."

He turned down a lane. He said, "All right, well, then maybe it's just me."

*

"Even though the facial nerve appears to have made it—" the doctor said with a pause, "we found the nerve had moved, what with the tumor pushing against it—" He let his hands drop and started his explanation again. This time, he smiled hesitantly, his face flushing strawberry-colored against his white eyebrows. He took a deep breath. "The tumor pushed into the nerve, and the nerve wound around it, taking the shape around the tumor, like, like a vine around a post . . ." He looked away and back. "It'll just take some time for the nerve to adjust, to get back to its regular state."

Freya squeezed the doctor's bicep tentatively and went in. Following her, Dr. Kane said, "His left eye opened during surgery. He wasn't able to see us; he wasn't awake, but now the eye's dried out. A little," he added.

"You didn't give him eyedrops?"

"I have them right here," he said like a man who was used to being accused of worse. "He won't be able to blink on his own until this nerve adjusts. You'll have to drop these liquid drops in." He held up the blue bottle. "You can experiment with the different kinds. This one is thick, gooey, but you can pick up other brands."

Her thin, twenty-one-year-old boy seemed like a bug trapped in a web with all the cables they had running to him. His mouth was open with a tube pushed down his throat. Another rubber tube separated under his septum, dividing into his nostrils. IVs, a heart monitor, bandages like two white pillows on either side of his head, and the rest of his head bruised, especially under the eye that stayed partly open, pasty, unmoving.

The doctor spoke a little more, but Freya couldn't understand. He told them of the visiting hours. Then, Dr. Kane left them alone with Reddy, who lay under a sheet, his white and blue hospital gown falling off his shoulder.

No one wanted to say it, but something had gone wrong. And no one wanted to say it because complaints didn't go over well in the best hospital in the country, the only hospital in the country that could work on Reddy.

Mark cracked his neck. "Hey," he said, "his arms are holding down that sheet like a paperclip." Freya looked in his direction.

"That's not funny," she said.

*

After Reddy looked for the mysterious girl in the hospital, after he'd smoked his cigarette and taken one last glance at the world from his old perspective, he passed right out in his bed. He didn't remember anyone waking him up but, in a dream, he had been in his bedroom at home and, tugging the chain to the lamp next to him, realized the lightbulb had blown out. He got up and flicked the switch on the wall, but

CHAPTER 1

that one didn't work either. He got scared because darkness always frightened him and went to the hallway. The light there didn't work either. He was just totally in the dark. The electricity was out. He touched everything on his way back to bed and covered his head with the sheets. He waited for the sun to rise. But this was a dream, and when he actually woke, a helicopter weed whacked around his head and he found his eyes wouldn't open. The sound thinned out into a ringing; it seemed to start from aboveground and drill down into him, startling him into a prickling consciousness. He sensed there was a strong connected to his hand, that he'd pulled the string, and the string rang a bell that hung suspended above him, but the string turned into an IV, stinging a point between his fingers, and the ringing came from somewhere inside his head. Something earth-covered plugged his throat, and when he gagged, the spill of saliva slipped between his lips. Reddy had had dreams like this before, where creatures sat on his chest, paralyzing him between two sheets, perhaps one of waking, one of dying.

He could control his breathing, but he couldn't hear his breathing above the ringing. He pushed air out, trying to gather energy from wherever it was stored to thrust his head to the side. The muscles in his neck strained. His eyelids pulled at the lashes. Gravity pinned him down. Finally, his head flung over. All at once, his limbs jumped.

But it didn't wake him. This had also happened in dreams. Tired now, he dozed back into a deep sleep.

This new nightmare edged him in at the elbows and knees. Reddy awoke several times to a cramped body. Days passed; he knew this much. One time, light appeared in one eye, but not the other. He tried to focus on lifting his head, which seemed to him like lifting a bowling ball with a popsicle stick.

Over time, he gained movement of his fingers and toes. When he was awake, he thought he was dying. He asked himself what really mattered. What really did? This tough question. When no one seemed to be around, he reached with his shaky arms up to his head and felt the two earmuff bandages, soft and hard at the same time. The mutations were gone; he was relieved. He dropped his arms and one fell, dangling off the bed.

*

Much time passed without change. Reddy sat up with the help of his mother's hands, unable to hear anything but the sound of bees in his ears or see more than a black, oily mist changing form across the surface of his eye.

They bumped soda and ice cream into his lips. The vanilla bubbled as he cried. He just couldn't stop crying. A napkin wiped his bristly chin, and they'd let him lie down again after the ice cream, even though he wanted more treats, especially more soda.

They'd been giving him ice chips to suck on. All of this made him cold, but the lower crescent of his stomach ached so hollowly with hunger, it would digest itself if he didn't do anything about it. He would take anything they put in his mouth. But every time the nurse's hands vanished, the ice chips vanished too, and he didn't know if she took them with her, or if she left them in a Dixie cup somewhere on a ledge.

His mother's hand dropped pills onto his tongue. She let him hold the water cup himself. Soon, a change in mood came over him, an electric haziness in his body and, when he came to, a strange pulling on his numb, frozen eyelid irritated the muscles in his face and pricked the sinews of his neck. He tried to touch it, but he found his arms were held down. The sensations stopped and started again, pulling upward, and then, so suddenly, ended with a hair-raising thrust.

They released his arms. His left eyelid had been sewn shut, and now he feared the medicine wasn't working well enough, because he had full feeling on the right side of his face. If they were going to sew his right eyelid, too, he would certainly feel the needle. But nobody did anything else. They propped him back against his pillows and left him alone, as far as he could tell, heavily medicated and pudgy-lipped.

His fingers padded along the eye. He moved up his rubbery scalp to the prickly stitches echoing his ears. Someone opened him up like a tuna can. It was funny how he didn't know he was crying unless his eyelid burned, how he couldn't be sure he was peeing if he didn't hear the sound of piss hitting water. The doctors must have pulled the cheek tumor out through his nose or mouth with a crochet needle, the kind with a hook on the end, because the tumor was gone, and he couldn't find any more sutures.

Instead of changing the bandages on his head, the nurse took them off. With the tumors gone and the bandages gone, he could get on his side, a comfortable position, but unfamiliar now, and when he sunk his weight into the pillow, the pillow gave out. His head went through it. He wanted another coke, another ice cream, and agonized over his sore dick but reminded himself, as he had been doing since he'd woken last, that the removal of the catheter meant it was time to go home soon.

His fingertips tensed and clawed around the bed.

Asleep again, scenes of terror came to him. A fight between his parents. Bill collectors calling. To avoid bankruptcy, his

CHAPTER 2

mother and father conspire to kill him. He hears this in his dream, his empty stomach turning inside out and swallowing him. A crochet needle puncturing his lungs. His lungs deflating. They look like handkerchiefs in his chest.

Someone squeezed his biceps. They forced him up from the bed. They pulled jeans up his legs and got his socks on. They got him standing, and he clamped a padded, flat shoulder. The curved knobby back under him buttoned his pants, shoved his heels into shoes so tight his socks bunched under his toes and around his ankles. Then, Reddy was speeding out of the room in a wheelchair. He gripped the vinyl armrests as it rolled him and slipped him around corners, bumping over inconsistencies in the floor. Eventually, the air went cold, and he was rumbled over pavement. He was put into a seat, one with a belt holding him firmly back. Someone stuffed a pillow behind his head. The familiar door handle, the giving, folded magazines that he sat on. A weightless soda cup bent under his shoe. This was his father's Volvo, and he could locate the electronic window button with ease. The breeze pushed against his hairline and whipped his shirt around. He pushed the button up, turning off the wind, and before long, the vehicle stopped vibrating.

When they got him in the door—after all those thirteen steps up the front that took forever—he recognized with deep comfort the damp smell of their home, an earthy scent like seeds and musk and felt like a wounded pet that the family could not bear to put down.

*

When Alex pulled out the top drawer to her aunt's dresser, the small antique lamp on top of it jiggled. There were rolled-up socks and silky peach-colored underpants big enough to set sail in. In the next drawer down, she found a stack of envelopes on its side, like files she could flip through, organized by the postmarked date from years ago until now, and each one of them sent by Alex's mother. She scanned one for her name.

And Pappa thinks she's the one who took it from the backyard.

This was the tractor, and yes, she had taken it.

It doesn't matter that he's a minister; he still has his favorites, you know. But we were lucky. He didn't have the evidence to pin it on her and without it, the detention center wouldn't take her.

Well, it was all true.

The clock in the kitchen sounded. She left the room as she found it, closing the door behind her, and hid the letters between her mattress and box spring to read later. Since her arrival, she'd hardly gone anywhere but to school and out to a restaurant that served burgers and fries with her aunt a few times. She decided to rest again in the front room even though it was cluttered with computer parts, broken monitors, and cords. She nudged in between the black sharp things near the bay window and watched people walk by. When she got too cold from being there, she sat on the itchy carpet with her legs in blue stretchy pants out in front of her like broken things.

Her grandfather didn't like her. She didn't know that.

Alex sat on her heels with a size-eleven shoebox full of carbon-copied prescriptions and typed-out papers. Sometimes she had this craving—an overwhelming sense that she wanted to consume something. She felt that with the letters, and now she felt that again, as if she could tear up these papers into tiny bits and eat them.

She tried to get it all organized and put away before the Porters came in. Her uncle shoved the door open, and Reddy and her aunt tripped through it. Reddy had been gone for three weeks. Aunt Freya got him down onto the carpet to take his shoes off, and once they were off, Reddy let go of his mother and ran away from her, knocking his shoulder against a shelf, cursing when he fell on his knees in the kitchen, while Aleksia scrambled to get up and get that shoebox back on a shelf.

"Good, you got pizza," her aunt said from the other room.

When she placed the plate in front of him, he hovered his hand over the liquefied cheese, his sewn-up twitching eye pointing toward the light. She could see the stitches and lashes up close now looking like the legs of a trapped bark beetle. Reddy ripped off a bite. He flung it back on the plate and pressed his fingers to his lip. The grease dripped down his chin to his shirt pocket. Alex looked at her uncle. Reddy ripped off another wide bite. He took the bread out of his mouth and touched around on the table, leaving the soggy thing on the placemat. "Mark, get that."

Uncle Mark shook his head.

"Brush it on the floor then."

Alex flicked it off the table.

"Pizza's his favorite food. He's all right."

Uncle Mark leaned back in his chair, pushing his plate away as he did so. "I've lost my appetite," he said. They looked at the sauce dripping from Reddy's fingers. "I don't want him eating at the table like that."

"Uncle Mark, do you still collect butterflies?" Alex said.

"No," he said.

"Why'd you stop?"

"I don't know."

"Was it because you joined the Navy?"

"No, dear," her aunt said. "He didn't start collecting butterflies until *after* the Navy."

"Uncle Mark, did you have to kill anyone in the Navy?"

"What? No," he said, but Alex thought he sounded unsure. He tipped forward in his chair. "But he can feel. I know he can't see, but can't he feel the—the fucking sauce on his—his fucking face? I'm sorry."

"If you have a problem, eat in the family room," her aunt said to him.

"I'll eat where I want to," he said, and left with his plate.

"The Navy people don't kill people, honey."

"I thought they did."

She leaned into the table and whispered, "He was just a cable repairman."

"I don't think I belong here," Aleksia said into the phone. She hid in the bathroom, sitting on the closed seat with her knees to her chest. "I need a ticket back right *now*."

"They're family."

"I don't think they are."

"Don't be strange."

"I'm not being strange." She started to shake. "I'm not being strange, Grandma."

"You're not coming home."

"What are you doing to me? What did I do?"

"Aleksia."

Without another word, Aleksia hung up, stood, and made like she would throw the cordless into the mirror. Instead, she screamed in her head and walked out, under control.

Aleksia and the Porters designed a routine surrounding Reddy's needs like one of those spiraling mathematical wormholes made on graph paper. Their routes penciled toward Reddy and then curved away from Reddy and, drawn out like that, the *toward* and *away* looked about the same. On Tuesday and Thursday nights, her aunt took care of him while Aleksia went to pottery class. Otherwise, Aleksia took him to the toilet twice a day and brought him lunch and dinner – pepperoni pizza and meat lover's pizza, respectively. *We spoil him*, her aunt said. *Pizza's his favorite food.* The more she said it, the truer it seemed.

The sunlight came at a sharp angle through the window, lighting up the blue and white bedspread, making shadows where it folded and tucked around his body. His one opened eye pointed forward at the dust floating easily through the light. When she jabbed him in the shoulder, he looked beyond her. She set the pizza box on his lap and he streaked the sheets with grease when he pushed it down his legs. She stood above him with her arms crossed while he ate, trying to block out the sounds, trying to understand what was going on inside him. He stared forward with that one eye.

When he stopped eating, he muttered something and pushed away the box. Curled on his side, he looked somehow like a seahorse. He slipped back into obscurity.

She wanted to give him something to do.

After Aleksia's third pottery class, she went into the supply closet in the back of the classroom. She had a craving. It wasn't that she wanted to eat the clay but, not being able to describe the desire even to herself, she decided it was most like hunger. Some mouth inside her chest -maybe it was her heart- salivated when her teacher, Claudia, stood on a chair, unwrapped a brick-sized chunk of it and held it up for the class to see. Watching her instructor wave it around like that made her crazy for it. Claudia set it on the table and hopped down saying that, *actually*, they wouldn't begin working directly with the clay for another week. As she walked beyond the table toward the chalkboard, her lecture went silent, her image went blurry and all Aleksia could see clearly was that brick of clay.

Waiting was Aleksia's least favorite thing to do.

Late that night, her aunt and uncle went to bed and she emptied her purse of the clay under the bathtub faucet where she sat with it, molding it and so on, until she satisfied the mouth in her heart.

The water turned gray and the glossy block slid in her hands. She had to let go, to stop thinking. The clay became big-bellied people in trench coats; it became penguins stuck to the slick white dike of the tub by webbed feet made of thumbprints. Sometimes, she cut it into pieces with her fingernails. Sometimes, she punched it into a bowl-shape with her fist. When she was done, she turned on the shower and cleaned up the film with face towels she found in the linen closet.

Aleksia snagged an apple from the kitchen. On her way back down the hall, Reddy rustled in his room. She took a bite of her apple and watched. He stood near his dresser, the yellow streetlight striping his chest and face through the blinds. She flipped on the lamp. His head turned up. He was surrounded by electronics and green things. She moved toward him by the two rusted lamps tossed together on their sides, their shades like hooped skirts at his knees. The double bed took up most of the space in the room. His elbow held him up against a metal filing cabinet with a cupful of pencils on it. On the opposite side of the bed, a black bike hung on a bike tree. National Geographic magazines were stacked on a sewing machine; a

CHAPTER 2

sticker-covered computer monitor was on the floor next to a box of CDs; and some kind of butterfly kite hung from the far corner ceiling like it had been caught there.

He got up heavily and set something on top of the dresser; then, he was reaching out toward her, seeming somehow like a baby bird fresh out of the shell working through the grass to pavement. With the apple in her mouth, she eased herself onto the bed, stepped across the top of it, and got down on the other side. He took the other direction. Reddy was scurrying now, a night creature scratching. Alex saw what he put on the dresser, an index card. She watched out for him as she picked it up, turned it over. On one side, a picture of a girl cut from a magazine catalogue wearing a bra and panties, on the other side, in thick childish letters, the words "Pleasure Card."

He hurried to the light switch, and the lamp went out. The skinny stripes stretched over everything, and instantly, she found herself in a three-pointed trap between Reddy, the dresser, and the wall. She put the card back. He sighed, opened the dresser drawer, felt around for the card, slipped it in and shut it. The way he did it, she believed for a moment he could see, if not with his eyes, then with something like a ghost in his body. She took the apple from her mouth and chucked it at him. It hit his hip and bounced to the bed.

"Fuck, damn it," he said, and mumbled, "what's going on?" She stepped backward into the hallway.

The following evening, she brought home anything green she could find from the Dollar Store -two bags full of sea glass candle holders, porcelain knickknacks and fairy lights. Going through his things, she pocketed the cellphone in his nightstand and found a box of Legos in the closet. She spread the Legos across a breakfast tray and placed it in his lap. She dropped his hand on it. He reached out with his fingers spread and pulled one Lego into his palm. He sat up and got another. Feeling around, he attached them. He created a skyscraper. With the book her mother gave her, Aleksia curled up next to him. He separated the different sizes into separate piles. From there, he made a rocket.

"Time to go to bed," Aunt Freya said from the hall.

Aleksia pulled away the tray. When their hands touched, she closed her eyes and behind her lids, glowing, she saw him – a better version of him. She grabbed his shoulders and forced him backwards, his knees bending at the bed. They fell together. She held him down.

"Alex," he whispered. She pulled his shirt up. He laughed. She covered his mouth. His eyelid slipped up and down. She wrote on his chest with her finger: *WHAT DO YOU WANT?*

"Maybe one of these days I could take him out." After dinner in the kitchen, Alex wrapped her arms around the back of her wooden chair and lifted her hips, adjusting the seat cushion with its thin looping strings that were always untying themselves. Her aunt ripped a paper towel off the roll. Her uncle looked at the soup in his spoon. "We'll take a walk. I'll hold his arm," she said.

"Aleksia." Aunt Freya blew upward in a sigh, so that her hair flew away from her face. "His nerves are swollen. That's the problem. And if you jostle anything . . ."

"I won't."

"We shouldn't even be letting him out of his room," her aunt said. "We should've gotten him a bedpan. I still think we should, Mark. Something serious could happen."

Mark set his spoon against his bowl lightly. "I don't want

you taking any chances with him, all right."

"If we'd known, I never would have let him move all that junk in there. That room is really full of junk," she said. "He doesn't need to end up in the hospital because he's sliced his leg open or cracked his head open. He doesn't need those books or computers, those radios, CDs, not that sewing machine. He can't even see." Her voice drifted, as if it were the first time she let those words pass her lips, as if she secretly came to the conclusion that Dr. Kane's time estimate of a six-month healing period was absolute bullshit. "The bicycle, we need to get that, too. That kite. The clock." Finally, she got up with a sniffle. "Mark, you still want ice cream?"

"I'll have some," he said, "in the TV room." He got up and went there. Aunt Freya took out bowls. "I know you want some, right?"

One chair at the table sat shorter than the others with a slick, rounded back. That's where Reddy had been the day they brought him home and he hadn't sat there since. In one window, blue curtains; in another, blinds. Nobody planned to stay there, Aleksia saw, but the Porters lived there for—what had her aunt said? Thirteen, fourteen years now?—in this temporary existence of second-hand furniture, the kind everyone could throw away at a second's notice of a better opportunity. There were dented decorations purchased along the way in the time (that read to Alex in her imagination) as the might-as-well-make-it-nice-while-we're-still-here time period. A calendar hung by a naked nail struck through an orange catfish, mouth opened, tail flipped on the wallpaper. Some of the butter knives had rounded handles and were perfectly weighted in your hand; some were perfectly flat tiny mirrors. She pilfered one of each kind. *The longer an object sits, the heavier it gets*, she thought. The objects layered throughout the house, one year under another like bodies in a grave to be dug up and re-layered with newer bodies. This made her think of home. It made her think of Tante Kirstin on top of her cousin, Levon, on top of her father. Is that how they did it? Three bodies deep? Was it in death-order, or order-of-importance? Her father explained it when she was little. Would they put Mamma on top of Pappa? She knew a body only stayed in the grave for ten years before it was dug out for someone else to go in. But what would they do with his body after ten years? And what if her mother died in the meantime? What happens to their bodies when they're taken out? Are they burned? Do they go to a dump? Are they put it in a river? And, during the winter, do they freeze underground, or do they stay pretty warm in there? How long does it take for the body to decompose? How long are her Pappa's fingernails now? Would someone steal Tante Kirstin's rings? Where would they put Aleksia's body? When would she be gone? Would it be soon? Would she outlive everyone?

Her aunt brought the tub of ice cream to the table with a bowl, a spoon, and a silver scooper, which she was pushing into the tub as she said, "it was nice of you, though, to think of Reddy. Shows real empathy and, your mother would say, *improvement* on your part."

*

Reddy woke to a tap on his shoulder. He thought Alex was there to feed him, not knowing the time of day, but instead she climbed in. Her body was warm. He tried not to move. She pushed herself into him. Finally, he let out a sigh and nudged her heavily as if moving in his sleep. His shoulder touched some part of her body. After a pause, the mattress dipped

CHAPTER 2

and her skin, warm, moist from a bath perhaps, pressed right against the side of his body, and his heart picked up so abruptly and stayed so fast, he thought his parents could hear it down the hall. She put her head on his chest. He smelled her breath as her wet hair slapped his neck. Electricity rushed through his knees. It almost hurt—not touching her. He pretended to be asleep and let out a groan and moved the arm that she was covering to catch a bit of her breast. She stirred, and he let his head drop away, so in case the lights were on, she couldn't read his face. He wanted her to grab him. He waited, trying to control his breath. She shifted and lifted her leg over his, and all he could feel was the hot weight of it. They lay still.

Afraid she'd lost interest in what she'd started, he moved his elbow and held her breast. She didn't move, as if she were the one sleeping now and, after an unbearable pause, rubbed herself against his thigh. And something like a star exploded in him. He shuddered. Electricity. A shock. The Big Bang. The Big Bang reversing. And everything went black, again. She lifted her head, lifted off the bed.

He said, "Alex." He didn't know if she had left. "I want you to take me out." There was no response.

He didn't move until he knew she'd left the room. Then, he got up and told himself to remember that, to always remember that.

*

The unemployment office opened at ten in the morning, Tuesdays and Thursdays. It was nine-fifty now and Mark guessed he was the twentieth person in line. Just before him stood a man named Jim who wore a plaid button-up shirt and a black cap that said across the top in red letters, "Jim." His lips and nose were wet and salmon-colored. He kept his lower lip drooping down, letting you see his pink tongue and letting the air pass through easily, as if he were tempting a fly.

Mark leaned against the brick wall, pushing it with his shoulder. Jim turned slightly toward him and started talking, and when he talked, he spit and sounded like he was talking through putty. Every so often, he pushed his thumb to his chin, drying up the bit of saliva or sweat that had gathered there.

"Fell off a John Deere forklift two months back." He held his hat under his armpit and smoothed out his red, wet hairs along his scalp. He put the hat back on, pushed his hands deep into his pockets, and rocked onto the heels of his boots. "Lifting pallets of rolled up rugs in a warehouse, Oriental. H and L Oriental Rugs. On the river. Could see the water out the top windows of the warehouse, if you're standing up top the forklift. Shouldn't have done it, but hey. Had to take a look.

Let me tell you." Jim looked into Mark's eyes, then his look fluttered away, as if a fly flew off and he watched it. "When I fell? I saw stars, almost like faeries, just zipping around my head." He wiped his chin with his thumb. "So, that's why."

The glass door opened, and two ladies with clipboards and white jackets came out. They asked men questions and were wanting their IDs. Mark pushed himself off the wall. Lately, his son got stuck to the walls, Freya had said. As if God ripped the house off the end of the row, grabbed it by the kitchen and basement, and shook it. Not that Mark believed in God. Freya did, and she said that's how the house probably was for Reddy, shaking so that he found himself stuck to walls and reaching for curtains.

Mark looked at Jim who was opening and closing his mouth. Then, it occurred to him in a flash. Perhaps he wasn't at the unemployment office. The ladies were wearing white coats, and Jim fell off a John Deere forklift. Mark crossed his arms and stepped out of line to look at the waist-level brick wall the city had pushed evenly into a dirt mound, with its official blue lettering and white background but, even in his slight inebriation, he had found the right place, this place squeezed into a mall of government office buildings, hygienic and bored-looking, cooped up together and surrounded by a big white parking lot like fat around a heart.

A young hippie-looking guy held the door open and waved in the first three men, and they ducked their heads as if they had to crawl under his arm. A woman with a short Japanese haircut, bobbed and so black it hinted at blue, made her way down the line, ripping off slips of paper and handing them to the men as she went. Mark's lungs were turning inside out. He opened his mouth to let the air in. He didn't have a story.

Jim had a story about a forklift and a river. But Mark didn't have anything to say for himself about why he was there and why he didn't have a job.

His knees began to shake, so he locked them in place, which only made the blood pump faster to his heart. There was no reason to bring up his short stint working at the church. He stopped going in and they stopped calling and he preferred to keep it that way.

The lady reached Jim, and he told her about the rugs and the forklift over on Riverside Drive where they got this warehouse. The woman perused his license, handed it back, and gave him a slip of paper. Mark stood still, holding in the smell of the cigarettes he smoked and the gin he drank in the station wagon before he'd gotten the nerve to get in line.

"Last pay stub," she said. He reached into his back pocket and pulled it out, unfolding it with his shaky fingers. She peered at the paper. "Three months ago."

Mark could feel his throat constricting now. He kept his lips pushed together. She asked for his ID and he gave that to her too. She traded it for the slip of paper. On it, it said, "34. You are number 34. Please wait patiently." He pinched the slip between two fingers, and she moved on. He didn't have a story.

One day at the auto parts store, his boss promoted him from parts delivery to parts management. This meant he would have to talk with the drivers all day long through a radio that sat on the desk in his boss's office in the main storage room. Because he couldn't figure out how to deny the offer (and he couldn't tell if it *was* an offer), he avoided his boss until, three weeks later, his boss assumed he'd accepted the job. The thought of pressing the button on the microphone and having his voice heard by people he couldn't see made his head spin. He dropped off his last exhaust manifold in South East that morning and never went back to work again.

The next day, the boss called and told him he was making a big mistake and said to just come back, that they would work it out, that nobody knew the storage room better than he did, but he had just lay there in bed holding the phone unable to explain himself.

This morning, he couldn't figure if he should wear a tie and button-up shirt to give the impression he was really making an effort, or if he should wear what he wanted to wear, his stained blue T-shirt that Freya hated so much and his jeans, which would make him look—as he felt—incapable of getting a job. He decided on the shirt and jeans. Freya didn't wake up when he left. She would've thanked him for going, and he couldn't stand the way she made everything hers all the time with all her false appreciation, so that it was as if he never thought of anything on his own. So, he was glad she didn't see him off. He stopped by McDonalds and got himself an Egg McMuffin with hash browns and ate it there in the parking lot. He had his car, if nothing else; he had his Volvo to rely on.

And now that it was warm out, he could wait until next year to get the heat fixed. But damn if it didn't get hot as soon as March hit.

Lately, he'd been feeling strange. A shadow was trying to crawl inside him and make him nod off. It reminded him of driving down Moffett Road in Alabama at night with only poplar trees to look at and when sleep was this seductive thing on the side of the road trying to pull him in. All he had to do was close his eyes for just a second. And that would be it.

Sooner or later, that shadow would take over. He hadn't had

a cigarette for six years and no gin either. This morning, he had both.

The hippie man opened the door and waved Jim and Mark in. The cold air went right up Mark's sleeves to his sweaty armpits. Instinctively, he crossed his arms.

The vinyl seats made a snoring sound as the three of them sat down, the man on one side of the desk, the two men on the other. The man touched a few things on the surface of his desk and moved around some papers. Facing Mark, there was a photograph of the man with his son. Both had long blonde hair pulled back in ponytails. There was something almost refreshing about the picture, about a father and son looking like two phases of the same life. And still, it made him want to smash the man's face in with the corner of the frame.

"I'm the fastest around," the man said, and Jim smiled over at Mark. "I do two at a time. Numbers?" They handed their numbers to him. He threw them in the trash bin, looked up, then scratched away on a clipboard as Jim explained about the forklift. Occasionally, the hippie man sighed or opened or closed a drawer. He said, "Good then," and passed a carbon copy of something to Jim. Jim took it and stared off.

"You?" The man scratched on a notepad, then flipped his hair over to the other side of his head. Mark dug his fists into the seat. "Mark Porter, right?" Mark nodded. He wanted to close his eyes, to nod off. "You're done." The man pointed with his pencil eraser at Jim who was holding his hat in his hands and chewing at his lower lip.

"He don't really talk much," Jim said, and Mark stiffened at the sound of a stranger talking about him.

The man's eyes peered up at the two. "You guys together?"

"I was standing in the line—" Jim started.

"No," Mark said. He shook his head. "I'm not with anybody." He felt Jim holding him with his eyes, but Mark just stared forward, gripping the vinyl of his seat by his knees.

"Jesus, what time is it? It's eleven, and we got how many left? Were you fired, laid off?"

"See he's a nervous wreck?" Jim said.

"Fired," the man said.

Mark took a deep breath and said, "Promoted." Then, he laughed and gasped. Once he started giggling, he couldn't stop. Nothing was funny and yet he couldn't stop laughing. In a high-pitched voice, he apologized, but it just pushed at his insides, made his side ache, bulged at his throat. He covered his mouth, bursting with heat. The laughter was violent, explosive, suffocating. He wasn't even making sound anymore, just sucking in at his hand. And then, it all shut down.

He wiped the tears from his face and breathed deeply. When he was able to see again, the man handed him a yellow paper.

"Okay. You stand in that line there, and you, Mr. Porter, over there."

They used the armrests to push themselves out of the chairs. There was a violent quivering under his skin. It made his heart vibrate. Jim, who was about a head shorter than Mark, looked at the yellow paper.

"I could go with you," Jim said.

"I have to get this money," Mark said.

"I mean if you have trouble talking." Jim moved his tongue around his mouth like a fish flipping in the sand. "I could go, too. I mean, what are you going to do?"

Mark tilted his chin toward his shoulder, then looked at his paper. Across the top, it said, "Application for Temporary Employment."

"See?" Jim said. "See? Mine says, 'Application for Unemployment *Compensation.*'" He came up to Mark's armpits. He grabbed Mark by his elbow. "It's just over here." Fluorescent lights flickered against the shiny gray walls.

"I have to get my money," Mark said again. "It's—it's what you call important." He paused, running over the words he just spoke in his head. *What you call important.*

"I know. I know how that is."

An argument broke out at the hippie man's desk and an unemployed man in a raspberry-colored suit screamed, "what kind of bullshit is this?" Then, he marched out the door and tried to slam it shut, only the door was on a pressurized arm-closer and had to go at its own pace. He circled around out front, smoking a cigarette like he meant to rip its insides out.

He folded the paper up into quarters and stuffed it next to the cigarettes in his shirt pocket. Then, he looked over the heads in line.

"I'm not cut out for this," Mark heard himself whisper, and Jim was talking over him, saying, "That's the problem. You can't just quit. Get wrongly fired or accused of something, maybe. Laid off, sure, but promoted and quit? What was it exactly made you quit, Mark?"

"Excuse me," Mark said. Then, he left Jim standing in line while he went directly to his station wagon.

He drove to the hospital parking lot and watched med students scurry in and out through the cafeteria doors into the courtyard. He didn't know what it was he planned on doing. He sipped on his gin and smoked cigarettes. As if he planned on doing anything. He loved gin just the same as his son loved pizza. Gin was his old friend. He thought of the picture on the hippie man's desk. He had always seen his son as this separate thing that didn't do anything but need maintenance.

He thought of the time during a M*A*S*H rerun two winters ago when Freya said, "life is too long. I don't understand why it just has to keep going when nothing's happening." Only two things stopped her from taking the pills she had in their medicine cabinet—and which pills she was talking about he didn't know and partly doubted they existed—but her two life-savers, she said, were Reddy and her fear of hell. But, she said, she was getting over her fears.

Well, the house might as well have been sucked up by a tornado and spit back out again, splintered and misshapen. She was afraid of what she might do, she said. She put herself in the psych ward for ten days and Reddy started hanging around more, snooping through family albums, grumbling about how this was all Mark's fault for—what did he say?—"for being as *in*active and *in*attentive as living room furniture."

Remembering that now, Mark's knee knocked into the steering column.

She was always saying things.

He rolled out of the hospital parking lot -the same hospital where Freya, Aleksia and Reddy had been yesterday. And, what happened? What did Freya say? That Aleksia had nearly kidnapped a kid? Could she have said that? He couldn't wrap his head around the story and hadn't thought about it even once all day. She told him when he was half-asleep, what did she expect? She was always saying things, and always saying things at all the wrong times.

He circled around the neighborhood in his station wagon, drinking his gin until rain misted his windshield. The light in the front room was on, then off. The pizza delivery boy came and went. Mark pulled into the driveway just as Aleksia was walking up the stairs in her raincoat. She stopped when she noticed him and waved. He felt that thing creeping up in him again.

He stepped out and yelled, "Hey!" then slammed his door shut. Her smile faded. "Where are the towels?"

"Sorry?"

"I want to know what you've been doing with the little towels." Using the iron handrail, he launched himself up the steps. "I know you're doing something, and I want to know what it is."

Shock passed over her face. Energy surged up his spine.

"I'm using them for something," she said.

"You're using them for something."

"That's right." She reached for the doorknob.

The rain pushed his hair down. "You feed Reddy yet?"

"I had class." She looked around. Her eyebrows knitted when she caught sight of the cigarettes in his front pocket. He lit one and kept it between his lips.

"Fine." Then, he walked right in with that lit cigarette pointing straight out in front of him. He called out to Freya, "well! I did it. And I'm home."

*

After Aleksia shook out her raincoat with its rubber sleeves and hood, she went through the door her uncle left open to see him hang his key ring on an exposed nail, the one that held up the hospital calendar, the one that was struck through the mouth of a wallpaper-catfish.

Alone in her room, she closed the door behind her and lifted the heavy window. Party voices hung above someone's yard, just below the twilight sky. The next-door neighbor's llama had been taken in, probably because of the rain earlier, which had stopped now, leaving the moist air cool after a hot day. Moments like these, alone in the US, she thought of her mother. Her mother would never leave Norway because the country matched her internal circadian rhythm, this universal or ethereal pulsing her mother was so dead set on praying to, but if her mother came to the US, they could rent a car, or get on a train and go across the whole continent together.

That would take about a week, she thought, and together, they'd release her mother of this depression, break her out of that Norwegian rhythm. This thought made her miss her father too, that small man, partly insane, wearing ragdoll clothing he made himself and speaking in poetry of impossible plans. (We could fly with newspaper wings; we'll make them like kites and fasten them to our arms; we'll jump from a treehouse platform and glide to the back deck. Aleksia, you can go first. Then, Mamma. No! We'll make a zipline from that tree there and run it to the attic window. Or wait, we'll just cross a swan with a cat with a human and ride its back, hold onto its ears. *I don't want it to have ears, Pappa.* It must have ears. There's no sense in going through all the scientific effort if it doesn't have ears. It won't hear us when we call. It'll run off and join a circus. *We could use the string-and-can phone, Pappa.* He sits forward in his chair, claps his hands: That's not a bad idea.)

Her mother warned her beforehand that her sister, Freya, would want to turn an eighteen-year-old (yes, Alex thought, speaking to her mother in her mind, everybody forgot about my birthday except Reddy) into a best friend. Alex tried to befriend her cousin instead. When she talked to Aunt Freya, she tried to smile because things were harder for her, but then Alex just holed up in her room thinking about how stupid her aunt was for complaining and circling throughout these rooms, wearing down the carpet.

Lying in this bed so often late into the afternoon and into nightfall, Alex would smoke joints and label her feelings, sense the itch of some emotion and get back there and scratch it. In all of this time, she found a big difference between being honest and telling the truth. She considered herself to be smart, no matter how stupid she could seem sometimes, no matter how much she hated herself for things like taking that little boy at the hospital from his mother.

The night before, she and Reddy had played in the bathtub until four in the morning not knowing only two hours later Aunt Freya would come banging on her door to wake her up to go to the hospital. Because Mark had taken the car, they had to catch a bus to Reddy's follow-up appointments. They met with doctors all day. Aleksia tried to read her book as she sat in waiting room after waiting room. It was the last appointment, she thought, when she started to crack.

Everyone knew she hated hospitals, hospitals and airports. Hatred crept up in her like one of those guys with the outward pointed shoes climbing a telephone pole. It wasn't right because hate led, inevitably, to bad behavior, but as much as she tried—lying in her bed at night concentrating on all those people she loved, like her grandma and her mother—the feeling wouldn't go away. It clung to her chest. She fought the urge to growl. Hospitals and airports were places you had to wait, and both had that pressure pushing at the sides of her skull. She tried to practice patience like this shaman guy talked about in the first chapter of this book but, as often as people talked about practicing patience, no one ever told her exactly *how* to practice it. It was as if she'd been told to play "Ode to Joy" by rubbing her forearms together. Being in this city, under these ignorant, lazy conditions, her mind drifted from subject to subject and, at particularly bad times, became paralyzed between them. Her English and Norwegian slipped away, leaving her with colors, impressions, gushed-out feelings. Her imagination seeped into her seat. It made her want to cut herself, again, or jump off that bridge so popular with her type. She let go of the book; she told herself, "Lift your head as if to bring it above water."

Her aunt started talking from the middle of an idea.

"And the worst part is I have to come back in a week and go to each doctor for the results." She picked up the flier Alex was using as a bookmark that read "Liminal Lounge." A pottery student gave it to her. "This looks interesting." She handed it back. After a long pause, her aunt said something about Timothy, Reddy's older estranged brother, being her favorite. "I know it's not right, but I'm honest. You put Reddy on a corner; he just stands there until you tell him where to go. He's nice around you but, believe me, he gets grouchy." She patted Reddy's hat. "Even when he went on trips with Emma, he called every night. Collect."

"Who's Emma?"

"Oh, his best friend. They love each other. It's really the sweetest thing."

"Yeah? Then, where is she?"

She didn't mean to say it like that, but really, where was she if they were so sweet?

"You'll see her. She comes by. Only friend he has left."

Her aunt picked up a magazine for herself and put it back down. A little boy screamed out.

"I shouldn't have said that about Timothy. It's just . . . with you here, I can say anything." She smiled.

"Because I'm bad."

"No," she said and caught Alex's eyes. "No. It's not because you're bad. Come on." She tapped Aleksia's knee and she accidentally recoiled. "Hey, I noticed you're a night person. Your mother, now she's a day person. I think it's okay, but Mark and I were wondering."

"Wondering what?"

"We just don't understand what you do during the night that you can't do during the day. That's all."

She thought of the photos she snapped of Reddy in the bathtub the night before. "Lots of stuff."

Aunt Freya looked off. "Yeah, well, okay."

"I'm a night person. It runs in the family. Mamma said all of us winter babies are night people. I was born in February."

Reddy was eating snacks in his wheelchair. He looked so sad there, Aleksia thought, so uncomfortable.

"The winter's hard. In the winter, I just don't know where my head's at."

"Yeah," Alex said. She sat up, trying to pop that spacey feeling. "I know eight people who've killed themselves in the past two years because they couldn't make it through winter. There was Levon, my *Onkel* Henrik, Kirstin—then my Tante Kirstin—Erik, and of course Pappa. Who else?" She thought for a moment, running through the months in her mind. "Erik, *then* Pappa." Thinking about it woke her up a little. "Oh!" She took her hand away from her aunt. "Then, this girl, Amy, I didn't know very well. From school."

"Daniel," Aunt Freya said.

"Right, Daniel." Daniel was another cousin.

"Everybody does it sooner or later, I guess."

"Not everybody. I'm not going to," Alex said. "I tried to tell Tante Kirstin—just run away. You don't have to jump into a river, just try something new." The little boy's balding mother looked at them. Aunt Freya's face went flat.

"But she didn't listen."

"She didn't listen."

Because his name had been called, her aunt rolled Reddy toward a door where a nurse took him away.

The boy had longish hair that curled up from the back of his neck. With wide eyes, he blew Aleksia a kiss. She tucked it away in her shirt pocket. He had dimples and long eye lashes, a pudgy chin folding in as he looked down.

"He's flirting," the mother said.

"Here." Aleksia offered her hand to him, touching his cheek lightly with her knuckle. She liked the smoothness of it. He didn't move away.

He said, "my mommy's got cancer."

His mother tilted her head. "He has to tell everyone."

"I'm five," he said.

Alex came around the row of seats to the boy. He scooted out of the seat, handing her a hollow red block. She was angry, so angry that life was this way, but she held that burning feeling in her chest. "He likes you," the woman said. Something might explode. "Kids know good people when they see them." She smiled. Her aunt and the woman struck up a conversation. Alex opened a book for the child. She sat close to him and, after some time, he pushed his head into her armpit while she read a story about dancing bees and pollen with her heart beating against her ribcage.

"What's your name?" he said, lifting his heavy head from her side.

"Alex." Maybe it was talking about all the death that made her head so hot.

"Do you like Lou Reed?"

"Of course," Alex said. Or maybe it was being in a hospital.

"Vi-cious," he said. "You hit me with a flo-wer." He pointed to a picture in the book. Or maybe her aunt was suffocating her. He snuggled back into her. She had wanted to go to New York City. They finished the book. Or Los Angeles. He banged two blocks together now. He banged two like cymbals. Alex grabbed two, did the same thing.

"Aaron, you stop that," his mother said. Alex shoved the blocks under the row of seats. Alex needed something to start or to end. Either, but not this. Not this waiting for something that you didn't want in the first place, so she took the boy by the hand.

"You going somewhere?" Aunt Freya said.

"Miss," his mother said, partly standing, her body frail and bent. "They . . . they might call us." The woman held onto the armrest. "*Please,*" she seemed to be saying, but she spoke too quietly for Alex to be certain.

She hurried the boy down a ramp. She had to hold his tiny hand tightly, tugging him upward each time he stumbled.

It was so surprisingly easy.

"I like ornchjuice," he said. "You carry me?"

She lifted him and held him against her chest, looking over her shoulder. He wiggled around. He sat on her arm because he liked to watch where they went.

"We'll find you some orange juice," Alex told him. The hall led to a series of other halls. She chose a direction past a row of framed photos. She could take him anywhere. He was so small.

CHAPTER 3

She couldn't be sure there would be any juice machines around. Her head felt puffy and hot again, full of pressure. She checked her pocket for change, having to move him from one side of her body to the other. She had two quarters. "Do you hate hospitals as much as I do, Aaron?"

"I don't know," he said.

"I hate them a lot."

"I like hospitals!" he said.

"I bet we have a lot in common. Wouldn't you rather be out there?" She held him up to a window to see a long park with a line of trees and thinking of it now made her cringe. "Wouldn't you rather go out there and play?"

"Let's play friends," he had said. "Do you like me?"

They parted from the window and took another turn. "Yes, very much." With one hand, she was pushing at her temple, massaging it. "Very much."

"I like you, too." He wrapped his arms around her neck. She could smell that child-smell emanating from his skin, something like sour milk, something like Cheerios. After a moment, he said, "But maybe we'll get lost!"

"You think I would get lost?" she said. "I'm an adult." She wasn't thinking right. She remembered once when her grandmother said that about her: *Aleksia, you're not thinking right.* "Adults don't get lost," she told the boy. *Aleksia, you're being strange.*

"I want down."

"No, you want to go to the park." She came around another corner where there was an elevator. Since his little body slid down her hip, she jumped, readjusting him. "You want to push the button?"

They took the elevator to the lobby and she let him down.

The boy looked dazed, wandering absentmindedly toward the elevator doors. A big blue sign advertised "Donuts for Donations." She had to snatch him by his coat collar. "This way, kiddo. We're going to share a doughnut," she told him. "Wouldn't you like a sugary doughnut?" He walked beside her to the table. Alex gave the lady the two quarters she had. "You can pick one out."

"Is this your little boy?" the woman said.

Alex said, "Yes." She said, "Of course."

"He's adorable."

Aaron bit his lip, looking up at her.

"Pick a doughnut, Aaron." He started walking in the direction of the elevator again. She caught him, led him to the plate of doughnuts. Aaron pointed out a big white powdered doughnut.

"What," she said, because she didn't like the way he was looking at her. She broke the doughnut in half and put his portion in his hand.

The ground was wet and, when they got out to the trees, across the long lawn, it started to rain. He ate a few bites of his doughnut. He said he didn't want the rest.

"Here." She threw it across the lawn. "I wouldn't make you eat it." They sat on a bench together. He swung his legs at the knees.

"One day I'll lose a tooth," he said.

"And what will happen then?"

"Then, the fairy comes down from the heaven and gives you the money."

"That's right," Alex said.

"Where's my mommy?" he said. "I want my mommy now. *Please.*"

CHAPTER 3

"I'm not sure, Aaron," she said, brushing away the powder from her jeans, and she told him how she wished she could be his mommy.

In a flash, he was at her feet. He kicked his shoes against the ground. She reached out to him.

He beat his fist against his chest screaming, "No! No! No!" Before her eyes, his face turned red. Her feet must have been a mile down. "I want to go home!"

"Stop it, Aaron."

He spit out sounds, unintelligible sounds.

She grabbed his head. "Stop it, Aaron. Stop." He wiggled away. When she reached for him again, he slapped her hand.

They took the elevator back up. She found a door with no sign on it. "Let's see if we can find that juice."

His lips pushed together. His little fists were stuffed into his little pockets.

"You still like me?" Alex said.

He shook his head.

She picked him up, found the ramp and went up it and then let him down. "I think you can walk the rest of the way yourself, don't you? I'm going back to the park to play."

The boy stopped. Alex didn't know why she had said this. Sometimes she acted out. This is what it's like, she thought, to be a dangerous human being. To be a danger to others. *I'm dangerous to others.* She looked down at him.

"What the hell is wrong with me?"

"I don't know," he said. He walked up the ramp ahead of her.

Aunt Freya flung her arms out.

"Where have you been?"

"I'm sorry." Alex followed the boy's slow tiny shoes.

"Well, come on," her aunt said.

Aaron ran to his mother and burrowed his head into her dress.

"Mommy!"

"What's wrong? What's wrong, honey?"

She led him by the hand away from Alex into a little room.

Alex re-lit her joint. She'd been smoking like this for a week, trying to erase that boy from her memory. Maybe she'd always been this way, or maybe she'd been this way since that night with Reddy. The weed helped her deal with the shame and confusion.

That night, all the lights had turned on by themselves and the bicycle tire spun, and the Pleasure Card flew out of the dresser, and the electronics buzzed on and broke.

She'd gone in there, and she shouldn't have done that either, but something happened. He came. And when he came, the lights turned on. She got up and no one was there. And then, everything in the room picked itself up and moved. And then it all dropped. It was like a star exploded. And she wanted to tell Aunt Freya, but she couldn't because she shouldn't have been in there, and now after the hospital incident, her aunt didn't want her alone with Reddy, and she shouldn't have touched Reddy like that, but she did stupid things. She was always doing stupid things. But he had communicated with her. And she went over it in her mind, again and again, trying to find a way to believe she had imagined it.

She put the joint out. It was like nothing she'd ever experienced. When it all stirred and everything lifted in the air, her voice trembled as she said, "Reddy, what do you want?" And he'd said, "Alex, I want you to take me out."

CHAPTER 3

Since then, she'd been trying to understand it. Now, as she jumped from thought to thought, she knew she had to make good on this. She had to do something right for the first time in her life. Not for herself, but for him. She sat up on the edge of her bed, then swung her weight up, gaining the energy to have another conversation with her aunt.

In the kitchen, a big black rotary phone sat heavy like a boot on the butcher block table. She leaned against this and touched the dull meat cleaver which sliced into the wood, left there, arrested mid-swing, like a joke everybody forgot about. Her aunt wore a pink scarf wrapped around her hair, and when Aleksia started talking, she spun around startled with a bag of ginger snaps in her hand.

"Well," her aunt began, "the doctors say he's getting better."

"He needs to get out of the house. He's going to go crazy in there," Aleksia said.

Something inside her aunt descended like a lead weight on a fishing line, deep and wavering to the bottom. Wrapping her robe around her tube-body, she went to the sink and started scrubbing the hell out of the dishes.

Alex didn't move.

"He is not leaving the house," she said, and on the word "not," her eyes flashed the same way they flashed when Aleksia returned with the boy at the hospital.

"I don't want to argue," Aleksia said. Her uncle walked in carrying a large box on his hand like a platter.

"I thought you went to bed," her aunt said.

"Huh? I'm looking for my Steve Martin 8-track."

"It's not in here," Aunt Freya said, lifting her eyebrows at her.

"I'm taking this ashtray." Mark picked something up off the top of the fridge.

"Mark?" her aunt said. "Can you do something about the rodents?"

He left without answering. To Aleksia, she said, "you know, he had these dreams of growing a garden in the backyard, one we could eat from so we didn't have to buy groceries anymore."

"Rodents?" Aleksia said.

"Don't worry. They don't come up the stairs."

Alex took a moment. "Do you think you'll ever let Reddy out, again?"

"What do you think?"

"I don't know, I only—"

"God, I can't stand this anymore, being in the middle—that's where Mark likes me—in limbo. He thinks it's safer there. Makes me want to die, honestly." She looked up. "It's like the middle of summer in Norway when time just stops and night never comes and the light gets into everything." She bunched her hands. "Shows off all its dinginess. I don't know what to do," she said with an emphasis on *I*. "His senses should be back by now. But he doesn't tell me how he feels. I ask him in my head every day, 'how do you feel?' and he won't answer me. As if we put him in this position. As if we cut his nerves ourselves."

"When you talk, Aunt Freya, you sound like you're talking to yourself and you're just making everyone around you listen to you doing it."

"Is that how I sound," she asked, only it wasn't a question.

"Yeah."

"I guess that's what happens when you're used to no one listening."

*

Alex held the cold keyring in her hand, having taken it so

gently off the nail, and stood in the kitchen in the light coming from above the sink. The keys went into her pocket and her hand cupped them. Then, she went in Reddy's room. He lay asleep on his side. She pushed his shoulder.

"*What?*" he said, and she flapped her hand over his mouth, holding him in place. He resigned.

The two, breathing hard and feeling heavy, three-legged it across the kitchen. Alex stopped. She held him tightly, got a smile ready. No footsteps followed. They got out the front door. She had to fasten his hand with a slap to curl his fingers around the iron rail. They went down, one step at a time. The night air filled their lungs and cleared their heads.

After the thirteenth step, he said, "are they looking?"

The lights were still out. She tapped his shoulder twice for *No*.

"You'll have to put the car in neutral—that's N. Am I talking too loud?"

No.

"The driveway is tilted. You'll just roll out onto the street if you keep the wheel turned. Don't turn on the headlights until we're down the street."

She got him in and left the door partway opened. A light turned on, but it was from the neighbor's place.

Inside the station wagon, she became suddenly frightened by the fact that her feet didn't reach the pedals and the seat wouldn't move if he was sitting on it. She tapped her toes rapidly. There were blankets in the back. With the blankets behind her, she could get her toes to touch the pedals. They rolled backwards—the interior light blaring green. In the street, she turned the ignition.

She dodged parked cars, her shoulders tense and pointing

toward her ears. Fumbling around with her left hand, she got the wiper-blades, then the lights. They closed their doors. The darkness held potential the way light, with all its specificity and all its decisions made, could not.

To get around in Oslo, she rode bikes and, for this reason, when the road curved, she leaned to the side. Reddy rolled down his window with the little switch, and Alex had to stop in the middle of the street to turn off the windshield wipers and adjust the blanket. There was a high school nearby. Ever so slowly, the swishing sound of the tires rolling beneath them, she drove and leaned toward it.

"How do I look?" He flipped down the visor as if to consult a mirror there, brushing his fingers through the short hair that had grown around the scars. He snapped the visor shut. "I want you to take these stitches out. My one eye is fucking blown, but this one? I really think I could see—maybe anyway. I think I see light through the cracks. Know what I mean?"

She didn't answer. Aleksia took a wide turn into the parking lot.

In the dim, yellowish glow of the headlights, rows and rows of white lines lay orderly across the black lot. She pulled Reddy close to her by the collar of his shirt and crawled over him. Beyond the parking spaces, there was a curb, and beyond the curb, a sidewalk and a football field. Beyond the football field, a forest. She put the car in drive for him, and the station wagon lurched.

He already had his foot jammed into the gas. He let off some and mastered it, driving steadily toward the curb, his head tilted back. When he reached the curb at about fifteen miles an hour, he pulled the wheel. Alex grabbed the seatbelt, latched it, and held her body in place with her feet on the dash and her knees locked. The left tires rolled up the curb lip. Then, the right ones too. He sped up. Station wagon parts clanked together like pans dropping from a cabinet. The scene thrust about. The silver metal bleachers. They loomed up, and he spun the wheel, heading across the field toward the goal. She kept the smeared yellow lights just in her view.

When she was five years old, she had surgery on her eyes because they were crossed. The next week, her father came to school and told the instructor that something horrible had happened, that her dog fell through the ice pond in the backyard and drowned. Alex didn't have a dog, or an ice pond, but the story was so sad, she cried anyway. He wrapped her little hand with his and brought her home to sit on the roof, because he didn't want her to miss the solar eclipse. But with her sensitive eyes, the light just burned. She must have told him this because he climbed down the roof and came back with sunglasses, mirrors, a shoebox, and a razorblade for cutting a hole in it. They made a solar eclipse box. That day, they clung to that roof, freezing and cuddling. Eventually, her mother came up with hot chocolate and cookies—which Alex remembered because she had dropped hers—and stayed until the sun came out from behind the darkness and had passed over the house.

Reddy held onto the wheel like a handrail and slowed down.

Fireflies blinked silently in the pine trees. They looked how xylophones sounded. They looked how beignets tasted. She wanted to write this on his chest, but he started driving again and swung the car around, shouting out, "We're going to run away!" They were like faeries, whispering under leaf lanterns.

In the mud, the car slid to a safe stop. They sighed together, the whole world still in one piece and, under the bulbs broadcasting heavenly brightness, she saw in this shadow-less space the way the light bled in through the cracks around the doors, and thought, for a moment, that she did know what he meant.

*

"Aleksia. *Aleksia.*" She woke on her back in her bed with her arms spread apart.

"Yes?"

"Can I open it?" her aunt said, already opening the door. "Hi."

"Please stop calling me Aleksia. It's Alex," she said.

"Okay," she said slowly. She glanced around the room. "Have you seen Mark?"

"Nope."

"It's three o'clock, about time to get out of bed. I made you lunch."

Alex rolled off the bed and put on her robe.

"I could use someone to talk to anyway."

In the kitchen, there was a ham sandwich and a handful of potato chips on a plate for her.

"Stayed up late last night, eh?"

"I took a walk," Alex said. "I borrowed Uncle Mark's keys and took a walk, locked the door behind me. Then, I got to that school and fell asleep."

"Fell *asleep*? How does one fall asleep like that?"

"I don't know. I wasn't feeling well. I woke up drenched."

"You weren't afraid?"

"I'm used to the darkness," she said, which was true.

"I'm just surprised I didn't hear you." Her aunt remained quiet for a moment. "You do that in Oslo?"

"No one stops me."

CHAPTER 3

"I don't know where he went."

"Uncle Mark?"

"I told him to take Reddy's old cellphone if he's going to start going out."

Reddy's cellphone was turned off and stuffed in a shoe in Aleksia's suitcase.

"It would be just like him to not tell me if he got a job." She turned the TV on. Alex never even noticed it in the kitchen. It was tiny and staticky, with a bent-up wire hanger on top of it. "I love this show." Alex finished her sandwich. Her aunt yelled at the TV, "once upon a time!" The man on the show echoed back, "once upon a time?" She gave herself a congratulatory smile. "I got it."

*

Mark set his white Styrofoam cup of coffee into the cup holder under his ashtray, lit a cigarette, pulled out onto Maudlin, and made his way to the highway. Without the sugar or milk, his coffee tasted dry. Already, it had spilled down the side of his hand and stained the cuff of his denim shirt when he got it out of the microwave. It was hot out, and if he used the AC, his car would overheat, so to keep himself from sweating, he kept all four windows down, making the seatbelts flip and flap in the wind.

This morning, he buttoned his shirt all the way to his neck and tucked it into his light blue jeans. He put on a belt too, one that matched his boots. In the dark closet, quietly, so as not to disturb Freya, he groped around, touching hangers and shoes and ties. He needed something else but didn't know what that something else was until his hand landed on it—up there above the winter sweaters—something soft like a Nerf ball. That was exactly what he needed today, his dark blue USS Scamp hat. He pulled it down over the tops of his ears, and when he looked in the mirror, he slid on his big flat nicotine-colored glasses. He hadn't seen that hat in years and didn't know how it ended up there, just above the sweaters. He squinted at the embroidered silver dolphins surrounded by the gold letters on his hat and whispered as he read aloud, "SSN-588." Today, he told himself, he was an attack submarine.

Now, he had spilled some of his coffee on his sleeve—but what a little thing to get one down on a day like this, a day when he had things to accomplish. He didn't even care that the weather changed three times this morning.

He sped sixty miles an hour down a tight little lane next to other people encased in shells doing the same thing. From a distance, Baltimore looked as gray, metallic, and industrial as a motor. Grease and rust, gears and belts, pipes up in the sky letting out exhaust. He was going to fix everything today. An endless white cloud washed out the colors so the place looked like someone tumbled it around with bleach and stones. Despite the city and traffic, he felt inspired and capable. Getting up early and drinking hot, black coffee had a way of making him feel that way.

He pulled off the exit into the depths of the machine and listened to the rattling engine of the VW bug ahead of him. He lit another cigarette. It tasted better than steak. The VW needed the timing checked, Mark thought. If he had a bug like that, he would take better care of it. Hell, he'd do it today. Today. How the hell did he feel today? Chipper. Why? Who knows?

He inspected the cigarette between his fingers and, ready for another puff, halfway between the steering wheel and his mouth, his station wagon leapt forward—tackled by

CHAPTER 3

something. He patted down his pants—he had dropped the cigarette— until it was between his fingers again. There was a honk. He threw his hands over his ears.

Holding the cigarette between his teeth now, Mark grabbed the rearview mirror. He adjusted it and wondered with only the smallest fraction of his brain why he had to adjust it, but the thought vanished at the sight of a red-faced man in a dented red pickup truck behind him, a truck with the words "Dick's Bricks Masonry and Contracts" painted across the hood in green and white letters. What was he supposed to do? The sign read, "NO TURN ON RED." There were no cars passing before them, but there was the bug first of all; he couldn't get past the bug and what—what did they expect him to do? He leaned back, his foot firmly on the brake. The horn cleared its throat and honked, again. Mark pointed at the light.

There was a crunch as the Volvo jumped again. Mark tightened his grip on the wheel. The truck pushed against his bumper. The brakes squealed. The back lifted up. Mark pressed deeper into the brakes, put his bodyweight into it. The tires burned. He broke a sweat. He let off the pedal, freed himself from the truck's bumper, and pulled closer to the bug. The pickup truck reversed. The guy had white knuckles and above them, small empty eyes. He grinned.

Mark hoped to God he wouldn't cry. The truck came right at him. A grown man doesn't cry. It hit him. The stereo system he'd brought crashed to the floor. It wasn't his fault he was a grown man. His glasses flung from his face to the dash. His head knocked into the ceiling.

The VW gently drove through the light. He was only doing the right thing. If you want to get the shit beat out of you, do the right thing. He would never leave again. He wanted to spend his last day ripping doctors' hearts out and bludgeoning them with mallets. But the doctors didn't give Reddy his disorder, he did. He and Freya. When the light turned green, Mark pushed into the gas, turned, got into the far-left lane, reached the speed limit, and remained that way. The truck gained yards on him. The driver lifted his chin, stuck his hand out the window, and raised his fucked-up middle fucking finger. His head lay back as if disconnected from his neck, and his mouth gaped open. Mark couldn't figure out what he was seeing, but then he did; the man was laughing at him.

There was construction a quarter mile down the road.

The next light turned yellow and Mark gunned it. He only had to get to the bank. The truck came up behind him, stuck to his bumper. He's going to push me, he kept thinking, but soon the "he" turned to "they." *They're going to push me.* He put on his blinker, glided into the next lane. The truck followed him. The asshole pulled into his bumper and tapped it. Tears spilled out, ran down Mark's face and over his lips. His coffee ran down his leg. There was a street ahead and a turning lane before it. He sped up, turned. The man kept on the road, slowed down like he might turn, too.

Instead, he kept on going.

Mark used McDonald's napkins to dab the coffee on his pantleg. He remembered how, as a kid, he'd run to the bathroom to cry. Sometimes, he wouldn't make it. Tears flowed along his face before he could get to the door. The way the tears formed, the way his cheeks dimpled like a bubbling pancake, and the way his chin moved as if it wanted to turn inside out, interested him. He liked to watch himself cry. He looked into the rearview mirror, stared into his red and blue watery eyes—the same eyes he had as a kid—and had a moment

CHAPTER 3

with himself.

If he'd had another second to think, he would've slammed the brakes. No, he would've thrown the coffee out the window, then slammed the brakes—and that round head would've been a plate of spaghetti tossed at a windshield. Mark pulled back onto the road and up one light to the bank. The red truck was gone now. When he got out, he checked his bumper. The tailpipe had turned into a snorkel.

Noticing the place empty, he could relax. He leaned against the wall, his back against it, catching his breath. He could feel the tellers staring at him. He slipped a pen from his shirt pocket and wrote on a scrap of paper and got behind the white line until the light at the fourth teller lit up. He didn't want to talk to them. The teller had blonde hair. She and Mark were the only white people in the place. Her mascara clumped together like tar and her face was painted three shades too orange. A flimsy gold-cross necklace hung around her neck and her silver-hoop earrings brushed her shoulders. He set his piece of paper atop the counter and pushed it across with his fingertips. She wore a pink halter top and when she leaned forward, just an inch to look at the note, Mark could see right down it. Her tan stopped, and from there on, she was as white and smooth as an abalone shell.

She scanned his face, then focused behind him.

"That's my account number," he said, hanging his arm at the elbow on the divider between the tellers. He put his finger down on the note and read it aloud. "I need two grand."

"You have an account here."

"That's right. That's the number."

"I'll need your ID."

He gave it to her and watched her bracelets jingle together

as she looked up his information on the computer. He couldn't be sure how much was in there after the monthly payments on the surgery and all the bills they had to pay since he'd lost his job. It was all the skimming-off-the-tops from his paychecks after everything else was paid each month. For six years, he saved with that job delivering car parts, but he'd been spending those scraps for a few months now, just to get by. So, he wasn't sure how much was in there.

The teller brushed her hair behind her pink-tan shoulder, and Mark tilted forward slightly to get another look.

"Mr. Porter."

"Yes," he said. A bit of electricity shot up his legs and into his abdomen. He waited for his money.

Her finger stood up, a spider leg over the mouse.

"You only have one hundred and fifty-nine dollars in this account." She turned to him. "Can I help you withdraw from another account?"

He tucked his chin under. "Oh—no, that's okay. That's fine. I'll take that." She counted out seven twenties and the rest and handed it to him.

When he pushed the door, it clacked against the wall. He tried to catch it and close it slowly, but he could feel them staring and everything was taking too long, so he let go and pulled the second door instead of pushing it like the sign said to do. When he got in his car, he adjusted and readjusted his side mirror. He bit off part of his fingernail, ripped it off the rest of the way, and threw it out the window. Then, he rolled the window up, said, "Fuck it," and twisted the dial of the air conditioner all the way to four, so that the sweaty hair sticking to his forehead turned to beef jerky.

He hated the highways and how crazy and circular and

confusing they were. No one had to make them that way. They did it to make their town look worthwhile from above. All the roads could've been straight. In Wilmer, Alabama, everything was easy and you could walk anywhere you wanted to go anyway. Here, you were right in the middle of everything, and still you had to drive twenty minutes to get anywhere. And everyone was unhappy. They kept it up each day, all the driving twenty minutes to every place that would've taken them a five-minute stroll if they lived in Wilmer, Alabama. And in Alabama, you ran into all the same people again and again. That never happened here. But no one wanted to live in Wilmer, Alabama. They all wanted to live packed in like pieces of trash at the dump, decomposing, stinking everything up.

Nowadays, a person couldn't do anything without being guilty about it, always having to think about who you're buying from and what you're supporting, and in Baltimore, there weren't any choices that Mark could see: Walmart, Target, Best Buy, Home Depot, Office Depot. And all the small businesses got boarded up and guys in big white shirts walked past them, meeting with others on the steps, and walking on in that way that they walk. A few businesses ran it all—told you what to eat and wear. Not like in Wilmer. In Wilmer, the people made the culture, not the businesses. Here, people gave themselves up and held their plates out for the slice of pie being served. Mark didn't want any of it. And all these new generations came into these neighborhoods and didn't know how the working class used to say what happened; the working class decided if a road was built. In Alabama, someone down the street opened a watermelon stand or a grocery store, and everyone shopped there and everyone was happy about it, but everywhere else, the only ones opening stores were foreigners who sent the money back home. Mark wouldn't know the first thing about opening a convenience store, and he was *an American.*

He drove to Virginia once and never told anyone about it. He ended up buying Christmas presents—sheets, towels, Nintendo games, and a *Fight Club* poster for Timothy because he liked anything with Brad Pitt in it—and driving around Potomac Mills Mall afterwards, trying to find his way to I-95, he found the same stores as around White Marsh Mall and, while he liked the familiarity of it, he was disappointed; each time he broke out of his situation, he got more of the same thing.

And, looking up, every time he was in town, he spotted three crazed people at once, two on the sidewalk out the side window and one through the windshield, and they were bony, living dead people carrying nothing around in their hands except Walmart bags of toiletries and cigarettes.

He knew a few roads, the ones he needed to get to the auto parts stores and the ones he needed to get to the hospital, and he didn't plan on learning any more than that.

Mobile's hospital wasn't sophisticated enough to deal with Reddy's condition; that's what a doctor told him. That's why they had to move. They put all the hospitals wherever people were packed in. Every day, cars backed up, one after the next in lines down the highway because someone crashed into someone else's car and killed the person inside it.

It started to rain, so he protected his stereo system with a Member's Only jacket before he brought it into the pawn shop. He stood behind a woman searching for her wedding ring. She wore a shirt the same color as her skin and it shocked him when he walked in. The stereo gained weight as he stood there, and every so often he hopped and pulled it up to rest on his

CHAPTER 3

belt buckle.

The lady in front of him shifted her weight, scratched her shoulder under her bra strap and pointed, saying, "Naw, don't think it's that one neither." She said something else and the men laughed. Mark was sick of being human. Her arms were empty, but she favored her left side in this exaggerated way as if carrying a purse of bricks over her shoulder. She rested her hand on her hip and said, "Nope, not that one neither."

"I think that might be it," she finally said. Mark circled his head upward, catching a chainsaw, a few plaques, weapons, and bikes. Bikes, he could bring in that old bike.

"Can I help who's next?" the man said. Mark stepped up, and the attendant walked off.

"Feel free to put that thing up on the case."

Mark slid his awkward long-fingered hands flat into his back pockets. He reminded himself of the good hat he was wearing today. He pretended to whistle a Johnny Mathis song that he couldn't remember the words to, just the melody, and *pretended* because he'd never learned how to whistle. The man came back.

"What do we have here?"

"Oh!" Mark pulled the jacket off, dusting the top of his system with his stained sleeve.

"Pretty old," the man said. "Does the 8-track work?"

"Uh, yup," Mark said. "And the record player, too. Needs a new needle. Good condition. I could show you. You could plug it in."

"I can give you seven dollars for both."

"It has AM/FM radio."

"I can give you seven dollars."

As Mark pulled away, the clouds above the lot seemed to

part.

The sun lit up the storefronts along the parkway, making them slick with sunshine, and Mark began to feel good again. The stores were situated so that they had their own roads running parallel with the main road, so when Mark remembered about the construction, he decided to cheat and pass everyone by. He passed the parked cars, looking for cops, but feeling lucky and clever today. He slowed at a stop sign and checked out the workers, drilling holes and building a brick wall between the parkway and the business road. Two men holding trowels gesticulated. One flung his hand toward the wall, the other toward a wheelbarrow. Mark let off the brake and saw then, in the loading lane alongside Lucky Larry's Easy Shoppe—a block up—the red truck. The air conditioner blew full blast. He headed for it. From this angle, he could see right in through the front windows of the store where the blister-faced man stood at the cash register, holding three or four hotdogs in one hand, a soda fountain drink in the other, still laughing. Mark put on his hazards, made sure the truck had the green and white Dick's Bricks logo painted across the front.

The fucker had no more important of a place to go than he did, and this was perfect proof of it. He stepped out of the station wagon. A pile of broken bricks sat next to a big black toolbox in the bed of the truck. Mark looked around. The drivers on the parkway couldn't see him because of the new brick wall. He picked up a brick, tossed it at the truck window. It bounced and hit the ground, leaving a white smudge. The man inside set his hotdogs on the counter carefully. Mark picked up another brick. The front door of the store swung open, and the man was coming toward him. Mark wound his

CHAPTER 3

arm up and this time *chucked* it at the window.

It caved like cellophane.

The man came around the front of the truck with his burnt-red fist raised. Mark, in an inspired moment—a second of thought, a bit of courageous doing—grabbed the metal handle of the toolbox.

Unfortunately, he underestimated the weight of it and the tools spilled, and he wasted time freeing his hand from it all.

The man stood over him. Mark scrambled for a wrench, got one, held it over his head backing himself into the passenger's side of his station wagon. His height always made people second-guess him. He slammed the door, scooted overtop the AM/FM/8-track/record player/stereo system, put on his seatbelt, and drove off.

He took a deep breath and found himself laughing and smacking his hands on the wheel to a song in his head.

Seconds later, the truck tagged behind him. Mark knew what it was he had to do. The truck tapped him. Mark turned down a side street completely *pumped*.

The truck kept driving, just like before. Mark's laughter cut out all that darkness in him. He checked his dark blue Scamp hat in the rearview mirror and saw the truck coming back for more, turning down the street. This was life. This was real, real life. He took a deep breath, threw the car in drive, and slammed into the gas. The car jumped and whirred. Then, the bull kicked under him. He let off and he was going fast, real fast. Warehouses blurred on either side of the road. Ditches, grass, and dirt disappeared completely.

The guy was at his back corner. The truck pulled up into his bumper. Up the hill, there was nothing but an orange construction site. He could make it. He could make something happen. The black ghost inside him filled his skin out like a suit. He said, "Fuck fuck fuck fuck," relaxing his grip on the wheel.

He swerved the station wagon into the truck. He smacked it, again.

It sent the truck belly-up into the ditch, with all wheels wanting for land, spinning sibilantly.

Something noxious came out of the A/C vents. Warm air blew out. Looking outside, Mark saw smoke rolling from under the station wagon hood, but he backed up before turning the engine off. He put his hand on his heart, as if he could control how hard it beat. From this angle, the man looked dead, his lips like slugs on the dashboard, and his neck bent in half as if given a hinge in the center.

It occurred to him that he'd seen this man twice in one day, just after thinking about how different Baltimore and Wilmer were.

Mark's father said that children should be seen and not heard. He thought about this now and wondered how he got to that thought, stuck in his station wagon, now with a cigarette burning in his hand and a red truck with a man in it, upside down, probably dead. Reddy's disorder only affected one out of forty-thousand births. He never could really understand what that meant. But it was rare. He could figure that much.

Both of his parents died in the same year, and it showed him something he never wanted to see: he hadn't loved them. He cried, and watched himself in the mirror, but he wasn't crying for them, and he wasn't crying because he'd miss them. He cried because he'd spent his whole life up to then being a good son and, now that they were dead, no one could say how good he was anymore. It was as if his mother and father had been filling him with shovelfuls of sand and each grain became him, the good kid, the son, Mark Porter.

He'd been the youngest of the family, the one his siblings hated, the one his parents babied and the only one who never wanted to leave Wilmer. Then, they died. The sand all spilled out, and when he looked around, he suddenly became responsible for a woman and two young boys. His parents gave him his identity, and when they left, they took it with them. He did everything he was supposed to do. A memory came to him: his father holding onto the seat of his bike, running beside him, his father's feet stomping and stomping, with Mark pedaling and steering, and then his father letting go. Mark, three years old, held the handlebars, horrified, betrayed, and he crashed into a boxelder tree. He didn't go near a bike again for a long time. But, deep down, he believed in the godlike perfection of his parents. One year after they died and a few months before he moved to Maryland, Mark did the same thing to Reddy, and the kid crashed right into the bar ditch.

They moved to Maryland for Reddy. He'd let go of the bike too soon. Looking back, he realized he'd done it on purpose.

*

Nothing frightened Mark more than the law. With an overheated radiator, the only thing he knew for sure was that he needed to hide that dead body. Sitting in his car, not far past the overturned truck, he circled through a series of unachievable plans, like calling the cops, running away from the scene and leaving his car there, walking to a gas station to get water for his radiator, and leaving both cars and the body inside one of them. He sat there, getting the nerve up, and once he convinced himself to get out of the station wagon, he moved quickly, efficiently, as if he might freeze if he didn't get back fast enough.

The man's body had folded in half and his thigh bulged out from the driver-side window. His head looked missing at first, bent at such an angle as if on that hinge. Mark released the upside-down door, having to lift the man's weight when he did it. The truck tilted toward the ditch; the body rolled out sideways; the legs tucked under onto Mark's shoes. Mark zipped up the Member's Only jacket he put on to protect his clothes from the blood and pulled the man under the armpits, further into the ditch. The truck leaned toward them, and Mark knew he couldn't lift this man, not fully, so all he could do was look out onto the road, make sure no one was coming,

CHAPTER 4

and drag the man, with his shoes making two trails through the gravel to the back of the station wagon. Mark let go with one hand to open up the back, but his keys were in the other pocket, so he had to switch hands. Then, unable to get the key ring out, he had to drop the body completely, this thing with a thick stripe of blood down its shirt and around the knees, its neck cut across the back so its head held on like a lid.

He got the door open and inched himself in backwards, yanking, finally pulling the guy in. He covered the body with army blankets.

He could dump it along the beach somewhere. He scratched that idea. There was a gravel lot out behind a shopping center, near the auto parts place where he used to work. He could drive to the center of it, open the back door, then, with his feet on the guy's shoulders, push him out and onto the ground. Then, just drive off.

But the car still wouldn't start. He got out and pushed it, the gravel crunching beneath the weight. He pushed it up a small hill that sloped down for a quarter mile. Then, he could hop in and steer. He wouldn't have killed a man on purpose, he told himself. Something made him do it. He simply wasn't that kind of person. The dark thing inside him, that anger that exposed itself in times of stress, subsided as he rolled to a stop in neutral. He smoked and took off his blood-painted jacket, tucking it under the seat.

But he got one chance at this life, and now he'd fucked it. To think, he spent most of his life trying to avoid this very thing—a permanent mistake—and the one day he goes out and tries to do something right, this happens. When he went through the guy's wallet, he found two hundred bucks and his driver's license. The guy's name was Jared.

When he folded the money, he saw Bart Simpson drawn next to Franklin in red.

Mark bought time, one minute to the next, holding those minutes like miniature babies in the cradle of his palm. The station wagon had finally cooled down enough to drive. He brought Jared to his favorite park. He could hear his own breathing, felt the paperweight of the death holding down the back of his mind. The sun rolled its way down, shining pink and yellow beneath the clouds, and fathers flipped burgers at the grills, while mothers, kids, and dogs kept track of each other. They spent their lives frivolously, unafraid, willing, and in states of constant confidence that every event would open up to an even greater one. The world unlocked for them, and all Mark could see was light around a doorframe.

Dogs barked. Misguided frisbees flew into trees. The smell of the burgers made his stomach fizzle. Everything around him spooled out. His dad once locked him in the downstairs coat closet for four days to think about something he'd done. He'd snatched him by the elbow and spanked him, opened the door and thrust him inside. But Mark was only seven and couldn't remember what he'd done – only that his dad was so tall and angry in his overalls that morning – so he sat on the floor holding his knees in, wearing his sleepshirt and underpants, just listening to his family go on without him. He searched pockets for peanuts, and he peed into a coffee can of skeleton keys.

It's possible he never learned a single lesson from punishment in all his life.

He loved his parents, he told himself, again. He had to say that now that they were dead. They may not have been great, but they were his.

CHAPTER 4

A white van pulled up next to him, and a big man got out with coolers he stacked up in the space between them. The man put up a handmade sign that read, "Fresh Crabs 4 Sale."

Mark got out, coming around the back of the station wagon.

"How much?" Mark said.

"What?"

"I'd like to buy a crab." He thumbed through the wad of bills in his hand.

"They by the pound, not by the crab, man." Then, the guy ripped off the lid of a five-gallon bucket, and inside it, the hand-sized crabs scrambled over each other, nipping air with their pinchers, scratching against the plastic. Mark looked down the road, across the small black lot, and then back at the crabs.

"They're still alive," Mark said.

"That's what makes them fresh," the guy said.

Mark spent fifty bucks on crabs.

He drove to Hyde Park, a green neighborhood with small, spaced-out houses on a peninsula, and parked under a tree with long spindly branches snaking down. Black water lapped against a floating dock. Little points of light skipped along the waves. He pulled the heavy, shifty buckets and coolers from the side of the station wagon, scooting them along the wood slats. He took out a smoke and smoked it. He wanted to start a garden and eat from it. He dumped out the buckets and coolers into the water. The tangerine moon lifted into the sky. When he took the cigarette from his lips, he got the paper wet. He watched each crab break the surface tension and plummet with a sideways tilt of its lightweight shell. And just as he had felt so calm sitting there cross-legged on the rocking dock, he felt just as inspired and instantly full of action. He put his smoke out, got in the car, and drove himself to The Second Awakening Protestant Church.

He slipped in through the back door that had been propped open to cool the kitchen down. Then, he walked in like he belonged there, went to Pastor Mike's office and slid that Simpsons bill right between the desk and the wall just above the trashcan where someone was certain to find it.

With his last bit of energy, he jetted off to Andy's Hardware.

But walking in, the fluorescent lights blaring on everything, men on metal ladders stocking or searching, customers explaining their situations and reading each aisle sign, he saw just before the garden center the refrigerator section, and going past the help desk, he heard a familiar putty voice and knew by the back of the head, the hair glowing orange, that it was Jim from the unemployment office. The inspired feeling rolled over, turned into a crawling anxiety. Mark kept his eyes pointed ahead and made it to the outside fenced-in area of plants, the smell of dirt and fertilizer somehow making him safe. A man in an apron talked to him about what was in season. They loaded up a flat cart and, avoiding the refrigerator section, he rolled it to the checkout line, where Jim was anyway. Mark turned his back, picked up a flashlight keychain. The woman in front of him got out of the way with her purchases and, once Mark moved forward, there was a tug at his sleeve.

"Ah hell, I know you."

Without speaking, Mark lifted a tomato plant onto the counter.

"You live near here?"

"Not really."

The lady held a scanner on a long cord and came around the register to scan the barcodes of all the pots.

CHAPTER 4

"You starting a garden, friend?" Jim said.

"I don't know what I'm doing," said Mark, handing the money to the cashier. He pushed the cart out to the lot and Jim stayed by his side.

"Let me help you with that," Jim said, once they were to the station wagon.

Mark stripped the black Andy's bags from his wrists. "I got it," he said.

Jim picked one up and opened the door.

"I said I got it." Mark pushed him away from the car.

He wiped his chin. "I wouldn't mind."

After some time of watching, Jim said again, "you live around here?"

"No." Mark shoved the plants in, some of them on their sides on top of Jared.

"I do. I live right over there." Jim pointed off to some ambiguous place. Mark threw in his new shovel and slammed the door. "Find yourself a job yet?" Jim said.

Mark didn't answer.

"Listen, I could use a ride."

"I have somewhere I have to be," Mark said.

"Which way you going?" Jim said.

"Home," Mark said.

"But I'm just right over here. Go ahead and give me a ride." His lower lip dropped.

"All right," Mark said. "Get in."

They drove a mile away with Jim talking the whole time about how he'd like to start a garden too, but he lived with his sister, this wild slut who he couldn't stand any longer, and the ground out back behind their brownstone was all dead and full of cigarette butts anyway. He stopped and lifted his nose.

"I hope you don't mind me saying -but you really reek." He squeezed his nose. "You need a shower."

Mark shifted. "Oh, yeah?"

"It's awful," he said. "God awful."

"I didn't realize."

Jim took off his seatbelt. "It's right here," he said. "Listen, I got a job."

Mark didn't say anything.

"Fact is, I got two jobs. I needed the money, so I threw myself off that forklift. So, I work on down by the docks until two each day, and if you're wanting to come on by Monday, I can get you a job working up there. How's that sound? You and me working together?"

Mark said it sounded good.

"Meet me in Canton, then. Nine o'clock. It's called Greene and Greene." Jim closed the door. Mark left, scraping the ass of the Volvo on a speed bump. He turned the radio on and up. Rock music. He didn't listen to rock, not punk rock or that alternative stuff—whatever that meant—but the classic rock; that wasn't bad, especially if it had some country in it. He especially liked the Eagles, Pete Seeger. Mark didn't realize it at first, but in his mind, he was at a bar talking to his new friend, Jim. He didn't actually want music on, just something to refill the air with sound. He kept his stare forward and vacantly imagined himself at a dock, out of place, everybody else knowing what to do. They could work together; that's what Jim had said—you and me. Something was occurring to him now as he pulled into the driveway—not that someone must have driven his car because the dial wasn't set to 102.3 as he had programmed it to, and not that the rearview mirror had to be adjusted this morning (because that wouldn't occur

CHAPTER 4

to him until it was too late), but that he might enjoy having a friend, that, hell, he already had a friend. Yes, he had a friend! His mouth opened in a smile of glee and his hands curled into happy fists on the word "friend." But what exactly did friends do? Suddenly, he was very nervous about Monday, blind-date nervous, job-interview nervous, dead-man-in-the-back-of-the-station-wagon nervous. *That* nervous.

*

Alex and Freya yammered in the kitchen when he came in holding two tomato plants. They looked up from the TV. Freya got out of her seat.

"You're getting my floor dirty!" she cried out, and Mark saw the two hills of soil that snowed around his shoes. "Get out with those! Now, I have to clean!" He had never been so glad to be home. She said a few other things, and he looked at his niece with her blonde hair up in a ponytail, still just a child even at eighteen, and his wife snatching a rag off the stovetop and the small dustpan from under the sink, the way her apron tied in a lazy bow down her backside over her denim skirt. Her brown shoes and navy socks. She turned around, standing up. "Aren't you going to listen to me? What's wrong with you?"

Dirt spilled in lines through his fingertips.

"I'm sorry," he said.

She paused, and something about his mood communicated itself to her. "It's okay. Just bring those outside. I'll clean it up."

In the dark, he loaded most of the plants into the backyard, tension tightening a cord around his neck. He went into their bedroom and closed the door to make it darker. He set his alarm to go off in two hours. He paid attention to certain number combinations. 12:34, for example. Freya came in around one and changed into her pajamas that she kept under her pillow. His hands gnarled. His knees clamped together. He stretched his fingers out. They ached and he hadn't even started digging yet. 1:11 a.m. The last number was 1:23.

When the alarm finally went off, Freya said, *"What's that?"* and dozed back to sleep with a twist of her body under the sheets. He stood in the hallway just outside Reddy's room, pausing. He turned back, squinting as if he'd dropped something by his feet. Then, the memory filled him up, made his heartbeats double.

He put on some boots, adjusted his headlamp, and went out to get his shovel. He knew the sound of the shovel cutting into the earth, with all its rocks and breaking roots, would be loud, but there was no law against nighttime gardening, and with all his plants surrounding him and the body in the car—so far away, around the front of the house—he could dig under the kitchen window and guard himself against suspicion. When he turned on the light in the basement, he heard the sound of nails clacking and scratching against the cement floor. He heard a thunk under the stairs and saw the last bit of a tail whip behind the shelves where he kept his records.

He'd forgotten about the rat poison he was supposed to buy.

After digging next to the oak tree for just a few minutes, he was already tired. His grip on the shovel handle burned. It was as if he expected to back out at any moment, as if he knew he wouldn't really dig a hole and put a body in it, but he reminded himself that, in this matter, he had no choice but to keep digging.

The next-door neighbor's llama, Cria, mwahed. All the time, the neighbor lady let it out, and the second it got into the backyard, it yelled its hollow raspy sound and the tall old black woman with the covered hair screamed, "Cria! What's the matter with you?"

*

At this very moment, as Mark hid from the llama, the body was barreling down the highway toward the Liminal Lounge half an hour away where it would sit for almost three hours unwatched while his niece and son bumbled their way across dance floors, bar stools, and bathroom stalls.

*

She would be home by five.

Downstairs, there were two bars, one running the length of the dancefloor, and the other up front. No one checked her passport at the door. They saw Reddy and seemed to recognize him and waved her in. The only thing she thought about was how good it felt to be her natural, unthinking self, to be in action, to be helping someone. The DJ's booth lit up purple and blue and hung in a box in the right corner. Holding Reddy by the elbow, she moved toward it, stepping along the outer rim of the dancefloor. Boy George played "Do You Really Want to Hurt Me?" and the DJ spliced it with some fusion jazz piece and a techno beat whizzing through it. She left Reddy in the dark space beneath the booth.

Twenty minutes later, she brought him back a beer pitcher, then squatted down, careful not to mess her dress, and drank some of it with him. He let his head rest against the wall. She tapped his shoulders and got up to take his coat off so she could sit on it, and when she did, she put her head on his shoulder. The bass rattled through them. She'd imagined some way they could dance, but it would be sloppy. She drank more beer, tapped his shoulders, and wandered off.

*

Mark sweated over the grave. He had his rhythm now and he could almost forget he was in his body—let his brain go, let the pain go, let the machine keep on digging without him. He felt as though the entire neighborhood could hear him. Shove, jump, scoop, and swing. Again. Shove, jump, scoop, and swing. And down and in to do it again. Into the ground—the sound of metal—and out again. Roots snapping and out, again. Dirt sprinkled into his hair. He shook his head, and down into the digging again. The llama's mwah had calmed to an ogle. Mark stopped and pointed the spotlight coming from his headlamp into the grave. It was wide, but not very deep. This was never going to work. That's what he kept thinking. *But I don't have a choice.* His teeth clamped. *I have to keep going.* Someone had to have seen the pickup truck by now. And seen all the blood. And the gravel trails leading to his tire marks. They would inspect them. He paused to rub his burning callouses. He would be so relieved to see the body tumble in. He took a deep breath and continued. When he was done, he could toss the dirt down and cover everything up, never worry about it again. It would be all gone.

"All gone!" was something Reddy used to say when they'd feed him as a kid. Mark liked this idea that eating something made it disappear. "All gone!" Reddy would lie, having half a sandwich left.

Mark didn't have a choice. He had to keep going. Some things you have choices about; some you don't and, grownups, of which he *was* one (he couldn't help the fact that he still forgot this), understood this about life. His father had always known exactly what to do, how to talk to people, how to control or comfort him. He wondered what his father would think if he were here right now watching him. He looked behind himself at the trunk of the oak tree as if someone were standing there. But it was nothing. He looked, again. No, it was nothing.

He died of cancer. Afterwards, his presence hung around in the corners and behind the doors of their Wilmer house watching, keeping an eye on things, making sure he took good care of his newest grandson. For that year, Mark couldn't undress or make love to his wife without his dad watching from the ceiling corner. When it became too much to deal with anymore, he pushed his father out. He stopped shuddering when he opened or closed a door; and when the air turned cool around him, he refused to react. *I am only a person, Dad*, he would think. Then, he would make love to his wife a little harder.

When the Porters moved to Baltimore, the ghost stayed in the old Porter home. Mark imagined his father imprinted on the fabric of that house the way well-known people and terrifying scenes weave themselves into places—into houses, over highways, across battlefields. Another reel burnt and repeated in that house long after they left it.

Reddy loved to be tossed in the air, and Freya loved to feign fear when her baby sprung above them all out of Mark's hands. That night, Freya, Mark, Timothy, and Reddy sat outside on the porch waiting for another tropical storm to come in. This was one of their favorite things to do, to turn on a battery-powered radio, grab a few drinks, and watch the rain come down. Mark had done this with his family, and his new family carried on the tradition in the same old house. To keep Reddy from falling off the front porch, they blocked off the stairs with a gate. Reddy stumbled around, walking from each one of them, showing off his McDonald's Happy Meal toy he'd gotten from Sunday School. He showed it to Timothy, who, always being such a good boy, humored him.

"That's so cool, Buglet! I've never seen one like it. Go show it to Mom!"

Reddy took his Hamburglar over to his mother, who said it was very nice.

"Go show it to your father, Reddy."

They had thick accents back then and didn't even know it until they moved to Baltimore and put the kids in school. Now, they talked just like everybody else, even Freya. When Reddy came over to Mark, Mark snatched him up.

"Hey, Reddy!" he called, and he jokingly said, "Gimme that! Give it to me!" Reddy's eyes filled up. "You don't want to give it to your old dad?" The waterworks came and he tried to wiggle out of his arms. "Okay, come on, Buglet. Okay," Mark said, and still sitting on the porch swing, he tossed Reddy up into the air. That's all it took to get him to laugh. Reddy's little face paused mid-expression but turned quickly to a smile, a smile Mark loved. Mark caught him, took a swing forward, tossed him up above him again. Freya screamed out and threw her hands over her mouth.

"Stop it, Mark! Stop it!"

"Higher!" Timothy said.

"I can't look." Freya turned her eyes to the wooden floor. She was so beautiful then, her hair so blonde, it was almost white, and her lips as pink as a little girl's toy, and she had dimples, just like Aleksia. Mark tossed him up again and, to make the whole thing more theatrical, he looked forward and rested his arms down for a second. He caught him. It was the fourth time that it didn't work out how he expected. Timothy had yelled, again, "Higher, Dad!"

"You want higher?" Mark stood up.

CHAPTER 4

Timothy jumped from his seat and yelled, "Yeah!" He was eight years old.

Little Reddy laughed until he was out of breath. Mark stood up. He was six-foot-five.

"Ready?" he said, as the rain poured down and lightning flashed across the porch. He geared up for the throw by bending his knees and gripping Reddy under the armpits. He hadn't taken into account the fact that he was taller now, not sitting on the swing. That was the whole problem. He tossed Reddy up. Reddy's scream cut off when his head and neck slammed into the porch ceiling. Mark caught him by the pant leg on the way down, but Reddy flipped forward before Mark could catch him all the way, and his chin knocked into Mark's knee. Mark had him before he could hit the floor. He pulled him up by the leg, then hurriedly set him down on his back. Reddy looked alarmed to see his father there above him. Mark expected him to break into a laugh.

"Is he all right?" Timothy said.

"Of course, he is," Mark said.

"What did you do?!" Freya screamed out. "Mark!"

"Nothing, he's fine," he said.

Then, looking down, Timothy said, "Buglet?"

Reddy didn't move; a little bit of blood spilled from his split lip. Mark put his hand on the front of Reddy's coveralls. His hand covered almost all of him. Then, Reddy's body went into a fit.

"What's he doing, Dad? What's wrong with him? Do something!"

Mark held him down first, then picked him up and held him to his chest.

"What's wrong with him, Dad? Why's he acting like that?"

Thunder cracked across the neighborhood.

"Give me the burglar. Give me the burglar," Mark said, and tried to get it between Reddy's teeth.

"It's one of those—those—it's a—" Freya didn't know the word for it. The word she searched for was "seizure."

"Dad! Why don't you do something?" Timothy kept saying.

And Mark remembered saying, "because I can't!"

*

Four in the morning, and not yet three feet down. He didn't give Reddy his disorder. He was born with it, and the genetic mutation passed down from the Olsen side of the family, not his. That day at the hospital, with the storm taking down powerlines around them, they found out that something was actually wrong with Reddy. Mark had knocked him so hard against the ceiling that a tumor moved into some part of his brain.

Mark reminded himself that if he'd never thrown him, the Porters might've found out too late about his disorder, not that there was much treatment, anyway, just a lot of delicate cutting. Three months later in a Mobile hospital, the doctors took out two tumors from Reddy's neck at the base of his skull.

The hole wasn't finished, and it was getting light out. Mark was going to have to haul the body into the basement. Over near the sliding door, behind the bush, something glowed white in the moonlight. Putting one hand on his knee because his back ached now, he knelt down and touched it. It was rough and spotted and damp. He picked it up and stood. A face towel. Aleksia's small window was just above him. Something about it made him smile. *Kids.* He'd make her pick them up and bleach them, and he would forgive her.

*

CHAPTER 4

Looking up from a cute guy who had been talking to her, it occurred to Alex that she needed to get back to Reddy. The lights of the DJ booth no longer glowed. A rush of fear came over her as she pulled herself through the limbs and strangling parts of people on the dancefloor, toward the corner where he should've been. But, getting there, other than the pitcher and stickiness around it, the space was cleared. She held onto the wall, moving herself toward the restrooms down a hall in back. She went to the men's which had only two guys in it, who didn't look surprised to see her in there. And that's where she found Reddy sitting next to the faucets and under the paper towel holder.

"You found your friend," a guy named Tyler said. He waited for her out by the curb. The other two guys, Randy and Bob, waited at their small, beaten-out aluminum car. White cotton-ball clouds fogged around the yellow lights, making the parking lot green. Alex held Reddy by the elbow. Drunks made it to their cars and, aside from slamming doors, she could only hear her eardrums rattling.

"Where is it you're going?" she asked.

"Not far. Maybe two miles. You're coming, right?"

Aleksia looked at the station wagon. It looked lonely. The one named Bob jabbed the one named Randy in the ribs because he'd fallen asleep standing up, his face down flat on the roof of their beer-can mobile. His head popped up. He had dressed himself like a tennis player, with red sweatbands around his wrists and one around his head, pushing his orange curly hair (the sorbet color of Flintstones push-pops) straight back off his shining forehead so that—even standing there— he looked like a motorcyclist speeding past all of them.

"We ready?" Randy said, and his eyelids flickered independently of one another. Reddy seemed like one of those boxing toys weighted at the bottom, tipping over. Aleksia bent her knees—her heels gritting toward him on the pavement—and clawed at the hem of his shirt until she got a good hold and he bounced back up. Randy said, "everybody in," as he jammed the key into the door panel. He brought the key to his face, then slid it down until it sunk into the keyhole.

Bob, along with Reddy, got the backseat where they had to curl their legs under to fit in. Randy drove and Alex sat on Tyler's lap. Randy said they were going to a secret bar, and they drove so slowly, someone made a joke about having to sneak up on the place. He tried to jam the transmission into third gear but missed. Reddy reached up front around the headrest and touched Tyler's neck. Alex took his inflexible fingers and flung them back. Randy leaned into his bucket seat, pressing his foot into the gas and shoving the shifter into third. The buildings blurred. Alex let go of the dash and swatted Reddy off again.

"He's worried," Tyler said. "He doesn't know where we're going." When he said this, Alex squeezed Tyler's knee between her thighs. This is exactly what she had come to America for and, in this wishy-washy moment, she knew it. Tyler tightened his hands around her pointy hips. "You can have a cigarette. They're on the dash." She took one out of the soft pack and punched in the car lighter.

"You know," she said, "I don't know why people ever kill themselves."

"I do!" said Randy. He stopped the car, bolted from it, and puked against the curb. Tyler moved Alex to his other knee, pushing her into the gear shifter. She wanted a guy who would move her around.

CHAPTER 4

After a moment, Tyler said, "You want to get out too?"

"Sure," she said, "this is what I live for."

The engine kept running, music blared, and the headlights made everything flat as paper. With the guys wrestling and dancing, she felt like she was watching a play at the theater. She lay on the hood, smoking a cigarette and exhaling it to the sky. Tyler seemed to swim up next to her, and they kissed, listening to the sounds of drunks around them, voices that seemed to get closer and louder. She pushed Tyler up.

"What's going on?"

"My friends are stupid," he said, and lay back into her with his tongue, but she pushed him off and sat up.

Randy had his white tennis shirt pulled over his head, his arms sticking out straight and zombie-like. Bob was watching, smirking.

"What are you doing?" Aleksia said.

Randy said, "Where is he?" reaching down toward the tire.

"Warmer." Bob giggled.

Randy pulled Reddy up by the neck of his polo. Reddy turned his head as if he could look for help. He was far taller and thicker than the two of those guys, but pudgy, helpless. Randy pulled him in front of the lights.

"What are you doing?" Alex said, again.

With one hand, Randy held Reddy by the neck. With the other, he made a fist.

"No."

"Come on! Blind boxing. Hey, it's equal," he said and released the spring of his arm and punched Reddy in the face.

"Stop it!" The engine roared. Alex jumped from the hood. "Stop it!" Reddy fell to the ground on his side. "You asshole! He can't defend himself." With her purse, she smacked Randy across the neck.

"You bitch." He snatched her by the hair. He had ahold of her earring now. He had her hair like the legs of a moth. She kept swinging her wings. He was going to pull the earring straight through her earlobe.

Tyler got off the hood. As he did this, the beer-can-car engine revved.

Randy let go. Alex held her damned ear. Then, as the engine purred, he took a moment to throw her against the pavement.

The car's wheels rolled. The boys turned around to see where Randy was looking.

The headlights brightened; smoke came from under the hood.

"Is it moving? Who's in there?" Randy said to no one.

"I didn't see anyone."

"No one," Tyler said. "There's no one in there."

The wheels spun in place. The smell of burnt rubber. The screeching mean sound of it, and then it lurched into action, twisting its way across the parking lot. A group of drunks jumped out of the way. It screeched as it zigzagged—a fiery dragon out of hell.

Then, it crashed itself into a light pole.

As if on a delay, the green streetlight buzzed out and everything went silent.

From the ground, Aleksia lifted her head to see her cousin on the pavement, trying to stand.

Smoke billowed into the lights.

Reddy whimpered. She reached down to his face. "Let's go home."

*

Mark stood in the kitchen fully dressed. His gaze landed

CHAPTER 4

on the meat cleaver wedged partway into the butcher-block table. It was five in the morning. They were still gone. Alex was gone. Jared's body was gone. The place was a mess. He walked to the front door, looked through the window. It began to drizzle. Tired of standing, he knelt to the carpet.

By the time they came in, Mark lay in his La-Z-Boy, passed out in an agitated nightmare of half-sleep.

"Shhhh . . ." he heard, along with the ping of the light switch flip in the kitchen. They creaked across linoleum. She filled a cup of water. Mark lay still. They left the kitchen and went to Reddy's room. Mark opened his eyes but didn't see anything moving. He waited. Five minutes later, Mark rushed to get up. He stood outside the door listening. He could rip her head off right now. He heard Reddy's giggle, that hollow, tongue-swallowing giggle. The knob turned, and Alex came out holding the door close to her body.

"You want to tell me what's going on?" She jumped at his voice, clung to the wall behind her.

"You're up." Makeup rained down her face.

"What'd you think?"

"We made it back," she said breathlessly. "We're okay. We're okay."

"You can't—you can't even know how fucking mad I am right now."

"I think I do. I'm sor—"

"I could almost, I could almost—"

"Freya," she said, out of breath. "Aunt . . ."

"Don't you—go to your room. You're leaving tomorrow."

She hurried down the hall and closed the door with a slam. She cried in gulps he could hear through the walls.

"Be quiet," he said firmly.

"I'm trying," she said. "I can't stop crying," she said, and she went on doing just that. "You don't love me. No one has ever loved me. Only Reddy loves me." Her cries became muffled and she screamed into a pillow, "I hate you!"

Mark left her. The body was still in the car. He got a wheelbarrow, rolled it outside, and wrestled the body out. Then, he wheeled it back into the basement with the tough meat of the legs sticking out. It was too close to morning to bury him now. Giving in to the fact that he would have to touch the body, he pulled and pushed on Jared's fatty shoulders, tucking a tarp around him. He tightened the tarp with packaging tape. He'd made a Jared-burrito. Mark looked around the basement for a good place to put the body. There was a small cave-like area under the stairs where Freya kept wrapping paper and bows and Christmas boxes she planned on reusing. He dug these out, kicking bags and boxes to the side. Once he dragged Jared in and climbed over him to get out, he tossed up all the bows and paper.

They covered the blue burrito.

Mark stuffed his socks under the basement door. The only way to get back to his room was through the front door of the house, and so he went that way.

*

The abandoned station wagon tilted in a parking spot like a shoe fallen from a phone line. Aleksia pulled Reddy into the back with the plants.

His face was bleeding, his body heavy. She toppled onto him, then pushed him to the side where he could spoon the tire well.

"Holy fuck," she whispered, catching her breath. "The plants are leaking." Her knee pressed into and slid off something underneath the blanket, dropping her to the carpet. She caught her balance and reached underneath to feel a forearm, a hand, fingernails.

"Get out, get out, get out, get out," she said and pulled Reddy by the ankles. She strapped him into the front seat by the seatbelt. He wasn't saying anything at all. Then she came around back and peaked under the blanket once more. She half-convinced herself this was her uncle spying on them. It wasn't.

When she got home, she closed and locked the door to her room. She blew her nose. She plotted. She listened to the basement door open and close. Her face sagged. At the slightest sound, she jumped. She had to pee, held it all morning until she heard her aunt and uncle leave. By this time, her clothes and books were packed. The house smelled. She came out of the bathroom seeing Reddy's opened door. His window had also been left open. It was ten-thirty. She looked at him lying there. A green bruise dirtied his cheek. He had two black eyes. He'd gained a lot of weight since she moved in. His cheeks were pudgy. His shirt came up, showing a rounded-out abdomen.

She watched him sleep. Something stapled her toes to the floor. In one thought, she wanted to get his gold sewing scissors and clip the stitches from his eye for him, then leave. In another thought, she wanted to take him with her. She'd thought of this all morning and never came to any conclusion. She lifted her foot and found herself going through his things, putting clothes into a blue bag she found. She couldn't move fast enough. She wasn't sure what she was doing, really. She found his scissors, put those in the bag. She had to get his prescriptions, which were kept in the kitchen. She woke him up. *BE QUIET,* she wrote on his chest. She pulled him up by his arm. He groaned. She got his shoes on. She listened for the Porters. She felt she was doing everything out of order.

She didn't know how she and Reddy would carry so much between them. She got him standing. She handed him his bag, slung it over his shoulder for him. They began walking and she got almost to the door when she remembered the pills. She squeezed his shoulder, opened the door, doing any little thing she could to make it all happen a little faster, but when she got to the kitchen, she couldn't at first find the pills. The smell—which she knew came from the dead man her uncle must have moved to the basement—filled her up. The pills were on the counter.

CHAPTER 5

They got down one step, and then another, and she closed the door, holding him in place, and they got down one more stair, and she wasn't sure where they would go, how they would get anywhere by walking, and then, down the street, pulling around the corner was the station wagon. She let go of Reddy.

The car screeched to a stop at the driveway and her aunt ran out, ran up the stairs, losing a shoe along the way, screaming out, "no, Reddy, no!" Mark came more slowly.

Reddy hugged his mother and the two lumbered back up the steps, Aunt Freya's eyes glaring, mean as ever. Mark slammed the car door shut and Alex dropped Reddy's bags on the little slab of a porch, along with his pills and, without speaking, passed her uncle on the steps and left.

*

The alley streetlight glowed beyond his fence. Mark let his shovel drop as he glanced at his son one last time. He lifted the poor boy's shoulder with his boot toe and rolled him over into the hole. Mark looked in with his headlamp. With a thud, Reddy landed on his side. His son looked petrified like one of those ten-thousand-year-old kids they find curled up in ice.

Mark bent over with his left hand on his knee and mentally reached for the shovel but found his arm didn't move. He could almost see his pale hand in this light moving toward the shovel handle, but his arm hung dead at his side. He rubbed it, swung it with his body, but it only flapped around, wouldn't take action. Something came to get him now and his knees melted, and he was going into the hole with his son, falling onto him, knocking chins and knees, falling through him even, into him, embodying him until he bolted upright in his bed.

In this blur of sleepiness, he squinted out the bedroom door to the lit-up hallway. Something black rushed across. A scurry sound followed it. He pushed the pins and needles in his arm, the pain seeping into his fingertips. The dead body in the basement.

Another black thing rushed past. A whisper brushed his face. He stopped breathing. Freya's bed slid away from him. With his arm tight and limp at his side, he threw his covers off.

When he got to the door, he heard a voice, raspy and cold.

"I can't sleep either," it said. "I'm worried."

He stood stiff. "Can you get me some—" she coughed, "some water?" He didn't turn around. Holding his hand to his heart, he went to the kitchen and filled a cup under the faucet. Freya sat up in bed when he brought it back to her, the cup shaking in his hand.

"Did you hear something?" he said.

She shook her head. "Just Reddy moving around." She drank the whole cup and set it aside.

"I'm all right," he heard himself say, as if she'd asked. "You going back to sleep?"

"I'm worried," she said with a swallow, "about Aleksia."

They tucked themselves back in, a hundred miles apart in their 12 by 12 room, and Mark said, "Let's try to sleep. Okay, honey?"

"Do you smell that?"

"It's nothing," he said.

"If you say so," she said.

He could have told her it was the dead rats in the walls – or that they were in a trash bag or rolled up in a tarp or even that he'd burned them, but he hadn't thought fast enough and too much time passed as he now spun up an explanation so, instead, out of fictitious spite, he said nothing. And, she said nothing.

They lay there together in thick silence until half-an-hour later when Mark smoothly took his covers off and got his legs out of the bed.

He stood, and she stood too, saying, "I might as well just stay up." She looked so small so far away.

The rain started with the sunrise and continued through the Sunday. She made coffee and eggs. Purple moons hung beneath her eyes. She wrote on a piece of loose-leaf paper, "I've lost my voice." As the day wore on, he watched basketball and kept an eye on her. Freya unlocked Reddy's door and fed the boy, and she made them dinner around eight o'clock when a storm came out of nowhere, rumbling and striking lightning around the neighborhood. Rain came down in sheets. The cable went out, and then the electricity. Freya lit candles, and in the spotted darkness, Mark saw shadows moving, scurrying, always scurrying, hunching behind the TV, passing over the treadmill, standing in the doorway.

"Check the breakers," she whispered hoarsely.

Mark got out of his easy chair and went creakily to the basement, fumbling around for the box. He found it, along with a flashlight they kept near it. He fiddled around but nothing happened. His foot knocked into the body. He didn't look down.

"Let's go to bed early," he said when he got back upstairs, reaching out for her hand next to a flat red candle. She blew it out, along with the others, and accepted his suggestion. They walked to the hallway, where he spun her around into him, held her tight against his body.

Her cheek pushed into his chest. She let go of the muscles in her neck and allowed him to cradle her head. A moment passed. He let go, and in their bedroom, he rolled his bed over to hers. They shared covers and fell asleep holding on.

*

Dearest Sophie,

I guess I should tell you right away. Aleksia's left us and didn't say where she ran off to. Mark caught her stealing the car Friday night, or, let me back up. She took Reddy, and if Mamma and Pappa haven't told you, he can't see or hear anymore, has one eye sewn shut to keep in the moisture because he lost control over the little muscle that makes us blink. And so, your little delinquent (I mean that in an endearing way) took Reddy and somehow drove that terrible, half-broken station wagon to a bar or somewhere where they were able to get drunk. Well, she managed to get the two of them home all in one piece, (except Reddy has two black eyes!) but Mark caught her. The next morning, he took me out to eat—this shabby Chinese food place that's open in the mornings—and he tried to convince me to evict your daughter. (As a side note, you might remember that Chinese place. No doubt we took you there. It has those sucking fish that hold onto the side of the tank by their mouths.)

I know it must seem weird that we should go out to eat on a morning like this, but it seemed the gas lines around Baltimore have been breaking. It isn't harmful and it's been in the news a lot lately. I opened all the windows, except in Alex's room (she wants to be called Alex now), since her door was locked, and I couldn't wake her. (She was hungover.) Aside from the smell, it was a nice morning, considering I think it's been raining for a year here, even through the summer.

You know, Sophie, I thought by spring you would've moved back into town, but Pappa says you've met someone. I didn't tell Alex, just in case you're worried. I think she's still upset about Robert's death, even though she never mentioned it with any gravity the whole time

CHAPTER 5

she was here. You and Robert seemed to have the relationship I always wanted with Mark but we're ghosts passing each other in the halls. Anyway, I've told you that and you must be dying to know about Aleksia.

I wanted to give her another chance, Soph. It's just things have been so crazy. I feel like one of those Chinese circus kids holding all those plates up on sticks like bouquets coming out of their hands. Any little move, any divided moment, and it'll all come crashing down so, I have to admit that, at this point I was about ready to let Mark take the lead.

He wanted to kick her out for stealing the car, and I gave a weak little argument and my chair fell over behind me at the restaurant because I got up too fast. And it seemed like my argument worked because he laughed (about the chair), and that put him in a better mood. And it seemed like he and I—after so long being fenced off from each other in these sort of divided mental plots—had come together in our own . . . don't want to say happiness . . . our togetherness.

But as soon as we got home, we found Alex at the top of the stairs. If you remember, we have thirteen concrete stairs which are very steep, and all the time I am almost falling down them with my groceries. But there they were, Aleksia and Reddy. She had her suitcase and some other things I suppose she bought around town or stole from us, and then she had Reddy by the jacket.

I don't think he knew what was happening to him. He looked pitiful. We pulled him inside to safety and she disappeared.

I'm sorry to tell you this way. I thought I'd rather write you directly instead of calling Mamma and Pappa and, I'd call you, except I don't think you have a phone up there in your cabin. Please let me know how you're doing. I think she'll be fine. I don't mean I'm not worried, and if my letter comes off apathetic, I apologize. It's only that things have been so crazy. If you want me to do anything, let me know even though I have to admit, I've already got a lot on my plates.

Mark starts a new job tomorrow. He hasn't told me where he's working yet. I've learned to restrain my suspicion—just because someone doesn't say something, it doesn't mean they're hiding something. He uses words so sparingly; you'd swear he had to pay for them. You know, when Mark and I were young, I thought we had wonderful conversations, but I look back now and see that, all that time, he was just nodding and I had all those conversations with by myself. I lost my voice again. It feels like it's bleeding in my throat when I talk. I think it might be from the gas. I need a hobby. Does Mamma still have all those Dutch quilts? I think quilting might be therapeutic.

My horoscope this week—can you believe I'm so desperate for direction? —said I should take a moment to think. I'm trying to do that. Looking around the kitchen, suddenly I feel like everything is just a scrap of something else, like the way those Existentialists believe—that nothing is connected to anything else, that there is no God at all, just causes and their effects, and that we're the ones pulling meaning out of everything. Know what I mean, Sophie? I don't mind writing this to you because I know it's right up your alley. Like really, we are all sacks of chemicals observing what's around us, just little points of light (the light is the soul, maybe) and—I don't know—light looking at other points of light, and we're all just looking. Now, I can't help but think of Reddy, who can't hear or see, and I wonder what sense will go next. Seems like he's just blinking out of this world, shrinking until he disappears (though he has gained a terrible amount of weight).

But, where was I? The coffeemaker needs to be cleaned. I don't know what to say. Maybe only humans create stories. Maybe stories don't exist. Maybe they just make us feel less alone. Maybe we attach one moment to the next and give the space between these moments meaning, reason, and purpose. Maybe we snip out all the irrelevant parts because they're inconvenient to the story. Like this coffeemaker. I'll completely forget about this coffeemaker.

I'm sewing scraps together. The sun doesn't care who wins a war. It doesn't believe in luck or love. We're just on this rather small planet revolving—what's the word? —elliptically around this enormous sun, with other planets moving so quickly in their lanes doing the same thing. Just think how small we are, Sophie. In some way, the imagination always pulls in on itself, turns inside out realizing how small we are, realizing how nothing nothingness is, only makes me come to the conclusion that we are actually huge, only makes it possible to imagine everything all at once. Infinity, I guess. I've gone off the deep end. I miss you. I'm unraveling.

I've got a lot more to say but since I'm clearly running out of paper, I'll reel it in. I love you with all my heart. Please, please do write back. You know I worry.

Yours Always,

Freya

(P.S. The article you found with this letter is one I've held onto for seven years now. I have never seemed to stop thinking about that poor girl and her poor mind and her poor baby. She lived down the street - fourteen and cute as a button, until this happened anyway.)

TEENAGER KILLS BABY

September 26, 1997. Baltimore. It's no surprise that fourteen-year-old Kaylee Shauna Reynolds lives on Maudlin Avenue between two meth houses and across from former whorehouse owner, Gabby Knight. With the grimness of the street, its naked lawns, boarded windows and its residents' history of illicit behavior, Reynolds and her single mother fit right in.

Monday morning, just after watching cartoons, Reynolds, a slight girl with a shy smile, walked a stroller over the broken sidewalk to Melvin Middle School where she attended her second eighth grade year. In the toy stroller, a real baby.

"We thought it was a plastic doll," says classmate Darren Rhodes who first noticed the girl lifting her Redskins sweatshirt in Earth Science class to breastfeed the infant. "She wouldn't talk to us."

Reynolds's instructor, Carmen Garcia, says the girl had been acting differently, eating less and wearing bigger clothes, but that "it was hard to gauge. They change so quickly over the summers, especially at this age."

Reynolds hid her pregnancy from family, friends and teachers for seven months, eventually giving birth prematurely Sunday night in her room while her mother watched *The Simpsons*. She didn't make a sound.

"She kept it secret. She's so skinny. I don't know how," says her mother Kailah Jean Reynolds who found out five days later when the principal called. "He said, 'We got a problem. Your girl is carrying around a dead baby.'"

On the evening of the child's birth, Kaylee, afraid her mother would kill her and her baby if she were caught, stuffed a sock in the infant's mouth to keep it quiet, accidentally asphyxiating the newborn. For an entire school week, she brought the deceased baby to class. She pretended to feed, coddle and scold it when she believed it to be crying.

"She didn't seem to understand the baby was dead," says Officer Kwon. "[Reynolds] needs a lot of psychological help

CHAPTER 5

and family support."

Dan Stanman, Melvin Middle School Child Psychologist, says this psychological dissociation has been reported repeatedly among teenage mothers. When faced with the traumatic situation, the young mother imagines a better outcome. "This is an extreme case of denial," said Stanman Friday night during the school's emergency parent meeting, "when one lives and acts as if life were exactly how one wishes it would be."

A small memorial was held for "Jane" Reynolds Saturday afternoon on Maudlin Avenue. The young mother, held temporarily for questioning and analysis, could not attend.

—*Baltimore Daily News* staff writer, Carl James.

VIRGO: All things gyrate with electrical impulses, says quantum physicist and aura-analyst Ronald Miller of Scotland. Even the bits of your coffee table, as they appear solid, are in fact made of the tiniest of tiny parts, quarks, and those quirky things never stop moving. Keep this in mind this week. While you organize your paperclips and check off menial tasks (use toilet, wash hands) from your to-do list, your aspects show much of your potential and productivity for the rest of the year relies upon your ability to appear still while your internal life gyrates. So, put this on the top of your list this week, my tidy, efficient Virgo: sit still and reflect. Don't worry. Unlike your living room furniture (I hope), you will eventually spring into action.

—*Zodiac Weekly*

*

The morning after the storm, the power was back on and the clocked blinked 12:00. Mark rushed to his watch on the dresser. Freya, already up, made breakfast in the kitchen but he passed her, not speaking, uncomfortable with the accidental commitment he made the night before by putting his bed next to hers. Outside, the mud puddle lawn slopped over the curb. He drove himself to the warehouse called Greene and Greene in Canton.

When Jim saw him walk up, he tossed a cigarette into a trashcan. He wore a cap and had his foot on a crate. He waved Mark in, and Mark followed the short man into the cool, dusty warehouse feeling awkward, unable to walk straight without touching things, conscious of the workers inspecting him. He already didn't want to be there.

He wanted to get it over with and get home. He wished now he'd spoken to Freya, said something to convince her to stay away from the basement. He looked around. Jim talked and spit, pointing at pallets, waving toward the breakroom, a small blue place with a picnic table and a microwave.

"Need to use the restroom?" Jim said at some point. Mark said he did.

He locked the door behind himself and took a breath, washing his hands with cold water and his wrists, rolling up his sleeves, then his face, and drying off the back of his neck with paper towels. Music turned on outside, and when Mark opened the door, Jim was gone.

He checked both directions, confused now about which way they had come from. Going left, he found the breakroom, felt himself searching for the exit past all these men, and once he found it, out into the sunlight, Jim was there to turn him around by the elbow, leading him back inside. By two o'clock,

CHAPTER 5

Mark had a handle on the forklift. He didn't talk to anyone, just did his job and found a little pleasure in it. This could be his last day of freedom, he kept thinking. The body came into his mind throughout the day. Around three, Jim slapped him with his cap.

"All done," he said. "See? See? Not bad." He grinned up at him, and Mark agreed that it had not been so bad. "We're going on over to the Crab Shack. That's what we do." He looked off. "All right. So, let's go." Jim patted him on the back as he stepped down. "You all right?"

"Oh, yeah," Mark said. "Definitely. Sure. Let's go to the Crab Shack."

It seemed to Mark that Jim understood him better than anyone else on the planet. If he'd never killed that man, he never would have met Jim and he never would have gotten this job. They drank four Michelob. Things happened for a reason, he guessed. Maybe everything was connected to everything else. When he got back home, he felt in control of his life, knowing a paycheck would arrive soon, that all he had to do was get to work, and so long as he kept showing up, he would get paid. He calculated the amount and came to realize he would make $575 a week, which was certainly good enough for him, especially if they offered insurance.

That night, Freya went to bed early and passed out deeply. He got himself down the basement steps, ready to get back into the swing of digging, still buzzed from the alcohol, still optimistic. He kicked aside the boxes, no longer afraid of Freya hearing him, and had to cover his nose and mouth. He pulled the body in the tarp toward the sliding door and left it there while he went out. The rain had washed the dirt back in the hole halfway. He lifted mud into piles. He felt wet himself, soaking wet for some reason. He would just dump Jared in there wearing that tarp. He could get the hole ready, then look around, drag the burrito, dump it in, rush the mud mound with his whole body, just tackle it until it all rolled over onto the corpse. He could pack it down, put all the plants on top of it. He dug, going over his plan, and when he got down into the hole himself, his back and biceps ached, and he rested before beginning again, lifting these shovelfuls over his head, the mud dripping into his hair.

Then, something wiggled at his feet, something alive. He jumped, struck the shovel into the dirt. The movement squirreled around his ankles. He stabbed with the shovel. It stopped with a crack. He shined the light down. Slowly, it began to whip about, again. A rat, soundless, now headless—and tailless—and as bloody and wet looking as a plate of pasta.

It had to be six feet down, he told himself. He was six-foot-five, which meant he still had awhile to go with that decapitated rat around his ankles. He cut into the earth. He pushed it aside. When he heard a door open and close which he thought was Freya, he crawled out. Soaking and muddy, he breathed into his hands, muffling the sound, listening.

"Cria? What's the matter with you?" his neighbor whispered. Mark didn't move. "Where you at?" A light flipped on. Oh my God, Mark thought, dropping his head back, resting his wrists on his hips. The moon, directly above him, was less than full. "Cria? Where'd you go?"

It occurred to him he hadn't seen the llama all night. He could hear the neighbor moving things around, a chair or something across concrete. He got himself into his basement and shut the door. The hard blue burrito laid at his feet. He slid down the glass door and sat, waiting.

CHAPTER 5

He smoked a cigarette and put it out on the basement floor. His neighbor came out four times in two hours. She wouldn't stop. He had no choice but to drag the burrito back to the wall and cover it with all those empty Christmas present bags and boxes of records, empty crates, and blankets. Emotion bled to his face as he wiped his forehead with the back of his hand. He walked back up the stairs and turned the light off.

*

Friday evening, a red '96 Toyota pickup truck found overturned on Road 317, South Baltimore. Jared Klingleman, 47, contractor for Dick's Bricks Masonry and Contracts missing from vehicle. All leads given to Officer Ken Warby.

Late Friday night, Randy Wilson of Washington Blvd arrested and charged with indecent exposure involving minors. Ken Warby.

Saturday morning, four East Baltimore men killed in road rage incident after downtown bar fight. Two suspects arrested. Ken Warby.

Saturday morning, Carol Hindle of Cabbal Drive indicted for illegal captivity of South American llama after offender's call to SPCA reporting its escape. Llama still loose. Ken Warby.

*

Over the next four days, Mark worked hard at Greene and Greene.Each evening he had the intention to bury the body, but something prevented him. One night, there was a barbeque at Jim's place. Another night, he fell asleep in his La-Z-Boy watching *Seinfeld.* By Friday morning, seven days after Jared's death and seven days after the crab emancipation, he was used to the body weighing on his conscience. He felt the same about hiding Jared as he did about replacing the storm windows. Throughout the week, a feather settled inside him and it whispered, "you're going to regret this."

"Hey, want to show you something. Follow me," Jim said. He pushed through a door, and Mark went behind him up a narrow flight of stairs that got darker the higher up they went. At the top, the stairs stopped at a slanted rubber hatch. Jim pointed his head into it and light came through. They emptied out onto the roof, a gray rough rectangle littered with butts and empties, and off to one side, there was the water, and off to the other, the downtown with its buildings and pointy churches and houses with roofs flaking like pastries. "This is my favorite place," he said. The wind picked up. Jim tried to light a smoke and Mark helped him, cupping his hands around the flame. Jim looked off, not talking. The wind and the height made Mark uncomfortable. He waited for Jim, who finally said, "you ever in the Army?"

"Navy," Mark said.

"That's right. I saw your hat." He inhaled his cigarette. "Man, I wish I'd gone. What's it like?" He rubbed his chin. Mark couldn't think of anything. He searched the scenery for memories. He thought of Taiwan.

"You ever meet any women?" Jim said.

"I did," Mark said, pushing his clammy hands into his pockets. "In Taiwan."

"Before you got married?"

"I wasn't married," Mark said, "not yet." He paused, wondering how much Jim wanted to hear.

"I sure do love this place," Jim said.

CHAPTER 5

"One time, the boys brought me to a cathouse," Mark said.

"Yeah?" Jim grinned.

"I went up to the third floor to this room and walked in, and there was this little girl waiting there in the bed for me."

"What'd she wear?"

"Something red and silky, I don't really remember."

"Oh, look!" Jim said, pointing with his cigarette to three cops on horseback. "Friday," he said. "Sorry, go on."

"The boys knew the whorehouse, and I didn't want to go, of course."

"Of course." Jim watched the horses and tried to blow smoke away from Mark, but the wind picked up the little shadow and brought it to him.

"But they set me up with this woman, third floor. She must've been fifteen. I couldn't tell, but she was pretty, and I was just twenty anyway. She didn't really speak any English and I'm sweating in my boots. She smiles from the bed."

"Then what?"

"I got in bed with her."

"All right! Hell, man, that's good. I don't know why I didn't join the fucking Navy. I bet it was the time of your life, wasn't it?"

"I didn't do anything." Mark said, and found himself walking back to the stairs. Jim followed.

"Nothing? You didn't do anything? You weren't even married yet!"

"It started raining." Mark lifted the rubber slab. "Let's go to the bar."

"What—was there a leak in the roof?"

"I don't know. I don't know." Mark stepped down; Jim closed the door.

127

"It's all right," Jim said finally. They stopped before re-entering the warehouse and looked at each other.

"I stayed up all night, staring out her window while she slept."

"It's all right," Jim said again sympathetically. He changed his voice, changed the subject. "Hey, I've been meaning to ask—c'you help me move tomorrow? Saturday? With that station wagon of yours?"

He said sure, that he'd help, and then closed his lips tightly, following Jim to the Crab Shack. He couldn't stop thinking about that Taiwanese girl with her brown legs and dark eyes, the bright makeup. They were children, really, kids. He'd been about Reddy's age. When he couldn't *perform,* she seemed relieved. He sat in a painted wooden chair next to the window where the ceiling met the floor and she sat cross-legged at his shoes, hugging his bare legs. He had the chance to hurt her and didn't. That's what he always told himself – like he deserved a medal for not being as bad as the next guy. The truth? He had the chance to hurt a girl and couldn't.

It was a long time ago. She believed in him. It was a long time ago. Was she even a full real person, anyway?

He didn't know her name anymore, but he missed her. Jim talked about moving the next day, about his landlord and his sister, Tanya, and Mark played scenes in his mind of the girl, wondering who she would be now, wondering if she'd made it out of the cathouse, wondering if she remembered him. After all, it was a long time ago.

*

He showed up outside Jim's place early the next day. A gray-haired man sat on the porch holding a leash. Mark stepped out of the station wagon and up to the porch with his hands in the back pockets.

CHAPTER 5

He said, "Jim around?" and tapped the bottom step with his Velcro shoe.

"Oh, I don't know." The man pointed the leash over his shoulder. "She won't let me in. Got herself locked in there crying."

Mark nodded and, in silence, looked down the street.

"Try it," the man said. "She got her purse stole." He lumbered his way up the three cement steps that were falling away from the patio and rang the bell. No one answered. "Told ya." He rang again, then leaned over the black railing, winding and unwinding that leash around his fist. His lip hung down like Jim's, and he had pink rings around his eyes like he'd sat near a fire too long. He wore sweatpants on his wire-hanger frame, a T-shirt, flip-flops, and Mark couldn't figure out who he was and why he was here.

"Where's Jim at?" Mark said.

"Where's Jim at?" the guy said mocking him.

"Where's Jim at?" Mark said again with more force.

"Their money was stole. You know Jim; you know he keeps cash."

"What happened?"

"Someone stole Tanya's purse—I think before she's going to deposit the cash this morning."

"From the house?"

"Can you believe it? She got all the way to the bank before she realized. Came back, it's gone. I wasn't here yet." He pointed toward the lawn with the leash, and Jim was crossing it carrying a twelve-pack of Miller Light.

"Mark," he said and, "Hey, Olin." Olin cracked his back. Jim handed Mark a beer.

"She won't let me in," Olin said. "I just want her to take care of Caleb a day or two."

"This is my pops," Jim said to Mark. He swished away a fly in his face. "She'll watch him." He walked off around the side of the rowhouse to see if he could get in around back. Mark heard the dog bark. Steel patios jutted out along the fronts of each small two-level brick house down the row. Because they were built on a hill, just like the row across the street, each patio took a step down from the last. Jim's place had three stairs going up to it, and a short white sidewalk cut straight through the dirt yard, which sloped down to the road.

"That your Volvo," Olin said. Before Mark could answer, the front door cracked, and Jim was back.

"Come on in," he said. Tanya sat in a sofa chair with a quilt over her shoulders. Her long hair parted down the center was dry but looked wet. She said hi to Mark, taking a swig of her 22-ounce Colt 45.

"You still mad?" Olin said. She pressed her black eyebrows flat. There were boxes and objects all over the floor, surrounding her with a cheap oval coffee table, a brown leather chair, and a blue and white checkered couch off to the side. Mark held his hips. He wondered how they would fit all this in his car.

"We have to be out in an hour or we're in trouble," Jim said, looking at Mark. Then, he was talking to his sister. "I hope you're done pouting now."

"What're they going to do, Jim?" she said, but didn't look at him. Mark was there in body but, in his mind, he was calculating whether, if Freya were to discover the body, she would call the cops, or never say a thing about it.

"You wanna stay with me you gotta watch Caleb," their dad said, and Mark watched all this like he might watch a puddle evaporate.

"I told you not to keep that dog," she said.

Jim gave Mark a little smile and got back into the conversation. Mark picked up a lamp, wound the cord around its base.

"I just want to know why you were bitchy to me," Olin said.

Tanya sighed and slapped both her fists into the armchair. She snagged the beer off the floor and downed it.

It was a bright day, made especially noticeable by the darkness of Jim's place. He left the lamp near the curb and went back in to retrieve a box called "Jim's boots." He didn't like to be around arguments, but couldn't help but listen to Jim say, "Stay with Dad," and watch as both Olin and Jim wiped their chins at the same time. Mark took a fan out to the curb. It was lighter than he expected. When he came back in this time, Olin was stood up, winding that leash around his fist. Mark hurried out with a box.

He heard him say, "Because she's a woman," with an emphasis on "she's."

Mark finished bringing all the boxes outside to the station wagon. He was so tired. He rested his hands on his knees, stepping up those last three steps one more time. He had a sudden desire to go swimming, to be sucked under cool water. He could hear arguing inside, something smashing, Jim's sister screaming. Bumps against the wall. Jim stumbled out.

"Damn it." He held the side of his face. "That's fine, then," he said to Mark. "She's going to stay with my dad, and I'm staying at the motel. Sorry, Mark, we'll have to divide all that stuff up, going separate ways now." Mark sat down, sighing, feeling the sweat run in cool tickles under his shirt. "We're leaving the rest of the stuff, the couch and all that."

Tanya came out with the dog in her arms, and the four of them—including the dog, minus Olin who took the bus—got into the front seat of the station wagon. By four o'clock that evening, Mark had divided their things and left Tanya at her father's place with all her stuff. Jim got back in the car. Mark smoked a cigarette.

"I want to take you out for a beer, Mark."

"That's all right. I just want to know where we're taking the rest of this stuff."

"Listen, Mark."

"Huh?"

"Listen, turn the engine off. Want a beer?" Mark didn't want one. "God, Mark. Tell you the truth, I couldn't stand her any longer. Just couldn't live with her again. Know what I'm saying? So I can listen to her and her boyfriend all night? No, thank you. Hey," he paused, obviously drunk. His slippery lips rolled into each other. "Let me take you out for a drink."

"Just tell me where you want this stuff," Mark said.

"That's the thing," Jim sat up. "Seeing as I got you the job and all, and you need the money, probably. I was thinking maybe I could—" He stopped. "You could—"

"Hey," Mark said.

"Yeah?"

"We're friends now," Mark said. He'd just realized that today they'd had a real experience together. "Stay at my place," Mark said. "It won't be any problem. We have an extra room now."

"You have an extra room?"

"It's a nice room."

"Really?" Jim said, and Mark thought Jim's eyes were watering up.

"Sure." Mark turned on the car and pulled out of the

driveway. "We'd love to have you."

*

Freya said she would not keep her voice down. She shattered a water glass. He had never seen her so mad about anything, and he couldn't help but see this as a premonition of future violence in this household. She held her hand to her chest, as she did often these days, ever since the laryngitis.

Freya's argument was that Aleksia might come back. Mark's argument was that he didn't *want* Aleksia back. Freya said it was a harsh world out there and that Aleksia might be in danger. Mark said the farther away Alex got from Baltimore, the safer she would be. Freya said, then why are *we* here? And he said, you know why.

He brought beer in from the kitchen to drink with Jim while they watched TV.

"Sorry about the smell," Mark said.

"Yeah, what is that?"

"We got dead rats in the walls," Mark told him.

"That happened at our place, too. They eat the poison and look for a good place to die."

Around eleven, Mark said, "We don't usually stay up so late," because he felt bad about Freya's position.

"I'm drunk anyway," Jim said holding his beer up. "Goodnight." He walked crookedly toward his new room.

Freya was asleep already. Mark was ruining this relationship. They were nearing their end and he hadn't seen it coming. He laced his boots extra tightly and adjusted the Velcro strap of his headlamp. He'd been blind for a long time. How mad she had been! How loud, how unlike her! Even with no voice! Now, he was downstairs moving boxes aside. He'd been a disappointing husband. He disappointed her, he kept telling himself. This wasn't the life she wanted to live. The sliding door slid open easily. He yanked the burrito by the packaging tape onto the bit of concrete outside the door.

He stood up, breathing hard, looking around. Jim had gone to sleep. Things were changing in the lives of the Porters. He yanked the burrito closer. They'd never brought a stranger in, and now that he'd added this element, the scales were tipped. Freya was angry. He pulled the body parallel to the hole and, just like in his dream, rolled it into the grave. He continued standing a moment under the oak tree, detached from his surroundings. The batteries of his headlamp died down. Now, he looked at the enormous dirt mound, his heart hurting in his chest, considering the permanent disaster he might have brought onto his relationship by bringing Jim into Freya's territory and not caring about the feelings she had for her niece. He hunched down lethargically, not ready to get dirty, but then the basement light turned on and he heard Freya call his name. Her slippered feet were at the top of the stairs.

He rammed the hill, pushed it forward, fell into the grave with it, and jumped out.

"Mark?" She squinted, held her hand to her chest. He threw his headlamp to the side, tackled the mound again—dirt against the side of his face, his boots digging sideways against the ground. He stood. She was at the door. "Mark?"

He clapped the dirt from his hands and slapped his chest.

"What are you doing?"

"Gardening, Freya. Gardening."

"But why?"

He shook dirt out of his hair and glanced down to see how well the hole had filled in. "I don't know," he said. It was only about a quarter full.

CHAPTER 5

"I just wanted to say . . ." She pulled her robe tighter around her. "I just wanted to say," and here she subdued a cough, "it's all right if Jim stays. I know we can't choose everything in life. I'm sorry I got mad."

"Are you coming to bed . . . soon?" she said with a swallow. She looked confusedly at the hole.

"I'll be right up."

She smiled. When she went up the stairs, he thought he noticed a little lift in her step. He pushed more dirt around with the shovel point and stepped into the grave to put some weight into the dirt. It was strange to think he would never see that blue tarp again. He stamped the dirt down. He stamped it down hard.

*

Dearest Sophie,

I'm glad to hear about your garden and those wonderful statues you've been making in Robert's memory. I do not think you have to concern yourself with Aleksia taking her own life. She didn't seem depressed to me, only angry and disappointed by the way we live here. Baltimore, you might guess, is not quite the America she expected.

I've allowed myself to continue with the mundane. I cried for days after Alex left, blowing my nose. The two of us had such good talks together, and now I have no one to tell the things churning in my mind. Then, yesterday, I had to say to myself, "Freya, you must get on with reality." I never did file a missing person's report with the police. Guessing from your letter, you wouldn't have wanted me to anyway, and that's good because Mark is so terribly terrified by anyone in uniform. I expected her to be right back at our place in a day or two. Mark's so bitter about her leaving before we had a chance to kick her out that he won't let me say her name. On that note, my laryngitis is worse than ever. My throat burns down into my lungs, and it was torture to say goodnight across that gulf between our beds.

Lately, we've had trouble with rats, too. Mark found one in the basement and he's been hearing them all the time lately, and once he said it, I realized I'd been hearing it, too. He put some rat poison down there. He says they've died inside the walls. I don't know how people get them out.

I still pray. Do you? You never cared for Pappa's religion like I did. You never bought into all this sacrificing yourself for Jesus. I always thought Pappa had a very American way of looking at God, as something to fear, when all I ever wanted to do was love Him. But I can't shake that fear of that scary God, the one putting all the Olsens in hell for killing themselves off. What I want to know is, do smokers go to hell, too, for dying of lung cancer? And overeaters, of obesity? Aren't these all forms of self-murder, even if they're slow ways of doing the same thing?

Speaking of hell, how is this man of yours you call Dante? If Mark were to die or leave me, I can't even imagine how I could adapt to another man. You've always been so . . . adaptable. It seems to me, when two people stay together, they form a single unit. They form to each other. I am formed to Mark as he is to me, and if I were to leave him, I would walk crookedly, missing such a big part, missing my leg, and it would take another twenty years just to fill back out into my original shape. If I even contain my own shape anymore.

It's taken me two entire TV shows to compose this short letter.

I'm lost in thought on this idea of leaving Mark—not that I would do it. Of course, I can't do it—with Reddy in his condition, and Mark would be so terribly lonely. I don't think he even knows how to cook or work the coffeemaker. You see, I have made myself

CHAPTER 5

irreplaceable.

And yet, I can't help but think about it, how nice a second life could be—if it were possible. I'm only dreaming. I am still so sorry about your Robert's sudden death. I know you've never stopped mourning him. Neither have I. But I must say that I admire this life of yours up in that cabin (and yes, your neighbors do seem like fine people) on the shore with your new lover (lover, a word I don't think I've ever used!). But, even in my slight jealousy, I know it is all under quite different circumstances than if it were me up there, burying bulbs and drinking wine on little sailboats. I understand, it is one thing to have been left a widow and quite another to leave your husband out of boredom. There, I said it. I'm bored.

Well, the carpet needs vacuuming, the bills need paying, and the gutter-cleaning crew is supposed to be here already. The back ones need to be replaced completely, and I hope these young boys have tall enough ladders because we have never bought much in the way of tools—except a wheelbarrow, and I don't even know why in hell we have that thing. Lately, Mark spends all his days at work and out with his new friends. In a way, I'm glad to have time to myself to do ordinary things.

I forgot to tell you; Reddy missed Alex so much after she left that he tried several times to get out of his room, at all times of the day. He seemed to know how to get around, how to get to the door, and for this reason, Mark and I had to lock him in at night. Mark took the latch off the fence outside and screwed it right to the doorframe. You see how much they loved each other?

All my best, sweetie. I'll let you know if we hear anything about Aleksia. There really isn't any more news, except to say that I miss you (but that isn't really news, now, is it?).

Yours,

Freya

STITCHES

*

Much time passed with little change. She took a walk to the convenience store to get their cash turned into money orders. Mr. Johansen, the landlord, needed the rent paid on the last Friday of the month, and for the past thirteen years, the Porters did this, even if the last Friday fell six days before the last day of the month. Circling back toward the house, she stopped at the fence of a basketball court to watch a group of black teenagers, sweaty and intense, as they slapped, darted with short sneaker squeaks, reaching up high on one side to drop the ball through the metal net. The bounce of it dribbling echoed fat oblong sounds off the court. A cool wind smacked against the fence and the boys stopped their game to gather up piles of extra clothing. Freya noticed the ball had rolled toward her. When a young man chased after it, she thought of Reddy. She wanted to tell this boy she had a son who played on this same court when he was their age, but the player didn't look up at her. He turned away with his ball and tossed it to someone, and the game began again.

    Mark was walking up the street. Dirt streaked his knees. He centered in, walked faster toward her, carrying nothing in his hands.

"There you are," he said.

"What's wrong?"

"I was looking for you. Come on." They walked together in a hurried pace. "The pizza boy's here and you've got all the money."

"Oh." They reached the little car at the curb of their house. The long-legged blonde boy wore his Dominoes hat to the side like one of those rappers, but when he got out and spoke, he had a middle-American accent.

"How you folks doing?" he said. Freya fumbled with the money. After the exchange, the boy zipped out of the driveway.

"Is he new?" she asked.

"He always comes," Mark said.

"He looked a little like Reddy, don't you think?"

Freya pulled junk mail and Alaskan cruise brochures from the mailbox. Mark said he had a surprise for her, a reason to celebrate.

"Follow me," he said. Inside, he set the pizza on the kitchen table. They had the house to themselves today because Jim was working his other job. "Look out the window, Freya." He pointed to just below the kitchen. "Can you believe it?" She opened the pizza box.

"What."

"Tomatoes. We've got tomatoes. I did it myself."

"It's too late to have tomatoes."

"It's not. Come late fall, I'll have squash, too."

Mark followed her into Reddy's room.

"I feel like a million bucks." He lit a cigarette, blew out the smoke. "Let's order ourselves some Chinese food."

She moved toward the bed and motioned toward Reddy

with the fork. "You want to help me out?"

"I'll just order the food."

He came back a few minutes later, pausing slightly at the door before he went to the window and raised the blinds. "We won't have to buy tomatoes for the rest of the year," he said calmly. "I can can them. That's what I used to do for Mr. Johnson." Freya looked at his back. "When I worked for him." He stood there for a long time in silence. Something had come over him. She folded up the messy paper plate when Reddy turned his face to the side. "Did I ever tell you about the journal they used to keep?" he said. "I was about sixteen, and his wife used to make us sandwiches for lunch and she showed it to me."

Freya listened.

"One notebook, that's all, Bible-sized, with every date in it on a skinny line, and next to each date was something like—" He picked up something on the dresser. "'Put peanut seeds in ground' or 'bought seed from somebody.' And every year, for thirty years, on the same date—May 4th—it said, 'Mabel died today.' Then, nothing else. And Mrs. Johnson wanted to entrust me with this journal—to keep up the records. I said I would. I carried it around for a long time, or maybe it was a month. I was young, but I was waiting for May 4th so I could write it in. I couldn't wait to write it in! Write about this woman Mabel I never knew, this lady that was part of their family and not mine."

But then, Mark said, one day he had been walking to work when he realized he didn't have it in his jacket pocket. He cut across a peanut field back to his house. He looked in his room. His mother hadn't seen it. He pushed her into the stove. It wasn't under the bed, nor in the closet. He retraced his steps.

He got to the spot where he started. The yellow house was far across the green and brown striped land. He turned back down the road.

"I walked for hours, down flat dirt roads, through backyards, just crying," he told her. "That one line," he said, "pulled the whole damned book together. That book and that land stitched four stories together. You know what I'm saying? Like it stitched them from underneath." He tried to gesture this movement, but Freya couldn't decipher it. "You gotta figure, being from the same family like that, they all looked alike. And here they were, just one coming out of the other like Russian dolls. 'Mabel died. May 4th.' Hey," he turned around, "I'm thinking after all this, we should move back to Alabama," he said.

"You're good at telling a story when you really try, you know that?" she said.

His eyes flashed at the wall beyond her. "Hand me your flip-flop." She handed it to him. He stepped onto the bed. Reddy's body leaned toward his foot. "Or wherever you want to move to. I don't care anymore. Mississippi's nice."

"How?" she said. He slapped a beetle on the wall.

"Got him." He showed her the bottom of the flip-flop - the small thing compacted like a car.

"Why are you acting crazy? We can't leave.Not with Reddy."

He smacked the flip-flop on the window ledge.

"I mean, we could leave *after* Reddy."

He flicked the beetle off the rubber soul into the yard and handed it back to her. Then, he sat down on the edge of the bed, leaning over with his elbows pushed into his thighs. He covered his face with his hands. With a new breath, he got up. "I've always been this way, Freya, and I don't know what to do."

"Like what? Like what, though?"

"I don't know. I've always just been kind of—"

"What."

"Wrong."

Freya didn't look at him over her sesame chicken dinner.

"Come on. I didn't mean it," he said. She opened the glossy Alaskan cruise pamphlets. "Come on."

"Which part?" she said. Whales, icebergs, and fishing boats swam around the text. "Which part didn't you mean?"

"Whichever part bothered you."

"You know I've never liked it here," she said with a turn of the page.

"I know."

She relented and they talked about the enormous prices for one-week excursions, talked about how they might come up with money. They pretended. She opened the window and placed herself next to it, searching the air for her favorite sounds—the sounds of mothers calling their children home for dinner. Having finally heard it from across the neighborhood, she got up and cracked open a beer.

*

Reddy didn't know how long he'd been locked in that room. When his mother came in to feed him, the door stayed open. Alex left the day she tried to take him with her, and since then he didn't know what to do with himself. Sometimes, he got out of bed to stretch, but he couldn't stand the pain in his muscles. He'd lost the flexibility and often fell over. He could tell his mother was coming by the thumping on the floor. She walked with quick, even thump-thumps. His dad's thumps were heavy and strong. Alex always walked so lightly, he never knew she was coming until she was there. And sometimes he couldn't tell who was walking. It seemed like a mix of his mom and dad. It must be both of them walking at the same time.

He smelled cigarette smoke and the fresh, broken-leaf scent of early autumn. He waited for the draft to settle, which meant his mother had left. Lately, every time he tried to get out—through the door, or once out the window—she stopped him. He had this idea that he could get out the window and drop to the ground outside.

The draft settled.

As he sat up, the fat he'd gained rolled in on itself. He'd been thinking about his tumors growing like deer populations—the more room they were given, the bigger they got. They expanded, filled the forests throughout his body, biting off tree leaves, multiplying as they pleased. The rise in population, a steady climb at first, curved up until it straightened into a deadly line. Critical mass. The forest had no more to give. They'd taken it all. Everything dies.

On his knees, he went to his dresser drawers, pouring his hands over objects he'd touched a thousand times now: the cool nubby ashtray he rubbed with his thumb; the tea candles; the finger footballs; the basketball trophy; the bendable rubber promotional key chains with the slightly raised logos; the mini stapler; the compass with its point and pencil; batteries he zapped his tongue on; his Pleasure Card the size of a baseball card, only thinner, more flimsy. Other drawers were full of clothes and linens. He liked to imagine green.His hands accepted all of these things, were ready for them before quite touching them, formed to them once held.

This was his new sight and, the feeling, mixed with the autumnal smells, fizzled in his chest, giving him an erection, the blood pumping and filling and, just as he reached into his sweatpants to release this pressure, he felt the quick even thumps and the sudden draft of his mother.

He jumped to standing and knocked his head into something metal and sharp. He hunched, holding his crotch. Now, there was a stomping on the floor. She grabbed his chin. He bent down further, his body tingling. He touched where his head hurt. His mother held his arms and tried to guide him to his bed but used too much force, and he knocked his shin into the frame and fell into it instead.

Rubbing his fingers together and touching his tongue to them, he realized he was bleeding, realized it tasted a lot like the battery tasted. He had gashed his forehead. She left and came back. His father came in. His mom dabbed his cut with a wet napkin. The cut was just above his opened eye, and trying to lift his eyebrow, he felt how deep the cut went. More stitches, he thought.

But no one brought him to the hospital. His mother bandaged it and gave him an ice pack to hold against it. After he slept a few hours, he woke remembering his magnifying glass collection and found it under his bed. He set his Pleasure Card atop the dresser, and with one hand, held the glass just above it. His body remembered it all, the wooden handle, the angle at which he stood, and posed this way, matching up with some former version of himself, he could almost see the girl in her department store panties.

Much later, maybe a day later, he sat up in bed messing with the tape of the bandage. Tremors in his bed, a draft, the smell of bubble gum and beer, thumps too complicated to couple off. He waited for poking and prodding of some kind. He tucked the sheet in around his legs. It wasn't until he made a move to get out of bed that someone scuttled around him too quickly, as if they were going to drop something, then put their hands on his shoulders and pressed him back into the bed. It seemed like they were dropping things.

"Mom?" he tried to say but didn't know how his voice came out. He felt like an animal, a bug maybe, lacking the vocal cords and the control of the sounds. The thumping stopped. It picked up again. He knew by the smell, this was a woman, and she wrapped her hand loosely around his bicep. He thought they were moving him somewhere, to a hospital -finally- to stay for the rest of his life. They packed his things. They were doctors, maybe. "Mom?" Now, he held her arm, too. She massaged him, patted his head, and got off the bed. The scurrying stopped and started again. He got off the left side of his bed with his hands out. Someone grabbed his arm. There was something in his hand. He didn't know what. He kicked. The person let go. Reddy set up to kick again, but when he did, he rammed his toes into bike spokes.

His hand went up to grab the handlebars, but in their place was the seat and the seat was rolling away.

He waved his hand through the air. They were taking his things.

The dresser was gone. The computer wasn't on the floor. The lamps weren't either. He needed all of his things. What if he wanted to go bike riding? He stood with his feet apart, his toes still throbbing, swishing his hands through the air.

But then again, he realized slowly, it was nice being able to move around.

The people left and he got himself to the window, stepping over objects that weren't there.

They took everything.

Everything but him.

CHAPTER 6

And his mother brought clothes for him to change into. As the never-ending night wore on, he expanded, filling himself out to all the corners of the room, fearing, and at the same time accepting, his own critical mass.

*

Mark and Jim got drunk on the roof of Greene and Greene next to a cool blue sunset. They slouched together against the door hatch to avoid the wind and smoked a lot of cigarettes. Jim talked about his other job and Mark couldn't think of much to say. The two leaned their heads back and looked up at the sky, swigging from their 22-ounce beers. Then, Jim got a phone call.

"It's for you," Jim said, and handed the little silver phone over.

"Mark," Freya said. "Can you hear me?"

"Yes," he said, plugging his other ear.

"Reddy's gone."

"What?" He looked to Jim, who was looking back at him.

"He left. He got out," she said.

"How?"

"I don't know. Come home. Please, come home right now."

He handed the phone back to Jim, not knowing how to turn it off, and told him he had an emergency. He had to leave.

Mark sped home. He found himself swerving and braking too quickly. Freya sat at the top of the stairs crying. She went back in when he got out of the car.

He rushed through the door with his keys in hand, and Freya sprang from the recliner, the plastic cordless phone hitting the carpet.

"Did you take Reddy's cellphone?" she said.

"Take his cellphone?"

"I searched everywhere. During our sale. And today. He must have it. Where is he?" Her forehead loomed over the rest of her face like a boulder ready to fall. He noticed the thinness of his own biceps as he held them. She snatched the phone off the floor. "Officer Kwon said he still hadn't shown up, and they searched for—" she looked at her wrist, "seven hours. They wouldn't have searched at all, except for his condition. Why didn't you tell me where you worked? I called Jim several times and he didn't answer."

"I don't know," Mark said.

"You make me pry. I don't like asking so many questions." Waving the phone around, her voice grew in pitch and volume. She screamed about how she always told him everything, so that he didn't have to ask. "I tell you so much and look at what I get. Look at you standing there. Look."

Mark tightened his grip on his biceps. The room swam around him.

"I was with the police all day."

"I know," he said, dizzily. She had cleaned the place. "Didn't you lock his door?" he asked.

"Of course, I did! I don't know. I woke up and he was gone—and you were gone. There was nothing I could do."

He dropped his arms. "You left the door unlocked?"

"I didn't. I didn't," she said, but she looked unsure. He bunched up the keys in his hand, and the haziness of the room quit. He suddenly could see his wife there with clarity, as if she'd been submerged in a bathtub and now all the water had gone down the drain.

"Let's go find him," he said.

"We can't leave. They might call and—and I don't HAVE a CELLPHONE."

CHAPTER 6

He apologized. He reasoned with her. "If the cops find him, they'll hold him. We'll stop back in. Or, I could go by myself."

"I'll go," she said. "I'll go with you. I've been stuck in this house all day."

They got in the car and drove slowly around the neighborhood.

Every so often, Freya said, "I just don't know. We won't know until we find out."

Mark agreed and wove through the streets and down alleys behind the brownstones. It began to drizzle. He remembered his father pushing his mother's casket on a cart down the blue carpeted church aisle toward the pastor. Little girls in black dresses sang next to the yellow piano. It must have been incredible for him to know, for once, he filled a spot no one else could fill. He had a place in the world. He loved her, and because he loved her, he earned the right to push the casket.

The Porters stared lamely out their windows.

"Every once in a while, I'm afraid I'm like that girl," Freya said, "the one with the dead baby, and that maybe Reddy's been dead all this time and we haven't known it. You ever think that? If it could happen to that girl, then couldn't it happen to us?"

"He's not dead," Mark said.

"I know."

"There's two of us," he assured her. "One of us would know."

That night, they couldn't sleep. Freya lit a candle she kept on her dresser next to her porcelain brushes. It was like a night before surgery.

"He may just come home," she said.

"Maybe," Mark said.

"I just keep thinking that."

"Someone could find him and bring him back," he said.

"He might've needed some air. We should've taken him out more."

"It's stuffy in that room," he said.

"I want to go home," she said.

*

Mark closed up another photo album and stacked it atop the others. He saw Reddy at every age and, occasionally, remembered he should be looking for a recent picture.

"You find him?" Jim said, coming in. He'd come home early to help.

"Nope."

"He's got to be nearby. You check the backyard?" He took a beer from the fridge and opened it.

Mark said he had, but he hadn't, so he got up and went around back, half-expecting to see Reddy sitting there with a tarp draped over his shoulders. When he came back in, Freya was at the table with Jim.

"Look at these," she said. She spread out a bunch of 8x10 photos. "I found them in Alex's room."

"Jim's room," Mark said.

"Look."

They were black and white pictures of Reddy.

"What was she thinking?" Freya said. "What the fuck was she doing with him?" In some shots, Reddy was naked in the bathtub, smiling. In one, he had bubbles on top of his head. In others, there were direct shots of his tumors, and then in others, of his stitches. Some had him lying in bed asleep with a pizza box on his lap, his head to the side as if he were dead. "Oh my God," Freya kept saying. "Oh my God. I can't look."

But Mark wanted to see them.

"She's sick. Isn't she sick? Something's wrong with that girl. Something's wrong with all of us." She stacked them up and put them back in a folder. "Here," she said. "Use this picture." She handed him a photo of Reddy taken three years ago. In it, he wore a patient's gown. Mark cut off the bottom of it. Now, it was just Reddy smiling. He taped it to a piece of white paper and wrote across the top of the flier, "MISSING." Underneath, he wrote in his best handwriting, "Reddy Porter, last seen September 3rd. He is both blind and deaf. Please bring him to a police station if you find him." Then, he put down their address and phone number.

"I sure hope you find him," Jim said. "Do you remember that guy a few months back they were searching for?"

"No," Mark said.

"I knew the guy. Single dad. Okay, I didn't know him personally, but he came to my work all the time to pick up supplies. Hit and run. And then the guy's missing. We put up posters at work. I could put up a poster there if you want."

"They ever find him?" Mark stood up, a quiver running through him.

"Found his truck, but never did find him." Jim swigged from his beer.

Freya said, "What if they don't find Reddy? What if, Mark?"

At The Copy Shop, Mark copied the flier a hundred times and bought two maps of Baltimore, one that kept the city all in one piece with a street index on the back; and the other, a flipbook, neighborhood by neighborhood. Looking at the flipbook, he felt as though he were about to climb into a mine, one of those with a hole so small only an oval of light could come through just under the opening, and any second, that opening could close and swallow him up. The map trembled in his fingers. He would be wary of new gardens. He would check the ports. He pushed his glasses up the bridge of his nose and folded up the map.

*

Stepping down the blue hallway, and passing Reddy's room, Freya caught the sounds of a whimper and a whisper and so stopped. Holding the collar of her nightgown, she gently pressed the door open. A body under the striped comforter moved. She let go of the nightgown and rushed in, turning the shoulder of the body.

Emma's green eyes dilated.

"His favorite smell is vanilla," she said. She wore Reddy's old baseball jersey and his white cap. Her straight hair was blue. For a moment, Freya could say nothing as Emma held her hand to her cheek. "His favorite book is *The Death of Ivan Ilyich*. He loves snow. So much. And he hated, hated baseball."

"How'd you get in here?" Freya tried to say gently. Emma nodded toward the window.

"We've been doing it since we were nine."

"But how?"

"Shimmy up the pole, get on the metal awning and then climb over with your fingertips. It's easier now that I'm taller." She sat up and used a pinch of the jersey to wipe her eyes.

"Obviously, you heard," Freya said, taking a seat on the bed. Emma nodded.

"I looked everywhere. All our secret places. The Cave of No Redemption, Punk Palace, Tom's Diner, the hidden cemetery in the mall parking lot." She shook her head. "After two days, I realized I wasn't looking for him," she whispered, "I was looking for a sign. So, I came here."

"He went blind after his last surgery."

CHAPTER 6

Emma's eyes went big.

"You already knew he was losing his hearing." Freya shrugged. "The doctor said it was temporary. For all we know, he regained his sight and walked out. Some of his clothes are gone, so that gives me hope, but we also had a yard sale," she said looking around the room, "so I don't know if those clothes were sold or what."

"He went blind? Like blind-blind?"

"Yes, blind-blind."

"Poor Reddy," she said softly. "The worst things happen to him."

Freya glanced across the bed to the floor at something green.

"Is that your luggage?"

Emma nodded.

"How did you possibly get that in?"

"We have a pulley system."

"Oh, Emma," she said and pulled her body to her own. "Let me make you some tea."

"Can I stay? Until we find him?"

Emma never seemed to stay with her family.

"Let's get up and talk about it." Freya tapped her on the leg and Emma, like a child, uncovered herself, and stepped off the bed, as if there were no other way to exit a bed than to stand right on top of it and hop off.

"Remember when he almost went regional with his V-sit-and-reach?" Emma half-laughed as Freya pulled the kettle off the stove. "He was so upset."

Freya poured the hot water into the cups and brought them to the table.

"You have always been his most loyal friend."

"He's my best friend," she said. "In the whole world."

Freya needed this pleasant conversation but, with half a cup of hot tea in her system, Emma changed moods and started the questions. So, *where's Timothy? Where's all Reddy's stuff? Who's Aleksia? Did she put in a Missing Person's Report? What did the cops say? Did they comb the river? Did they call the hospitals? Doesn't Timothy have a right to know? Where's Aleksia now? Are his clothes all here? Are his pills gone?*

Freya picked up the empty teacups and washed them in the sink.

"I'm really overwhelming sometimes. I'm sorry," Emma said. She had the ball cap on backwards now. "I always do that to people. I'm too much *me* all the time."

"I didn't call Tim because," she found herself pausing, "he can't help from San Francisco—"

"Sure, he can!" Emma interrupted. "And, he has a right to know, you know?" She stopped. "I'm sorry."

After a moment, Freya said, "I can't take another person treating me like I'm incompetent. I'm not incompetent, I'm poor."

The two were quiet.

"I'm sorry," Freya whispered. She leaned forward against the counter looking into the sink.

"You're not incompetent. Look, no one thinks that." Emma was at her side, touching her arm. "You're not incompetent. I don't think that, and Timothy doesn't think that. He loves you."

"You know why Tim left, don't you?"

"Yeah, I get it."

"I never cared who he loved."

"I know. I know. It's okay."

"It was God who cared. Not me. He knew how I felt, and he

left anyway."

"I'm sure he had to work some things out."

"Thank you," she said. Her mind went blank.

"It's okay," Emma said. "It's okay. We'll find him. Or he'll come home. Reddy hates being far away."

"That's true." Freya led them back toward the table. "Thank you. Now, tell me about you."

Emma started to wring her hands. "I have a girlfriend now. She works with animals. Vegan, and everything. I work at the mall selling coffee at the bookstore."

"That's nice."

"If it's okay," Emma said quickly, "I don't really like talking about myself."

"Emma," Freya said. "You can stay."

Around three, Freya woke from a nap on her back in bed with the blankets at her ankles and her nightgown tangled across her chest, pulling at the threads of a dream. Just moments before, she had been -what was that feeling? Happy. True happiness, and sixteen years old. Staring into the room as if into the ocean, she held hands and ran through a field with a girl her age. They wore dresses and fell into the grass. This wasn't a dream. This was a memory. They placed blue cornflowers on their eyes and breasts and navels. It was *that* memory, she thought, that one. When Freya remembered this one in particular, she didn't believe any words were ever spoken. Words were too sloppy to contain the slippery, and words were too short and mean to hold the fire that burned between their mouths. Instead of words for that time in the field, she held it as truth that a girl could make her heart beat in her teeth and in her chin, and that she had -during that time- abandoned herself, as if one could inhale touch, as if one could feed on hard candies and rose water alone.

Maybe, as they ran across the field, they giggled the way in movies girls giggle while running across fields in dresses, as if all a girl could do with the world was laugh at it.

The images came back like a stack of photos thrown in the air, but the images were strongly vignetted; she may have been creating fiction: the girl married off young to a sailor in another country. No, that was her own story. She couldn't approach the memory without it fleeing. She turned her head toward the window. The girl fell to her knees, helpless and pink in Freya's arms. Trembling, Freya told her she could no longer meet her, could no longer touch her, yet, as she said it, she pulled the girl's hair from her face and kissed her leaking eyelids. She'd been born to be with a man, Freya told her. The girl vomited into the grass and forbade them from ever seeing or talking to one another, again, with or without the field. "Don't dare," she had said on her hands and knees, or something to that effect, "ever put my name in your mouth, again."

It felt unfair that she should think about this girl she *admired*; Reddy wasn't in his room. Her husband was out looking for him. Reddy disappeared. Anything could have happened to him.

Freya adjusted her nightgown and aimed to let go of this red-hot thing crawling from the tissues of her breasts. She found a pair of metal scissors atop the old sewing table. She leveled them with her ear. The sound of the blade, a violent mating call, a scream across the ethers. Her white hair fell in lengths. *I've always felt,* she thought, *like a human trapped inside a woman's body.* She snipped, cut, chopped. Perhaps, since that girl, she had never had a day of passion in her whole life. And now she had a bob with bangs running jagged across her pink-tan forehead. She twisted the loose hair together, tied it in a knot and put it in the pocket of a red and gold brocade pillow her mother had given her. In the mirror, again, she stopped and sat on the bed, legs spread, hands on her knees.

All these years, she'd held that girl in the warmest, most secret section of her heart. No one knew.No one would ever know. Keeping the girl secret, kept her *hers*. The world could take everything, Freya's money, Freya's self-respect, Freya's dignity, but it could never take *her*.

*

A black bird skimmed along the white sky overhead and down the center of Maple Street as if on a current. When it landed in a flash atop a chain-link fence, Mark let his elbows and hat catch the shock. Until this meeting, he thunked his boots heavily through the rain in his drenched red and gray Alabama Crimson Tide sweater, sloshing in three-pointed sidewalk puddles, observing himself, always observing himself—though it exhausted him, but he couldn't stop if he tried—through the eyes of the rowhouse windows. He'd been at this for hours, but the bird paused him mid-worry. A spirit existed in there, however mean, encased by feathers and meat. He remembered the weight of a crow in his hand. He pelted them with BBs back then, out in the woods with a skip over a log and a twist around a branch. When he caught more than one, he tied them together by the ankles in a necklace of birds and brought them home (not far because his adventures stayed in the yard) to his father. Blue-black feathers were pulled out in handfuls at the yellow oilcloth tablecloth and flipped in the wind across the grass, landing sometimes straight as needles in a pincushion or flags in the moon. He hovered at his dad's belt buckle while, above him, tiny breasts wrapped in squares of foil were gently set on the grill. They were cut into miniature steaks, round and brown; he served them to the twelve green army men posing and sometimes falling along the picnic table.

The crow lifted a wing and looked under it. With a shake and a shrug, it made off, leaving Mark to traipse along the sidewalk alone.

This was his new job—finding Reddy. Considering the circumstances, Mr. Greene at the warehouse let him work half-days. His thumb stuck through the center of his tape dispenser. He pulled a piece off, stuck it to the top of a flier, and pressed it against a glass door. Then, like every other time, he spun around, descended the steps, and climbed to the next rowhouse.

He took a break for his peanut-butter sandwich with the coffee he kept burning hot in his thermos. He felt compelled to keep working today. Glancing back at what he'd accomplished, he crossed the busy street to another blunt row of houses poking through the mist. Yellow and hot pink posters clung to the bricks of a CVS and the Street Church windows and every electrical post and bench on the other side of the street, even taped to the back of No Parking signs. This morning, his socks had gotten wet in a puddle. He'd worked every day for four days. He bit off a piece of tape, slid it across the flier with his fingernail, and pressed it to the door. In the middle of his flier, Reddy's photograph looked back at him.

He took five steps, pulled out his staple gun. With his fingers spread wide apart, he held it to a wooden post and shot it through and through.

The sun dipped beneath the clouds, and now a guy stepped away from a stone wall and into the sidewalk to say, "I just want to talk to you," making gestures from inside his pockets so his jacket moved around.

Mark didn't want to talk but, not seeing a way around this guy without touching him, he said, "Talk then. What do you want from me?"

And the guy said back, "I just want to talk to you a second." *What do you want from me?* Mark kept thinking. Mark led with his shoulder, pushing past him. The guy followed until, Mark figured, they reached the end of his territory where he presumably drifted back to his post.

A black line checked off every neighborhood surrounding him on the map, and so it was time to get on the bus. He'd never felt like a somebody, only a sack full of colored feelings lined with skin and given structure by bones like two poles spread with fabric between them. But nothing else. A woman sat next to him with a child. Feelings dragged out with the tide and swam back. Preferences changed on a whim. He used to like classic rock. He didn't know what he liked anymore. *What do you want from me?* Couldn't that guy see? Mark lived small, as small as a person could live. Mark held his elbows and pulled his knees in like a box broken down for recycling. Mark said sorry for making you look at him. Mark said sorry if he talked too quietly. Mark said sorry if he spoke at all. Mark lived with less presence than a crow on a fence. So, what did they want from him?

But now in four days stretched out across a map, people noticed. They asked about his son with such concern in their high-pitched careful voices, he thought maybe he was a *somebody*, a somebody who didn't ask to be a somebody—not out of humility but uncertainty—a somebody that maybe could take up space, who had his own square to stand on, a square that could support his weight from underneath; a somebody who could point his shoulder in the direction he wanted; a somebody who deserved to walk the sidewalk. The convenience store cashier called him by name today. The librarians softly clamped a stack of soggy fliers in their sober hands and tacked one to a corkboard before he even finished stuttering through his explanation. He took the form of a somebody and now—as if they molded his image from the outside by the pure act of their eyes touching his—he could pop four staples in a flier so fast it sounded like an AK-47 going off. He could fold up a map and call it a day. He could sleep at night.

"You should come home tonight," Mark said. "I'm going to be on the news."

"No shit," Jim said, unplugging his seatbelt.

"It'll be on at five, and then again at eleven."

Jim said he wouldn't miss it for anything, and Mark dropped him off at his new job.

Earlier that day, Mark walked into a crowd at The Copy Shop. It seemed like everyone there wanted to touch a poor sinner as he stepped up the aisle from the back door. The frenzy included a camera crew and a woman with a mic in the center of it. A five-foot-high cardboard replica of Reddy's face stood by the restrooms, and Mark's heart ballooned against his lungs and his arms steadied him, hovering away from his body, as if at any moment, long lost friends might jump out from an aisle to scream "Surprise!" and serve him cake.

CHAPTER 6

He didn't remember breathing, just some concept of talking and the way the owner, Fred, pulled him into the eye by the elbow, saying, "These people want to help you, Mark."

The lady with the stiff hair asked some questions, and then Fred gave Mark five hundred fliers for free, and before he knew it, like a shot in the hospital, it was over. But now, Jim hadn't come back, and all he could do was think about something Fred said as he pushed Mark from the media gyroscope and out the door: *Don't worry. We'll dig him up somewhere!* And how it had occurred to Mark, crying into his box of fliers, that everyone knew Reddy was dead but him.

"It'll be on again at eleven," Mark said to Freya now. "Maybe we should tape it."

"You sold the VHS player," she said. He pointed his toes outward, looked between his feet. She was right. "Where's Emma? It's late." Freya said she was closing the store tonight. He turned his head to her. "I don't know why you did that to your pretty hair," he said.

"You thought my hair was pretty? You never said."

"Sure, I did."

"I'm sure you didn't."

At eleven, they watched it again and Jim missed it and the first thing he said when he sauntered in at midnight was, "did I miss it?" Freya made a gesture like she was going to bed.

"What's wrong?" Jim said, when he saw that Mark had trouble looking at him. "I was out with Sandy—you know her? From the Crab Shack? Anyway, the important thing is they find Red." He motioned toward the TV set with his hat and Mark shut it off with the remote. Jim put his hat back on like he was getting up.

"You think he's dead?" Mark said.

"What?"

"What do you think? You'd tell me, right? If you thought someone—or something even—killed him?"

"I—" Jim stood up. "How the hell should I know? What if—" He lowered his voice. "What if Freya heard you talk like that? She cries every night. I can hear her."

"I know that. Of course, I know that."

"Sorry. I know you know that. Who knows? It's like Freya says all the time. 'We won't know until you find out.'"

"I'm not going to take that job." When Mark dropped Jim off in the afternoon, it was at Dick's Bricks. Jim said they were hiring. Mark squinted at the logo on the building and said slowly, "Dick's Bricks," like he'd never heard of it.

"No one said you had to take it," he said with a little bite to his words. Then, he went toward the kitchen. "Want a beer?"

Mark said he did. When Jim came back with two opened Budweisers, Mark said, "Can I tell you something?" He sat at the other end of the couch and rested his elbows on his knees with the bottle hanging down between them. "If I told you something, you'd listen?"

"You can tell me anything. We're friends."

"Damn," Mark said to himself. "I can't do it. It just doesn't feel right." He drank as much as he could drink in one long swill which was about half of it.

"What does it have to do with?"

"Something I was thinking about."

"Does it have to do with work?"

"Sort of."

"Come on. What's it about?"

"I'm telling you it's something on my mind. Something that's been there most of the day."

"Something bothering you, Mark?" Now, Jim had his elbows on his knees and his beer between his legs, too. "I've really liked living here." He rubbed the saliva from his chin and looked up with his droopy, pasty eyes.

"That has nothing to do with it."

"I know I don't always come home on time. In fact, I often don't come home at all." He pushed his heel with his boot. "I don't know what's wrong with me. All this—" He carried his boots to the front door. "It doesn't mean I don't appreciate it, though."

"Well, I'm glad."

"I really do." He smiled a wet, pink smile. "I could really live here, you know. It's like home. I don't have anything against you. No reason to leave unless . . ."

"I feel the same way," Mark said, waving Jim's concerns from the air. "You've been a real good friend. I'm embarrassed to say it, but it's true."

"Don't be embarrassed," Jim said with the roll of his eyes. Mark finished off his beer and got two more from the fridge. "I know, and I'm thinking if I'm not home from now on by a decent hour, then I just won't come home at all. I don't want to wake you. I'll just wait outside until I know you're up, if I have to."

"It's all right, man. It's really all right."

Jim looked relieved. "I'll do whatever." Mark didn't know what to say. They'd gotten off the track he'd set for them. The two drank like buddies and finished their beers in silence while Mark put together exactly how he wanted to say what he had to say. He pulled out his record player and put on something to kill the silence. Ever since he'd seen the sign for Dick's Bricks, something had been eating at his heart like ants on cheese. He got a record from the basement, brought it up, put it on.

"Hey, I like that record," Jim said.

"Jim, I have something to ask you."

"What's that?"

"I have something to ask you . . . now." Jefferson Starship started playing. "What would you say is the worst thing you ever done?"

"The worst thing?"

"Out of all the things in your life."

Jim laughed.

"I'm serious."

Jim got serious. "All right. All right, I got it." They huddled near the speakers. "You got something to tell me, is it?"

"I do."

"Whatever it is, it can't be that bad."

"I don't know." Mark said, pulling his fingers from the sockets to pop them. "I don't know."

"Remember that day you helped me move?"

"Yeah," Mark whispered.

"And my sister lost that money?"

"Going to the bank."

"Yeah." Jim's chest inflated. "You see?"

Mark looked at him.

"What I'm saying is—I took it." He showed his gums. "I know it was my sister. But she was, you know what she was." Mark gave him a rolling nod. "So, I'm done. What about you?"

CHAPTER 6

"Me?" He couldn't think of anything. Jim's dumb eyes opened like clamshells. Mark was sinking into them. The music played. He thought he heard Freya up, but he didn't. Now, he had on those blinders horses wear so they see in only one direction—and that was toward Jim—and if he wanted to see anything else, he'd have to break something. "The worst thing I ever done," he said, "is a lot worse than that."

"Really? What is it?" Jim's trap hung open. Mark slapped a hand on Jim's knee. "Let's have a smoke."

Downstairs, Jim offered that it was a nice night. "Cold, though."

Mark made a sound like *humph* and nodded wholeheartedly. He might have said that it's usually colder in September, but what he was thinking was that he was just a man who was willingly taking one step closer and then another toward a fiery pit.

"I killed someone."

"What?"

"I killed someone."

"Holy shit."

"I know. And I buried him over there."

"Over there?" Jim's eyes turned gray. "Holy shit." He rubbed his hands together and breathed into them. "You killed someone."

"Yes." Mark didn't feel cold at all. He heavily followed all the movements: Jim stuffing his lighter into the back pocket of his jeans, his cheeks puffing out. He kept looking between his hands and the place Mark said the person was buried, so Mark did, too.

"When'd you do it?"

"A while ago."

"Who was he? What happened? Jesus."

"The thing is—" Mark let his eyes off him. "It was a, you know, it's not like I . . . I didn't mean to, but he just—he was just, you know, when I found him so I . . ." He pointed with his lit cigarette, and Jim looked again to where the body was buried.

"You killed someone. Holy shit."

"Now, I *might've* killed him," Mark said conspiratorially. "I shouldn't have said I killed him. I'm not entirely sure. It was an accident." He pointed with his smoke. "I can tell you that much, and that he was, you know, he wasn't *alive* anymore when I found him, but maybe I did it. Damn it, I don't know."

"You don't know?" Jim pressed his palms into his eye sockets and sniffled loudly, getting himself together. "Does Freya know about . . . about what happened? I mean . . ."

Mark shook his head, "Uh-uh."

"Tell you the truth," and here Jim looked down between his shoes as a tear landed on the lit-up cement, "I wish you hadn't told me. I like you, and now you put me in a real awkward situation." He waved toward the mound. "Why would you do that? I just don't know what to think. I don't understand."

Mark stood there like he was stuck.

"Awful situation," Jim said. "Just awful."

They stood quietly.

"Jim." Mark said. "Jim, hey," and he tried to laugh.

"How can you do that?"

"Do what?"

"Laugh. Laugh, when . . ."

"Because I'm kidding, Jim."

"You're joking?"

"I'm joking."

CHAPTER 6

"You're joking." Jim looked out to the mound. "But," he said, and he shook his head, "you seemed so, so serious, so . . . like you said you wanted to tell me something, and now we're here and you tell me this, and people don't kid about that, Mark, and now you're saying you're joking? Just like that? You looked like you were afraid, Mark."

"I'm not afraid—what's there to be afraid of?"

Jim seemed to think about this.

"You were there when I bought the plants, remember? It's just a garden. I was kidding you."

"I don't know. You really made me believe you."

"I wanted to—I don't know."

Jim sighed. Mark tried again.

"When I gave you that ride, did I seem like a guy who just," and here, he got quiet again, "murdered someone?"

He seemed to think about this, too. Jim walked toward the mound.

"Jim? Come on."

Jim's eyes went skittish like a spectator at a stock car race. "I got a lot on my mind right now." He lifted his foot and put his cigarette out on the sole of his shoe. "I missed your news show. Sandy and I had to talk. I said I was sorry."

"No," Mark said. "You didn't say you were sorry."

Jim's eyes stopped. "I'm sorry, then."

Mark nodded.

"I can take a joke." Jim looked down at the dirt and foliage. "If it's a joke," he said, "let's dig it up."

"That's ridiculous. There's nothing to dig."

"Then it doesn't matter," Jim said. He saw something on the patio. It was the shovel.

"Jim, come on."

167

"If he's in here, your wife needs to know."

"No."

"I can't just stand by—"

Mark whispered, "Reddy's not in there. Not Reddy. Somebody else." And then, louder, he said, "Jim, my tomatoes."

Mark grabbed the handle and pulled on it. They froze in the dark. In their silence, an upstairs window screeched and slammed. Mark leaned in.

"How long do you think it would take you to dig to the bottom?"

Jim let go of the shovel and marched into the house.

*

She locked the window and the door. She had a knife on her. She pulled it out, pressed the button to the switchblade. Then, she closed it and pressed it, again and again. Click-snap-click. Click-snap-click. With it in her fist, she swung through the air, practicing a stab. When it came out weak, the knife clipped back into her pocket. Someone walked by, closed a door. Someone else was still creaking around the hallway.

"Emma?" Reddy's dad was on the other side of the door."Emma, are you in there?" he whispered. The doorknob clicked from side to side. She held the wall, her fingers on the pages Reddy stuck there, her left hand on the knife. More creaks as he walked away. It would be self-defense, she told herself, but could she do it, she needed to know. She backed away from the door. The knob clicked, again, and then she heard the soft sound of the rough metal hatch lock sliding to lock her in.

She bumped into the wall. She unlocked the window, pulled her suitcase toward her, and threw it out over the grave and, holding onto the weak pulley system, made the jump. Her ankle exploded in her sock. She hobbled toward the suitcase. The light in the basement turned on. With the sprain, she booked it toward the gate, slamming it open. The sliding door slid behind her. She fled down the alley with motion sensor lights revealing her path yard by yard. Ahead, a mattress stood against a fence. She waited. Tears blurred her view. There was nothing louder than her own breath. She saw the gate door slowly close.

Because she was left-handed, and had to keep her hand on the blade, she called her girlfriend with her right hand.

Her girlfriend answered.

"What's wrong?"

Emma tried to talk.

"Babe, what's wrong?"

"Reddy."

"What? Where are you?"

"In an alley. Reddy."

"Did they find him?"

"He's," and here she broke down, "He's dead."

"I'm sorry, Emma. I'm so sorry."

"He's dead. He's dead. He was my best friend."

"I know. I know."

Emma bit her lip and tried to think. "Listen.Listen, I need you to come here and pick me up and follow me home."

"Anything," her girlfriend said. "Anything."

"My car is parked in front of their house."

*

She lit a match and slowly moved it across the table, over two plates of omelets.

"Ouch!" Reddy sibilated, pulling his hand back. Aleksia lit her cigarette. "Something bit me," he said in a whisper. Buddy Holly played "Peggy Sue" from the jukebox on their table. Reddy found his fork and napkin. Aleksia handed him the catsup and helped him squeeze it on his eggs. "Thank you," he said beneath the music. The waitresses in their powder-blue dress uniforms and tags that had embossed names like Crystal, Stefanie, and Nicki bustled back and forth across the tiles, pouring coffee and wiping down tables. Aleksia pointed the burning cherry toward her wrist, watching her cousin eat. Just as it singed, Reddy's plastic cup tossed itself into the aisle, sending water and ice cubes slipping across the checkered floor.

He paused, then continued eating while a hurried waitress mopped it up without his knowing. Aleksia put out her cigarette, staring out to her car, but really looking inside her brain for ideas of what was to come.

CHAPTER 7

Sept. 12th, 2004

Dear Mamma,

I hope you like this postcard. It's sort of a joke. Virginia at Night. I took Reddy from Aunt and Uncle. If you really love me, you won't tell. They had him locked in his room when I found him. They only fed him pizza. I couldn't stand the thought of another person dying.

I miss you. I miss Pappa, too. Don't worry, I know what I'm doing and we're having a good time.

Sorry.
I mean it—
Don't be mad,
Aleksia

*

Her knees squeezed his hips as she leaned toward the bedside table. Then, her hand was on his face and metal tapped his cheek. He held his breath, bracing against the first snip at his eyelashes and a tug on his lid. When he flinched, she stopped and told him again to hold still by writing the letters on his chest.

This position, this action, drove him wild—the loving violence of it. He rested his hands on her thighs, his breath picking up, wanting to move her down, almost incapable of stopping himself. She unthreaded. His eye burned like fuck. She snipped the last stitch.

His eyelid pulled up. Light came in as if from under a door. Alex sat back and now Reddy was only interested in himself—the burn, the light. She grabbed his cheek, massaging it. He adjusted to the white-yellow light, propping himself higher against the headboard. He reached his hand into the blind silence for her face and thought now he could see it. But he could only pad his fingers along the L of her jaw.

He tried to say, "Light."

She tapped his shoulder for "yes." She bounced around on him. He held her biceps laughing. Then, she got off him, leaving her hand on his chest. When he tickled her wrist, she yanked it away—disappeared somewhere in the room.

All night—he expected it was night—he experimented with the light, trying to use his face muscles to close his eyelid, which was about as easy as puppeteering a marionette in another room, or writing upside down and backwards, or picking up a car with his tongue. He lived somewhere near his body, but not within it. With all his strength, he could not control his eyelid. He told Alex this. They taped it shut with an X.

The following day, Alex had gotten him into her stolen car—a Chrysler, she'd said, although she spelled it wrong—and started driving. So silent, so dark, like traveling with his head stuffed inside a black pillow that was stuffed inside another blacker pillow, that was stuffed inside an even bigger blacker pillow, but the environment translated itself to him through his organs—the rumbling of the car, and through his skin—the movement of air, the seat beneath him, the soft constriction of sneakers, the smooth dash, the glove compartment button, the pamphlets inside it. His back felt as if he'd been sleeping on a bed of apples. Simply being in a car seat was a marvelous relief.

The X on his eye pulled at his skin and eyelashes so he fucked with it, hopeful to see some landscape. When he took it off, he saw black. He was surprised to get a sense of black and white at all. When he first lost his sight, he often imagined color, and when there wasn't color, there was an imaginary black, but over time, it wasn't a color of any kind. It was just a nothing. A nothing incomparable to any other nothing. It was as easy to look out of his eyeballs as it was to look out of his knees. They were far now, so far. So far no one could find them out there in the infinite obscurity, banging down a highway through the galaxy, past the Milky Way where even radio waves couldn't reach.

He'd never felt so free and at peace.

The air turned cool and wet, slapping at his face. He pushed more into his sore cheek, massaging the area where the tumor used to be. He could not get enough of this fresh air. He wanted everything at once—to open his arms and take in the world, to hug it, to eat it, to fuck it. He reeled in the experience. He tried to hear, but the sounds were hidden in a place he could not go. He pulled inwardly, pushed outwardly, sensing by the space passing under them that he now had time he never had in all that lying around at home.

The next time he woke, he waited impatiently for his mother to bring him pizza. He rolled over, lurching off the bed.

He'd touched a warm body, and it all came back. Now, he crawled up, laughing at himself. *What an idiot*, he might have said aloud. He got under the covers, resting his arm gently over her. If he had the privilege, he would have played some morning jazz for her from his MP3 player. When he was locked up (for that's how he thought of it now, out here in Freedomville), he passed the hours playing memory games. Could he remember everything in his room? Could he remember the states in alphabetical order? Could he remember all the lyrics to "It's the End of the World as We Know It (And I Feel Fine)?" The answer was no—just the "Leonard Bernstein" part, which everybody knows, and he wondered if he would ever know any more of it, again, or if those four syllables would punch inside him forever. If he relaxed, music plucked effortlessly along the strings of his brainwaves. Sometimes it was jazz, sometimes Laurie Anderson, other times Mazzy Star, Radiohead, or The Strokes. He opened a window to a poem about snow he'd written in high school for his girlfriend. He went over it iamb by iamb.

Reddy unpeeled the new tape from his eye.

Just light, but it agitated the chemicals in his brain, waking everything up to be developed. Alex did things that did not include him. This gave him the sinking feeling that she didn't care for him as much as he cared for her. A week had happened in two days. She was taking advantage of him. He just couldn't figure out *how*. There was no reason anyone would want to spend time with him.

Finally, they got on the road again, stopped for bean burritos that they ate outside, standing up. He became conscious of the nutrients entering his body, breaking into smaller parts, and spreading out like missionaries to carry out duties. Their disciplined work aligned him. It was easier to smile. The back pain he'd had for so long vanished and he stood straight like a man with integrity, a guy who could look in the mirror one day, a guy pulled by a string at the crown of his head and liked by God. He kept the tape off, waiting for the *possible*, he told himself.

He asked if they were running to Mexico.

Her response: *NEW.*

The wind had sand in it. He cupped his opened eye.

Down the highway, she drove over a rumble strip and stopped. Suddenly, Reddy had it in his mind they'd been pulled over. He grabbed his knees, waiting. This was a stolen vehicle.

She didn't have a license. Nothing happened. They started driving again.

What the fuck was that? he said.

She tapped him twice for "no."

No? What the hell does "no" mean?

She didn't answer.

What do you want from me? he said. He crossed his leg and put his head against the shaking window, anxiety-induced dizziness overcoming him, wanting to get wherever in hell it was they were going. He feared the permanence of this situation. They would have to stay on the run and his health would only get worse and, along the way, she would toss him like a sandbag from a hot air balloon.

Are you going to kill me?

She tapped him once.

Put me out of my misery, he said, *like a half-dead deer.*

One tap, again.

At some stop somewhere she wrote: FIND YOUR CENTER. He thought about this awhile, looking for his center, trying to place it inside his belly. No matter how hard he tried, his center ran away. His center moved where she moved. If he could, he would stitch her to him, down the seams of their shirts, down the seams of their pants.

*

High noon in the sunlit silver car, Aleksia turned the music up and swam her hand out the window. The highway had struck straight out from her for quite a while, but now it rolled into overexposed, burned-out hills and wound its way closer to Albuquerque.

When she had taken the Greyhound bus to New York City, she picked up a trucker's atlas at a pit stop. She lugged the atlas around in a backpack to bars. It taught her everything she needed to know about the American highway system, but mostly that it *was* a system and not so complicated. She now left it open on the seat between them, although she barely referenced it; she had memorized the route to Albuquerque and to Casa Blanca, where Carl Dusty Crow, the writer of this life-altering book, lived.

Getting the car in New Jersey had been effortless; it could have only been the plan of a divine being and certainly was a blazing, illuminated, neon sign from heaven that she was on the right path toward her destiny. She waited in the dark by the payphones at 7-11 with her backpack on and her arms akimbo until an old woman and man left their vehicle running in the lot. Aleksia dashed to it, got in, adjusted the seat, and drove off. Like, no problem at all.

Now, she took an exit for I-25 into town. A naked mountain burned pink by the sunset lifted up half the city, the half she was coasting down.

In New York, she spent time thinking about her Pappa, how she never saw his body. Maybe it would have been easier if she'd seen his body. He'd been a woodworker and had built himself a coffin. He sawed off his arm. Then, dressed in clingwrap, he got in the coffin and went to bed. She repeated the story to herself a few times a day ever since it happened.

The artist in the studio next door found him—which wasn't challenging, because the rooms were divided by sheets and quilts—and brought him to the hospital where everybody said he died that night. Her mom never had a funeral, though, only a party where all these people showed up whom Alex had never met before (Pappa's work was famous; he wasn't), wearing glittered masks and velvet blazers and gowns, performing what looked like improvised ceremonies. A woman in a green dress braided Alex's hair and put petals on her tongue. This was her way of honoring him. The attendees paid Aleksia a lot of attention, as if this weren't her father's funeral but her coronation and she would be crowned with a ring of golden nails, so she couldn't feel her sadness, only her madness as they crossed into her headspace and encouraged her to sing a song she didn't know. In her New York dreams, Pappa mixed in with the crowd at the subway station, one-armed and masked, a hacksaw slung over his back. He was a special man. She found herself trying to catch his face. She found herself looking for *everybody*.

Because suicide was contagious, her mother had to go as far north as she could and would have to live on the coast with the reindeer to not catch it. And she did just that.

Aleksia wanted to meet Carl Dusty Crow in person. She wanted him to see her progress, how she improved her soul and her behavior. He could see these sorts of things just by looking at a person.

Alex used Reddy's ID to rent a $38 motel room where she had a laboriously long conversation with him, writing out, letter by letter on his back, words to inspire him, words to make him want the same thing she wanted—Crow's help—but he seemed annoyed by the idea. He said, "So, he's some sort of new-age guru?" and "God, you're like gushing over this guy."

The following morning, she put on a white dress that went to her knees, and drove them to Casa Blanca, a town an hour west of the Sandia Mountains. To the left of the highway there was a white gas station with a Subway attached to it. On the other side of the highway, red boulders scraped the sky, chipped out by wind and surrounded by blond grass bent and flickering.

Inside the gas station, she found Carl Dusty Crow's book on display. She lifted it up to the cashier, a thin woman in a shirt that said "Bebe" in fake diamonds across her bosom, and asked if he was around.

The lady rubbed a tiny potted cactus with a blue rag. She had to open her elbows wide to get around her breasts. She set it on the counter with the others.

"Do you know where we could find this guy?" Alex said, again.

"He left." The woman brushed her straight hair, which had the weight of fabric, over her shoulder. "He doesn't live here anymore."

Alex dropped her arms, looking out the front windows to Reddy.

"Too many people came looking for him. He had to leave, had to move up north."

"My cousin is really sick," Alex began. "I mean, really, really sick."

The woman gave her a look, then reached behind herself for the phone. "You can call the hospital."

"No, no, see . . . he's been to hospitals. He's dying."

The lady pressed a button on the register, making receipt paper spool out. Then, she drew on the back of it a crude map of how to get to another convenience store where Alex could find Carl Dusty Crow.

Eventually, the paved road turned into a gravel road, and the gravel road turned into a dirt road. It stayed this way for quite some time before turning into a paved road again. The needle on the fuel gauge bounced around with the bumps and she couldn't quite tell how much was left in there. She saw a hand-painted sign advertising gas two miles away. The

CHAPTER 7

Chrysler gurgled. She thought this might be the place on the map where she could find Carl Dusty Crow. The car died. Getting out, she walked against the bit of breeze that tinted the constant, humming silence of the earth with a whistle across the flats of her ears and finally blew a piece of paper to her leg. She peeled it off. In black marker, it read, "Out of Order." Coming upon the station, she found it abandoned.

*

Unless the place was closed—which it was by six every evening—George John kept the door opened because the air stayed in place otherwise and he liked good air-flow in his Shop & Go, even if it was only 65 degrees out. At least it was sunny. Lately, some big clouds had been coming in, blowing over mostly, but dragging black shadows over the pavement. He peered out from his convenience store window and watched a young blonde woman tug at the hem of a sickly-looking guy's jacket. He was about two feet taller, and his hair had the same yellow to it but without the shine. It looked dried and split like a dog's. She rolled a suitcase behind her, lifting the colorless dust from the ground. The young man looked around, his head wobbly, almost disconnected from the rest of his body. The girl got behind as they approached George's door.

With her hands on his shoulders, she pushed him in, saying, "stay."

"Where are we?" the guy asked in a hollow voice. Massive scars shaped like scythes were drawn around the outlines of his ears on both sides.

George picked up the catalogue on the counter in front of him. At the time, other than the scars and their whiteness, there wasn't much to think about these two. He was considering whether to order the Laguna patches. He already tried selling shot glasses and stickers, the kind with the desert sunset on them, and they took a long time to sell, but he eventually ran out of them, so he couldn't make the decision. Tourists hardly made it out this way, but when they did—usually by accident—they liked to buy something to prove they made it.

The girl pitter-pattered up and down the aisles. Because there wasn't a car out front, he wondered if someone was coming to pick them up. His convenience store/gas station/variety shop/bus station/post office was a mile from anywhere, and the only thing a mile away was another gas station that his friend Rodney owned and lost money on two months ago. George, himself, had to get a ride from fifteen miles away to get here each morning.

The girl picked up a 99-cent bag of Fritos, a bag pregnant with air from the elevation changes the delivery truck went through to get all the way there from Plano, Texas. She considered one of his dolls. Once she saw the dust in the doll's hair, she would put it back next to the others. The boy she came with never got his answer. They didn't know where they were.

George set down his catalogue and said, "Paguate." He thought a moment and let them know they were about seven miles north of Laguna. They were technically within Paguate limits although, from this place, it must look just like they were nowhere.

George had been shaving his head every spring since his twenties. As he rubbed it now, he realized he needed a new shave. He wore a blood-red western shirt with an off-white fringe that ran across the chest. He wore the same thing as yesterday because it wasn't dirty yet, along with a rusty horse belt buckle that hung almost upside-down at the top of his stiff Levi's.

The girl looked up with those Fritos in her hand, saying, "he can't hear you." Then, she noticed the blue booth in the back by the payphone and restrooms and went over to it, letting go of her suitcase and bag at the table.

"Where are you from?" he said over the aisles. She said she was from Norway and had driven all the way across the country to come here. Then, she asked if he had anything she could carry gasoline in.

"Oh," he said. "You ran out of gas."

"Maybe a kilometer that way," she said.

The girl walked straight over to the red gas cans as if she knew psychically where they were and said, "Can I use this? How much is this?" Looking back, even that was strange to him.

"Depends on whether or not you're going to put any gas in it."

She took the container and walked past the boy outside.

When she came back, she asked George something, but he didn't hear her and told her so. She seemed to notice his prescription glasses. He tilted his head back and she held up the inflated Fritos bag.

"There's no price," she said. He said he would give it to her for fifty cents. "Goo-oood," she said and brought her friend over to the booth, mumbling along the way. She sat him down carefully. He crept his hand along the wall and rested his head against it. She asked if her friend could stay for a while. He said it was all right.

"Do you know a guy named Carl Dusty Crow?" Her eyes were a watery blue and her lips, he noticed, fairytale pink.

He nodded, and that's when he began to understand why

these Norwegians had traveled thousands of miles to come to Paguate. He would call Carl and get him over here, he told the girl. Her face lit up. She clapped her hands.

"Thank you, thank you, thank you!"

Ever since Carl wrote this new-age book on shamanism, borrowing tribal beliefs and mixing them with Western science, health, and religion, he thought he was *hot shit* and white girls kept showing up saying they had no culture and needed a bit of theirs. This couple seemed different, though. They seemed exotic. George read the book when it came out, and it had some good things in it, things he thought Carl took right from his mouth. Now, Carl got all the attention, got free books sent to him, free plane tickets to big cities, and the only people interested in his stuff were white, upper-class American women looking for a scrap of something to hang onto. When he was lucky, he could sell them some turquoise something or other. But George had to admit, Carl had some good stuff in there, stuff the two of them had never even talked about in their long talks at Bibo Bar, stuff divinely inspired, and whenever he thought of his old friend, Carl, he heard a strange whizzing in his ear, made him think of a shaker, made him think Carl really did have powers. He never told Carl that, though.

"What's your boyfriend's name?" George asked.

"Reddy. I'm Alex," she said, and then, with her red gas can—that she was obviously borrowing since she didn't pay for it—she zipped out the doorway as single-mindedly as a dragonfly. George watched her through the window. Her hair blew across her face.

When she was out of sight, he eased from behind the counter and walked slowly, almost quietly, down the aisle, one boot and then the next. He stopped a few feet short of the blue booth. The boy, Reddy, must have been in his early twenties, as tall as George himself. His eyes darted from side to side like he was having a nightmare in there. His breath picked up. He made whiny sounds.

"Calm," said George. "Calm." Reddy rocked forward and back with his hands locked between his legs under the table. He closed one eye but left the other open, and George couldn't stand to look at him anymore, but he tried it one more time, lifting his hands up slowly with his palms toward the floor, gathering earth energy like Carl taught him. "Calm." He pushed the flat of his hands down in front of his chest, exhaling.

George stopped because he thought he heard the FedEx guy outside, but it was just a car that pulled off the road for a second and drove off. The thing about colonizers assuming he was spiritual was that he was, in fact, spiritual, but all his life, he was the kind of guy that didn't like to fit a stereotype. The fact that the young guy was clearly blind was a good thing. He had beliefs. He thought maybe he could help, but he sure as hell wasn't going to sell out like Carl. He had mixed feelings about the whole thing. When he looked back at the booth, Reddy took a deep breath and deflated in the corner. Something had happened. This trick of Carl's worked.

*

Carl Dusty Crow (in school his last name was John just like everybody else) showed up not long after George called. He stepped out of his little yellow car with his walking stick and slammed the door. It didn't have any bumpers or license plates, and George asked him about that once. Carl said he didn't need them. George had a hard time telling when Carl was joking.

Carl's black lab jumped out through the busted-out back windshield. When the dog hit the ground, its balls plunged into the dirt.

Carl came in talking.

"You won't believe what just happened."

"Tell me."

Sunglasses covered the top half of his face. He had sensitive eyes. He took them off, saying, "My old lady is walking, again."

"That's great," George said. "That's great."

"Great diet and a ceremony or two, yeah."

"That's really great."

George introduced Reddy. "I don't know much, but this girl came looking for you, a girl from Norway, and she dropped off this guy who's blind and deaf."

"That's tough," he said, but got to business. "Boy, what have you done to yourself? This isn't as great as you thought it would be, is it?"

George stood back -is that what Carl thought? This guy did this to himself?

Reddy sighed. Then, very loudly, he said, "I don't know."

"Whoa."

"See?" George said, "See? He's like a blackhole. Look at him." Carl stopped himself and wagged his eyebrows. He looked over at George who was, perhaps, in shock. "Can you leave us alone?"

His heart plummeted. "What—"

"George."

"I'm the one who found him."

George walked back to the front register and then decided to go outside. He didn't want to act like a child in front of him. All George ever wanted to do was just love *him*. They were the same age, went to the same high school, worked for the same construction crew until they were twenty-four. They were like brothers, and it wasn't until Carl started making miracles that George ever knew there had been any difference between them.

A few trucks passed by, and a carload of drunk teenagers piled into the store and George sold them two six packs. Outside again, he looked down the road for the girl. After some time, he grew concerned. Finally, Carl walked out briskly, not using his cane.

"What happened in there? What happened?" George implored.

"We'll see," Carl said with an air of mystery. Then, he shrugged. "I can't get anything out of him. He's hard as a rock. Tell the young lady I'm sorry." He smiled, but he repeated, "I can't get anything out of him." He got in his car. "Meet me at Bibo Bar tonight."

George finished his ice cream and, sitting across from the boy, reached out and touched his hand. The boy didn't move. George said out loud, "I love you."

Reddy didn't say anything back. His eyelids were closed, but then he opened them both. He wasn't looking at George, exactly, but more like *through* him. A breeze went up George's sleeve. The air thinned.

"Reddy," he said. The guy remained quietly staring into him.

But, in an instant, the store turned dim as sunset. A shadow of a cloud licked across the parking lot. A sound came from the front, a tat-tat-tat-tat-tat. And then, again: tat-tat-tat-tat-tat.

It was the register. The register was freaking out.

Dolls started shaking. Tat-tat-tat-tat-tat.

Cigarette packs flung off the wall like cards from a deck. At once, the glass animals along the front windowsill crashed. George jumped from his seat to brace the gondola shelving with his long arms. The fluorescent light tubes running along the ceiling buzzed.

"Stop!" George said, aiming this at Reddy. "Stop!" The coffee in the pot boiled. The pages of his catalogue flipped. With all his might, he tried, again. "Stop!"

The lights buzzed out.

The register dinged and shut up.

And then, in the silence, a gunshot. George hit the ground. The gondola shelving crashed behind him.

Another bang.

His heart jumped. A series of shots fired off. He crawled. He covered his head. He thought it was that group of teenagers coming back to rob the place. He waited for voices, but there were none.

Nothing moved but his heart in his chest.

Silence. His breath. His heart. His breath. And then, suddenly, another *bang*.

A pop-bang. A bang-pop-bang that seemed closer, canned.

Above aisle two, he saw a poof of dust. He came out from under the coffeemaker where he'd landed with his arms up. Another—*pop*! —and he jumped back. But it didn't seem like a gunshot. He knew the sound of a gunshot. He came around the endcap.

Like bodies after a blast, a mess of deflated Fritos bags were spread widely down the aisle.

He turned his head to the sound of tires crunching along the gravel. It was the girl, Alex. The cloud finished its pass across the lot and moved on. George stood inside unmoving, dust floating past him and throughout the store. Reddy sat in his booth staring. The girl came in with her gas can swinging.

"Hey!"

*

It all went so fast. She didn't see the cashier reaching over the counter when she walked in, but he flung his body back holding a gun, *shaking* the gun at the end of his long arms, stepping away from her, backward toward the coffee machine.

"Out!" he said, pointing it at her, pointing it at Reddy. He wiped his face with the inside of his elbow.

"What?"

"Out!" And he held the gun with both hands, again.

Aleksia rushed to Reddy, dropping the gas can along the way. She pulled him up. "Come on, come on, come on."

"Get him out of here!" the man said and yelled a bunch of other stuff as she gathered her cousin. She didn't want her back to the guy but didn't have a choice; she just expected that gun to go off, a bullet to stab her in the neck.

"Come on, Reddy. Let's go," she kept saying, half-carrying him and their things through the trashed store. She remembered that. All the broken things. They got outside. She got him in the car. She sped a mile down the road to a pull-off and stopped.

On his back, she wrote, *WHAT WAS THAT?*

"When," he said.

NOW, she wrote.

He shrugged. "Nothing." Then, "What's going on?"

She didn't want to spell it out.

"What's going on?"

The jagged mountains ahead cut into the scenery. She wouldn't get to meet the shaman. She had three gallons of gas. She pulled her head from her hands. *I'm too young for this,* she thought, and reached over to Reddy's face. His hair had gotten longer. It stuck to his forehead. She pressed it behind his ear. He'd done something remarkable today. She just didn't know what.

"Tell me! Where are we?" he said, and she laughed, a big gulp of a laugh, the kind with tears in it. She pressed the power button on the radio. Reddy jumped. It blared a station between stations.

She turned it off. She held still, surveying him.

"Are you there?" she said aloud, half-expecting him to hear her with the ghost in his body.

He didn't move.

"You're a special kind," she whispered, taking his hand in hers. She consulted the map. It was over now. No one could fix him. Not doctors. Not God. She hated permanent things. Lifting her shoulders to her ears, she thought, *we could go anywhere*. The Taos Gorge. She turned the car around and headed back the way they came.

Coming over a small hill, she saw a line across the road and ran over it.

"Fuuuuck," she said. A six-foot rattlesnake. *Rattlesnakes were real!* Reddy adjusted himself in the seat. She didn't know what happened in that gas station. What she did know was that, on her walk, a group of sketchy guys accosted her, told her to get in the car. She considered it. When she saw the car door already opened for her before the wheels even stopped, there was pressure on her shoulder, a pressure gently pulling her away. Stepping back, she'd said, "I'll walk." As the car drove away, a guy in the backseat set a shotgun on the car windowsill. The barrel peered back at her and the guy pulled the trigger.

CHAPTER 7

Bullets shot right through the billboard behind her.

Even now, as the sun slid toward the horizon, her ears still rang. A train could be heard in the distance. "I've always wanted to go to the desert," she said softly to herself. "It's romantic. All this untouched land. You can be free out here. No one can hurt you out here. Maybe animals. Maybe animals can hurt you. I'm an animal." They'd been driving for an hour with no music, so she continued talking to herself. "There are a few places," she mumbled. "The desert. The bottom of a big body of water. No one tells the fish what to do. To be blameless. To be seen for who you are instead of who you should be. Like a fish. No one tells the fish it should have done better. No one sends the fish to live with relatives. *Antarctica,* you could move there. Yeah, if you want to eat ice all day. Where there's no poverty. No laws. There's no poverty where there's no money. Actually, that's true. There's no poverty where there's no money. Eat ice all day. You're so stupid sometimes, Aleksia. You can't live in Antarctica. I'm so stupid," she whispered, "I hurt my own feelings."

She took in the scenery for a while. "I want a cigarette," she said, and got a cigarette and smoked it. Reddy stared forward. Seemed like he was blinking both eyes now. "Being vulnerable. That's the fucking problem with me. I'm trying to work on that. I think I could be a good person one day. But that's the problem. I was born wrong." She stopped for the train. "I was born wrong." She looked at Reddy. "Why are you like this? It's like I'm carrying a universe in a capsule, and I don't even get to open it." *That was a good way of putting that.* "I'm carrying a universe in a capsule, and I can't even open it." *Maybe holding it is better.* "I'm holding a universe in a capsule, and I can't even open it." The train passed and they carried on. She thought more for some time. "Because I like thinking. I like my brain. It's my favorite body part," she said, drifting into the statement and into a gas station parking lot.

There was no explanation for it—only magic, or godly interference, for why they made it to a gas station without running out of fuel, and everything else that happened soon after.

*

The grit-spark of a lighter. The smell of weed burning. A glass set on a table.

It was possible he heard something that day on their drive. Steps stepped along carpet. It had sounded like a record playing backward on high speed. On the road, a truck rushed past. But maybe he'd heard it through his skin. A tick-tick-tick of the fan prickling his arms. The droning—but like talking—across his brainwaves. Ghost whispers. A lullaby. A poem. He'd set his head back in the car seat turning the sounds into words. "Fuzzy morning song. 'Twas morning song! Inside, I'm wearing a soul and believe I'm eloping it? Sharing a soul and fallopian. Shouldering a purse in your soul and I can't even open it." It was complete nonsense.

Lying down now, somewhere comfortable, he moved his hand back and forth across his chest.

Swish.

Swish.

Swish.

He didn't want to move. A tear slipped down his temple into his ear.

"Hello?" he whispered to himself and threw his hands to his face, clasped them as if in prayer. He tapped each lobe. Cleared his throat. "Are you there?" he said a bit louder. The step-step-steps. The sound of her tap on his shoulder. He snatched her hand.

"Stop it," she said, as if to herself.

"Alex." He let go and tapped his earlobes again. "Say something. Say anything."

"Can you hear me?" she said. "Strawberry Pie. Pink Cactus," she droned. "Orangutan Rodeo. Um. Rainbow Pumpernickel. Cake Spackle. Can you, Reddy? Can you hear me?"

"Strawberry Pie," he said. "Pink Cactus. Orangutan Rodeo." She laughed and jumped onto the bed. "Whoa, whoa. Don't jump. Don't jump."

"Strawberry Pie," she said. "Pink Cactus."

"Orangutan Rodeo?"

She threw herself down and pulled his arm out so she could rest her head on his bicep. "Are you hearing me with your ears?"

"Say it high-pitched."

"Like this?" she said, "Strawberry Pie? Pink Cactus?"

"Now, low."

"Strawberry pie, pink cactus."

"I hear everything."

"You hear everything?"

"Can you hear this?" She lifted his shirt and gave him a raspberry.

"Stop! You're so immature!"

"This?" and she kept going.

"Yeah," he said.

He kept laughing, and she was saying, "Stop, stop, now I can't stop," and laughing right along with him.

They took another deep breath and fell into silence.

"So," he said, "How long was I out?"

And they erupted into laughter, again.

"About six months."

"So, what . . ."

"Stop talking. Stop! I'm laughing too hard. My side hurts."

"So, what did I miss?"

*

"...and then when we were in Tennessee, this thing happened," she said now, and passed him the joint. They were on the floor of the motel room, shoulders overlapping, the radio playing country, and she was telling him about the entire trip, and he could eat her voice up. *Please don't ever let this end,* he thought. *Please.* She said he had magical powers, and the more he smoked, the more plausible this seemed. She rolled over, probably onto her elbows. He could feel her breath when she talked, feel the heat off her skin.

"I wish we were near the ocean. Uhhhh . . ." She groaned as she got up. "I'm ordering pizza."

"You better not," he said. She laughed, coming back, pushing him, resting her head on his chest. Breathing. Breathing on him.

"Chinese, then?" she said.

"I don't want anything," he said with his hands in her hair, "not right now. I didn't know you smoked pot."

"Only because I'm too young to buy—oh! Yeah, you could—you could get us alcohol."

"I don't know," he said. "What if . . ."

"Yeah! Yeah!"

He announced his blindness at the front door of the liquor store. A woman led him through the aisles.

"How did you get here?" she said.

"Oh, I walked," he said.

CHAPTER 7

And he carried the tequila out all on his own!

Hours later, saturated with tequila and stuffed with chicken fried rice, the cousins lounged on the motel stairs. Aleksia had her head in Reddy's lap. They smoked cigarettes and took swills from the bottle.

"It's like looking into someone's eyes," she said. "You know? Like that shock? That's what it feels like looking at the Milky Way right now, like sinking into something so intoxicating, it must be forbidden."

"Reminds me of a supernova," he said.

"What's that?"

"It's the last flash of light from a dying star."

"That sounds intoxicating, too. What if you could try to see?"

"Great idea," he said.

"I'm serious."

"Like I haven't thought of that. Okay, yeah, let's try. What do you suggest? That I push my eyes out, like, really hard? Or that I try to suck the images in through my pupils?"

She shifted her head in his lap. "Fuck, I don't know. Either one."

But as he sat there, his back against the door, the expanded metal of the stairs cutting into him underneath, he found himself putting his hands out in front of his face. Ghosts rushed him and vanished. The pressure behind his eyes pushed as he struggled to see these fuzzy black things against blacker black. Another ghost-smack, and he gasped.

He took the bottle from her and drank some more. He pointed his head down. A smear of grass-color in the middle of his vision, surrounded by darkness.

"I think," he said, "maybe you're right."

"Really?"

"Is your jacket green?" he said. "And maybe sparkling?"

She sat up saying, "Yes! Yes! It's green!"

He couldn't be sure he was seeing through his eyeballs. Maybe he was seeing with his soul.

"What about the stars?"

He tilted his head up. "I don't think so." She put her hands on either side of his head.

"That way. See them?"

Detached sparkles. Diamonds on pavement. He looked. They seemed smeared with Vaseline. They seemed to be in a kaleidoscope, just like his feelings. "I see you, maybe, but you're blurry. I don't know, I could be imagining it."

"I'm blurry?" she laughed. "I'm blurry?!? I think you're seeing, Reddy. I think this is really real."

Reddy didn't want to sleep ever again. The sun blossomed over the horizon, painting the stairwell peach and cream.

"You know what," she said in the sleepiness of the morning, "we should never forget this. Ever. We need to remember this for the rest of our lives. Let's make a pact." She sat up, cross-legged before him.

"Okay," he said, exhaling. She took the joint.

"As long as we shall live," she started and inhaled, "Reddy and Aleksia will remember this moment."

"Deal," he said.

"No, you have to say it back to me," she said, holding her breath. "Wait. We need a special handshake no one knows but us."

"Okay."

She grabbed his wrist. He grabbed hers. They slid palms until they hooked fingers and pulled until the last finger let

CHAPTER 7

go.

"Perfect."

"So, now can I go?"

"Yes."

"As long as we shall live…"

"Reddy and Aleksia will remember this moment."

"Reddy and Aleksia will remember this moment."

"Deal," she said, and exhaled. An electric shock smacked his lips. She kissed him.

Quite blitzed, and a bit groggy, they went back to their room and listened to radio shows until they finally drifted off as content as children on blankets at the beach.

A vacuum cleaner hummed in another room. When it turned off, he heard voices and a door slam. He turned off the radio and watched the fan above him circle, following one blade at a time until he was spun. Sunlight dusted Aleksia's eyelashes. Sitting up, he saw himself in the mirror, and then went to it, turning his head side to side. Standing there, he knew profoundly there were two Reddys: the real whole one he'd embodied for half a year, and then this one that split off in that instance, as if he were cut through from the top by a hot wire—the image of the one looking back at the other. Fire burned through his chest, so he broke away to open the curtains and lift the blinds. He found his legs hard to move. A red and yellow striped rug covered the small bench he sat on to inspect the room. Her hair waterfalled from the bed. Her little feet cuddled each other. She woke just before check-out when he was rummaging through their bags for his pills.

"What are you doing?"

"Being self-sufficient," he said.

"You haven't taken those for three days."

He had the orange bottle in his hand. "I haven't?"

She rolled over like she was heading back to bed. "No, you're fine now." He poured the pills back into the container and put on his clothes—a familiar, nostalgic feeling coming over him—not that he hadn't put on clothes in all his darkdream, but now it was somehow different, to be able to see the colors, and to hear the shirt over his ears—to be responsible—and to see what clothes she had picked out for him, to touch the little suitcase he hadn't seen since she moved in. And it went on and on. The possibilities gracefully unfolding before him. He had the urge to call his mom.

They went outside together, dumping their first load of things into the car. When they arrived at the trunk, she asked him to get the rest of the stuff from their room and he was happy to do it. He only wanted to do things for her. He moved faster than he knew he could on his way to the door and gathered their things from the floor and table. When he picked up their toothbrushes, he wasn't sure which was his. He was in the bathroom and couldn't help but look in the mirror again. Now, he split into three: the whole, the half, and the half cut into another half—Aleksia's idea of him. He needed a shave and had gained twenty pounds, some—no, a lot of it—on his face, some on his chest, stomach, and thighs, like a girl. He had an ass now. He was ugly. He had another chin, and he pushed it toward his chest to see just how noticeable it was. The zipper on his corduroy pants bulged outward under his belt buckle. He wanted to hit himself in the face, but he slid down the bathroom wall and fucked with his tight belt, which grew tighter as he sat there. But he had to get up, so he did, and he had to shake it off, so he did that, too. Everything was good! He pulled up the song "Feeling Groovy" in his mind and whistled along. Everything would be easy now.

*

The raindrops sprinkled down, and Freya watched them come at a slant, hitting the side of the rowhouse. Mark left that morning for the tenth day of his search. Jim stopped living with them for no reason, even after paying rent. He didn't ask for any money back, just hurriedly took his things and left them alone. Emma spent all her time with her girlfriend and hadn't even seen Freya's new haircut.

Watching Oprah, she held her hot cup. She had the place to herself. Life wasn't horrible, she told herself. There were things to enjoy even on one's own, even in the midst of worry and tragedy, like the way the coffee mug burned a bit at the soft parts of her palms. But then there was always the waiting, the anticipation of a phone call telling her that Reddy could not be found, that there were different levels of disappearance. One could be gone from view, lost from everyone else but still exist somewhere on the planet, however untethered. One could be lost from themselves, but still exist somewhere, however dissociated. Or one could simply vanish with total completion—cutting open a gingerbread cookie-shape from the fabric of reality and walking right through it, to be as gone as having never existed in the first place. But that couldn't be, she thought. Every person who ever lived in all of history was still on the planet. So, Reddy was somewhere – even if he were underground or floating in the guts of a whale. The unpredictable events of her life tugged her along on a leash and decided for her if she would move into happiness or away from it, into all those gray, subtle emotions no one ever names but she would try now, blowing across her coffee: rubatosis, sonder, monachopsis, chrysalism. Short words for big things, with so many longer feelings shading the in-between. This wasn't a new thought, just something she circled back to, heeling like a dog steadfast in its patience, its standstill, as if living in this perception of her world was the only one to live in.

She put down her coffee and picked it up. A little white cloud danced above it. The air was nice. She noticed the wallpaper. Blue toy boats. Imagine, toy boats in the kitchen. Why did everything always have to be out of place, inconsistent, just off to the right, anachronistic? She went to the door, put on her shoes. The stand of mailboxes by the yellow painted curb looked to her like a birdhouse with locks on all the doors, made to look identical to the rowhouses facing them. Each door had its own miniature key. She pushed hers in 216 and pulled out her folded wad of papers and envelopes. She never liked to slide the rubber band off the bundle until she was sitting at the table. She wanted to hold off for as long as she could and to flip through each piece individually to pass the time. Inside, she refilled her mug. From the counter, she could see a letter unlike the rest, separating itself from the bills. She added sugar and cream to the coffee, wanting to sit down right there on the floor, sit down like she had been sitting in the shower lately. She recounted her loss of energy, trying to understand when it began.

Sitting on the kitchen floor now, her back against the cabinet, she pointed out the moment in Reddy's empty room, and thought this must have been when the energy evaporated, but then, reaching back through the year and then through the *years*, she—oh, but never mind. She didn't have the energy to fulfill the thoughts with words. She did not care, one way or another. When she crossed a busy street, she didn't care if a truck hit her. She did not care if she ate the wrong foods. And perhaps, she had to admit, she had projected this onto Reddy, and maybe—but where was she going? It was an interesting thought. She stared at the floorboards. Is it possible it was a new thought? No, it was nothing. She didn't mind the idea of going to a doctor only to find she had less than a week to live. Living was the trouble, not being dead, and sitting in her kitchen with this pile of envelopes, pregnant with potential, she realized she had never been afraid of death and this had been a glitch in her system. She longed for death, always had, could hardly wait for it.

She wished something would happen to her. At one time she sewed meaning into her life with religion, but even that thread broke, and she couldn't place when that happened either, only that she no longer had the energy to care about heaven or hell or discipline or Jesus. Afterall, how much had Jesus cared for her when He told her to push away the girl she loved –or when He told her to save Timothy from temptation?

She remembered a young woman at the post office who asked the teller for permission to send cash in a box to Africa. Into the box, she dropped Jesus pamphlets. The teller said it was okay, and the young woman, happy with herself, spun off, and Freya found herself wondering if the woman would send that money to those *poor* Africans if she'd never heard of Jesus. The question really was, could she be good without Jesus? Did she learn through her own hardships how to sacrifice—or had the idea only been passed down to her? If we could prove Jesus never existed, could these people ever find a way to do the right thing without Him? Jesus only had himself, after all, a short man on a tall planet, and maybe that's all we have, too—ourselves to look to for guidance, and maybe it was wrong to rely on him all the time, without actually learning anything on our own. If natural science and human experience weren't important to God, then why have brains—why have any organs at all?

It was not that she judged the woman. They were all just people.

Freya saw a tiny light in her own abdomen. It was like a candle run down to its base, flickering out one second and coming back alive the next. Why do people live when all that exists is *the instinct to exist*? They live only because they can't bear the thought of dying. But what should happen between birth and death? There was art, but even that was about pain. And there were flowers, but Freya'd had enough of flowers, even the blue ones. She'd seen Alabama, Maryland, California, and Norway, and really, after a while, with all that traveling, one town was not all that different from the next. They had buildings. They had people and streets that needed repairing. All the humans had the same kinds of characteristics—noses, legs, arms, and eyes—and they all liked to wear clothes, be entertained, involve themselves in religions; the planet had all the same races she'd ever seen—people with hair or without, thin or fat, short or tall—and still all just *people*, just variations of each other. She felt now that she was standing on the top of a building looking down. The possibilities *were not* endless. What did that statement mean, anyway? The possibilities were full of ends. There were a countable number of persons on the planet, as there were a countable number of elements. You could vary the types of food you ate, mixing up the ingredients in a different way, but it was still *food*. You could not give up *eating*. Every. Single. Day. Would anything new ever happen again?

She did not want to live and no longer believed that anyone else wanted her to either. Humans lived and subsisted on this planet, lonely for connection. She was lonely, too. She got herself up and, grabbing a book she had on the counter, chose a page at random. It read, "this is the paradox. The doctor tells you in order to get more energy you must *use* more energy." She put it down, slightly moved by its relevance to her state of mind and decided to take a walk at the mall.

She took the bus so she could look at people. The bus driver, arriving late, rushed off from each stop. He became a bus driver when he grew up. She held onto the cold bar next to her with the coffee in her stomach pushing up into her throat. On the one hand, humans were fragile little beings in soft clothes, with hair and arms and legs. On the other, they could survive car wrecks. They could survive long sicknesses. She heard once of a woman who woke from a thirty-year coma and didn't know a single day had passed. Thirty years and not a single mistake made. At a stop, a thick man got on, rolling a walker and holding it in front of her when he sat down. She gripped the bar again as they sped off and, catching this man's eye, he smiled showing two long teeth, each one on the right side of his mouth, and she wondered why it was that she was who she was, and she was not him.

How was it possible that she had all her own teeth? His smile vanished, and sneaking peeks at all the passengers behind her, and the one who sat beside her listening to a discman, she came to realize that no one was happy. Happiness was a myth. They owned bodies running on minimal energy that continued moving them around, and so they had to walk, to eat, to work, to shit, and keep going until the energy ran out.

They endured: a man with his head in his cracked hands; a woman with frazzled hair under a kerchief; a teenager on a cellphone, angry with her child crying in its stroller. Everyone trying not to die, no one wanting to live.

The electrified neon of the mall and the music and the loudspeaker advertisements combined in her a less dismal state. The rose-colored floor with its ramps and plastic plants, crowded with people, and she gave them distance in order to watch her feet. She edged along the right side of the storefronts, hanging behind a group of children and mothers until she could overtake them. She'd left her purse at home, so could swing her arms to get both sides of her body working together, but this had to be done consciously because both arms wanted to swing forward at once. Around the corner, more children hung around a water fountain with stone ledges and a place to drop pennies. She sat there invisibly. A burning ache in the upper part of her back hunched her over her knees, the weight of her breasts pressing against her chest, making it hard to breathe, when a pink bouncy ball bumped into her shoe.

She picked it up, rubbery in her fingers, and looked around for the child who lost it. Crawling in overalls, he stopped at her feet. He stood in surprise, having followed the trail to this stranger, and she handed it over. Released, surrendered to his next moment in time, the boy ran toward a jungle gym and climbed the hollowed-out plastic cubbies to the slide. When he went down, a look of disappointment flashed over his face. He had to push himself down with sneakers and hands. But then, he went up and did it again.

There were humans, holding inside their skin a bunch of bones and chemicals, and then there was everything else, the spaces between them, the space between bodies. And all these living things walking around in their structures, through doors, and out again, this time with food or bags or drinks. If you could see them all from above, all the tops of their heads, all of the phones that must ring at once across the nation, all of the hellos spoken together, all of the doors slammed, all of the cash registers opened, all the cars starting at once, all the goodbye kisses, all the orgasms, all the toilets flushing—and if all these humans were to grow taller—their heads would hit the ceilings, but one would still never be more special than another.

Each person feels special, and yet not one person is. These humans remain the same, circling, wearing down the carpet, hoping for something meaningful to come along, something spectacular, out-of-this-world. Bouncing balls and plastic plants: civilization and the evidence of progress. A birthday party, a trampoline. A newspaper article about *them*. She held her elbows, still hunched over, and began to cry. Someone had to be Freya Porter, but why her? The sobs convulsed inside her, and she couldn't find anywhere in her disjointed, repetitive thoughts a reason to live. The child on the slide would, before long, be a tired man on a bus. And the jungle gym would be thrown in a dump. The storefronts would change, and eventually, the whole mall, an entire mile of outlet stores, would be boarded up, abandoned or demolished like everything else.

She could not find an answer. And she could not wait any longer.

Freya took the bus home and walked in. Empty-handed, she stood in the living room with the TV off. Then, she went to the hallway, improvising her path, led only by the rhythmic beating in her chest. She looked in Jim's old room, Alex's old room, picking up the oval mirror on the dresser top. The leftover scents of Alex and Jim communicated something to her. This communication lifted off the dresser and the bed and the carpet and the bedside table and gathered together in an almost perceptible spirit, which moved before her like a piece of paper in a changing breeze. It came to her and filled in her skin. She padded along the wall to the next room, Reddy's, with its double bed.

In her own bedroom, she tugged her duffle bag from the bottom of the closet and, in a disorganized manner, sitting on the floor, stuffed into it panties and a nightgown, along with beauty things from her vanity. It took her a long time to gather the energy even to zip it shut, and more time to get the suitcase from under her bed, which, over a long hour, she filled with clothes and pictures. She opened the windows, turning the house cool again. When she couldn't think of anything else to bring with her, she dragged the luggage to the front door and took the time to go through the mail. This habit engaged in her a short-sighted sense of responsibility and purpose. She shoved it off, determined to follow through with her plans.

But then she noticed the small green envelope with her name on it. She ripped it open. With one hand, she felt for the slick wood around her seat cushion, and with the other, she put her fingers into the letter and spread the page flat onto the table. It was from Emma. As she read each word, her heels pushed harder on the floor, leaning her back, hesitating, stretching away from the end of the note. After she read it, she turned on the TV to get rid of the silence. There was a commercial on she'd seen a hundred times. It was for a new kind of toilet scrubber with a disposable head. It had a catchy tune. When the game show came back on, the crowd cheered.

CHAPTER 7

Mark's big TV sat on a TV dinner stand. She stood in front of it. She had the butcher knife above her head. It slammed into the glass. The TV fell off to the side, crashing and bending. In her slippers, she stomped her foot into it until it cut her, and she glanced around for more things to break. She swung it into the porcelain angels and jogged her way to the front room, dropping the knife to the carpet, and pulling, tugging on the curtains until they ripped down onto her with the rods, and she shoved all that away from her toward the door. She slid her hand along the bookshelf, knocking the books down. Then, she fell to the floor and let herself scream.

There was a line of blood down her ankle from the TV. In the kitchen, she threw the chairs over and kicked the table. She opened the cabinets, emptied them of their dishes, breaking each one—one at a time—on the faucet. And she looked out the window to the plants below the oak tree, slicked by rain. Once she got out to them, she ripped them out of the ground like hair from a scalp.

To Reddy, she said she was sorry. She told him she loved him. She took a cornflower from the grass and placed it on the grave.

*

The heavy car dropped the cousins down steep hills with trees and bushes flashing past, reaching as high as a Baltimore building, with greens in every stage of growth; it flung them wildly around turns through Abiquiu, where blue and yellow rafters smacked paddles into the river. Families in floral lined up for photos. Aleksia popped a tape from the stereo, and now they listened to the weather report about Hurricane Ivan sucking its way through Florida. Oh! To hear the news! To know what was happening in the world! She had her left leg bent, foot on the seat, fresh skin open to the air like a girl without a care in the world. A girl who might throw his clothes out the window. A girl his mother would worry over.

They passed signs, and Reddy said them aloud. *Wildlife Center. Boneyard Road. Arroyo Something.*

"You can drive if you want," she said, nonchalantly.

"Nah," he said back. The highway relaxed into an open landscape, opened to fresh, fertile fields, a lavender mist blanketing the shrubs. "Hi, cow," he said, as he'd made it a point to greet roadside animals for the past six hours. "Hi, horsey." Perhaps, he needed to hear his voice. He slouched into his seat. "Oh, hi, goats." In the distance, the hills crumbled behind layers of mud-brick houses, flat as cakes. He'd seen yurts before lunch. The cousins ate sandwiches and crunchy pickles. He'd seen trailers and ancient school buses. Kids running shoeless. He could live anywhere. Be anyone. He could get himself mixed up in anything he wanted. He could tell her to stop the car, and here, or maybe right here, his new life would begin. Day one, on that rock precipice. He could drink hot coffee at dawn, whiskey at sunset, reading popular novels and watching her (because, of course there was always a her, and she was right there beside him) fall asleep with a stray cat draped across her arms. This experience of seeing and hearing, smelling and salivating, feeling and touching was beyond explaining, but he wanted to make a profession of writing (now that he was free!) and so he tried anyway.

"Hello, eagle." Never in his life had he taken the question, "Am I dreaming?" with greater consideration than he had today—but how cruel would that be? And now, looking up through the open window, head set against the frame, wind pressed into his cheek, and eyes up at the sky, he witnessed the persistence of the clouds spreading out on the wind. A dream had never been persistent. He pulled his head back in, breathing in that orgasmic place, the place where senses and poetics combined. They passed a naked white tree with branches clawing upward. They switched out the shame of their incestuous relationship for the thrill of their romance. Slowing into town, the light posts were decorated with flower baskets. Luminaria spread out evenly along roof ledges waiting for a light. Their love was too big to be wasted. Shoppers came out of stores carrying kids. Bicyclists rang bells. Dogs made friends. It was divine intervention—*Hello, dogs*—a wish granted. So, he would not question it. He would not shame it.

And he would not try to explain or excuse it. He only wanted to love it.

"Light me a cigarette," she said. He put two in his mouth, lit both, and handed one over. "Thanks."

"I want to be a writer," he said.

"Yeah, I think you'd be really good at that," she said.

"I hope. What about you?"

"Me? I want to have goats. But I'm okay just being me, I guess." She drew a line with her cigarette across the plains. "I think I'll be good doing this for a long time."

"Yeah."

Just north of town, on the brink of sunset, they reached the Gorge.

"This is it," she said and parked. Sightseers walked along the sidewalk, taking photos and eating snacks. "We aren't going to be like the people who made us," she said, as they walked the sidewalk. It turned into a bridge—a sight so wide and busy on the eyes, it dizzied him as much as the motel room fan. A car went past, rumbling it all. He gripped the metal railing. And reaching dead center, it was as if he floated above the river below, which must have been massive but looked like a stream. He could hear it gushing, ramming rocks. It hurt him later to think how friendly it had seemed.

"Tempting, isn't it?" she said, leaning over. They'd been on solid ground the whole way, but now they hovered over a gash in the land. "I can almost understand." The wind bounced against their ears. "I wonder how far your superpowers go," she said, with a playful emphasis on "superpowers."

"You're still thinking about that?"

"We should test it sometime."

Reddy looked down.

"Like, if something happened to me, what would you do?" She bit her lip. She put her hand up on his shoulder. "Not right now, but sometime."

"If it's even real, it's not something I meant to do—or know how to do. You know what false causality is? Just because one thing happens after another thing, it doesn't mean that thing caused that other thing," he said. "If I eat a hot dog and then get hit by a bus, it doesn't mean the hot dog killed me."

"Whatever," she said. And then, as the clouds turned pink, "I miss my dad." She talked about her father and their Aunt Kirstin, and her voice moved gracefully through the details. The wind splashed their hair around. Cars passed. Tourists quieted down. "It doesn't seem real that people can die. It will never make sense to me." He asked her why she came to the States. "I didn't want to come," is all she said. He told her what it was like to be in that room—to not know anything, to not know how many months passed. She told him how alone she felt.

"What's your ideal relationship?" she said suddenly, or at least, it seemed sudden to him.

"I, I don't know. Someone nice," he said.

"Hmm." She swung her hips to the railing and back out again. "I don't know what I want either. A guy who's kind of soft, kind of hard? Wants me. Wants family. Wants to travel. Wants kids. Lots of kids. But, most of all, won't put up with my bullshit."

All Reddy could say was, "Yeah."

She stopped moving and looked over, again, as if stunned. She stopped for so long in this position, he couldn't tell if something was wrong with her, or if something was wrong with him.

"In my next life," she started, pressing her belly into the

railing, again, her hair dangling down as she looked over, "I just want a shot at innocence."

The wide colorful gorge surrounded them. He carefully watched her frail wrists. He couldn't stop staring at her. *Tempting, isn't it?*

"Hey, let's etch our names on it," he said.

"Yeah, okay. Yeah," she said.

Reddy pulled out a credit card and scratched into the gray railing, *A & R.*

"Perfect," she said. "We'll be here forever." The river shined like a knife.

"Let's head back. Get a hotel," he said, and then he followed her toward the car. "I just don't want to be forgotten."

"Maybe that's all I want, too."

"Yeah. How do you feel?" he said.

"I'm good. You?"

"Bit of a headache," he said. "But happy."

*

The dull headache clenched the back of his skull. *Don't let this happen. Don't let this happen.* By morning, he was made out of cooked egg. His face cramped and ached, and when he pushed on the side of his nose, it crackled. *One day*, he thought, *one fucking day. That's it?* But then again, if he only had one day, there was no other way he would have rather spent it. He should be thankful. That thought made him think of his old best friend, Emma. She lost her whole family by being adopted, but even strangers would tell her how thankful she should be. She resented all of them. That's how he felt right now. He had to be thankful for having a glimpse of what everyone else had all the damned time. *Fuck, it was a lot of pressure.* This headache wasn't permanent. He repeated this as

CHAPTER 8

a mantra. *It doesn't have to be. Not everything is permanent.*

On the hotel room nightstand, he found a note from Aleksia. The words had holes in them. He twisted his head to the side to read around his blind spots as they multiplied and widened. It read: Downstairs. Check out is noon.

Too tired to put on fresh clothes, he left in his undershirt and sweatpants.

In the hall, two short ladies in striking white uniforms spoke Spanish, and he couldn't tell which voice belonged to which lady. Reaching the stairwell beyond them, he tuned into their conversation. It came in and out. They pushed a cart up to a room and went in.

Not hardboiled egg or even scrambled, but the egg you crack into a pan and let sit and bubble until it's rubbery and dry. He felt like twelve eggs spilled into a pan, cooked and cooled, boneless and bloodless. His legs and arms, his fingers and hips—all made of egg. He couldn't help but touch a part of his swollen face. His headache knocked. In the hallway, he looked in a mirror sideways. Partly, he wanted to hide from Alex; he also wanted to know what she was doing without him.

This one change in his face fractured him, again. The half that was split in half, split again. Standing there, something rushed inside him—that old familiar feeling—from his left to his right. His knees were bending like taffy. He pressed his palm to the mirror, holding himself up. He wanted Alex, and she didn't want him.

A tall, older man came through a door wearing Velcro shoes, closing the door with his luggage in his hand. Reddy turned around, letting his head rest on the mirror, looking at the man, not speaking, only breathing.

"You okay?" the man said. Reddy stared. The man went

away. Reddy let his fingers walk down the wall so he could get to the floor. He would have to crawl to her. He tried to force a smile on his face because his muscles tightened in his cheeks. He remembered being on top of her the night before—after the Gorge—how she liked it, how her nipples stood up. He bit them like pencil erasers. After she orgasmed, she wrapped herself in a towel and stood away from the bed, tilting her head quizzically.

"Nothing happened," she said. She looked past him, blinking, and after a moment, hid away in the shower.

Make me happy, he kept thinking, putting one hand down and then the other, dragging along on his knees. Someone on this planet could make him happy. Self-sufficiency was a myth. He pulled himself up to standing. He could walk to her. He would walk straight. From the small lobby, where a white-haired woman behind the counter was saying something to him, he saw a tiled area with lights which seemed far away, like he was roller skating for the first time, trying to get from one post to another. His hands reached before him as he walked, his legs stepping heavily.

He heard the buzzing and rings of slot machines and, as soon as he got to one, he latched onto it, lifting his head to look around at the swirling lights pouring down.

She wasn't there. The place looked empty of humans. Light came in from the front windows. He couldn't see over the two aisles of machines. He crept along. Getting around the corner, he saw a spark of her. When she noticed him, she put in a coin and pulled a lever.

He didn't think he could move. He didn't think he could scream—*that something was wrong, something was so wrong, something was the worst kind of wrong.* She went to the next machine beside her, away from him. Her hair shined and curved around her ear, sticking to her neck. She caught him staring. Out of the corner of his eye, he saw her jet off in another direction. He lagged behind in this small place that seemed to get bigger with every step he made. Around the corner, there was a young man, short, strong, and capable.

Reddy rested his head against a dividing wall. Pink-tinted images came to mind. He took the risk of lifting his head to see if she was still there in the light, his vision tunneling, then set it back gently.

There had been no foreshadowing. He saw the blood in his head. His parents swam in it. They were just people, and he had come into their lives like a twister, pulling toward him everything within reach. He sucked in his mother, his father, their money, their lives, their careers. Then, he saw the hospital and all the doctors, and he was the tornado with all its strength, taking everything toward himself. All the history was his. All the attention was his. He never had enough. Nothing satisfied him. They gave him toys for having tumors. Then, the tumors turned on him, started to eat him, to make him hungrier. And as the pain turned more striking, so that he thought he might hit the carpet like a dead man from a chair, he broke a sweat and hummed to see if he was still hearing. He wanted to go home now. He was ready for it to be over. He didn't want to be guilty. He'd always been guilty. As if he'd faked his illness. Everyone knew it. Alex knew it. He touched his chin. He'd been drooling.

Alex started a conversation with the young guy, playing with a barrette in her hair, and Reddy couldn't help but see how damned pretty she was. He didn't want to hear the conversation—the giggle she made for the guy. Seeing her like that, like some child he couldn't force to grow, made him want to smash something. Why didn't she love him? But he didn't have the energy for it, and a moment later, he cracked. His eggy, wobbling knees gave out, and he flopped to the floor.

*

Reddy had his hand to his head. Aleksia had her foot to the pedal. It took all day to get going. Now, it was nighttime and there was nothing much to see. It was about 30 degrees out. She cranked the heat until her face and lips rubbed together like newspaper pages. She had to do this because Reddy kept opening the window.

Aleksia never tried a latte from a machine before, but she needed to stay up all night, so she filled up a tall flimsy twenty-two ounce cup with the sticky vanilla drink she got from the truck stop and drank a quarter of it on her way out to the car.

The greenish tint to Reddy's face looked worse beneath the gas station lights. He looked at her as she got into the seat.

"I have to use the restroom," he said. He scratched the back of his head. "I don't think I can walk. Not by myself."

Aleksia put her coffee on the floor near the pedals. She didn't want to talk about it.

She walked him in through the two front doors, and he walked the way he used to—as if the whole world slanted. One foot stepped on another. He breathed hard. The guy behind the counter looked them up and down. The bathroom was over three aisles away and in the far back. He used her for balance, and he was such a great weight on her, she could barely hold herself up.

They came around the third aisle. She shrank under him, her legs like snappable chopsticks. She jumped to move his arm. He wasn't saying anything. It was like trying to get a slug to stand. Then, she faltered. She stepped on her own toes, and they both went elbows first into a line of shot glasses.

She ducked. He grabbed at her to get up. She managed to catch him and get them standing before the entire aisle tipped over. But the shot glasses had crashed to the ground, and the man behind the counter was coming toward them.

She brought Reddy to the women's restroom and put him in the handicapped stall, while she sat in a little chair by the mirrors and thought about what to do.

The man would think he was drunk. Reddy's disorder was too rare for anyone to believe her, and she didn't have any papers of importance if they called the cops. But why would he call the cops over some shot glasses? She didn't want to talk to anyone. She could wire them money for the shot glasses. If there had been a window large enough in the restroom, she would've pushed her slug through it.

She waited for him to finish up in the stall. She had her passport and she had his ID, but she didn't have a license, and technically, she had kidnapped him. *And the car, oh god the car.* She splashed water on her face.

They finished in the restroom and Alex helped him out. He had his arm around her shoulder. She kept her head down and took a different aisle toward the front doors. A teenager was sweeping up the glass, and the man wasn't behind the counter anymore. Just as they passed the teenager, he turned to say something to a woman at the soda machine. They got to the doors, stepped through, and the teenager must have seen them because she heard someone yell out, "Wait a minute!"

They picked up the pace and made their way to the car.

Alex grabbed her latte, turned the ignition, and they blasted off.

In a matter of hours, she had started drinking French Vanilla crap from a truck stop and had picked up smoking cigarettes the way she thought people ought to smoke them, one right after another. She lost count already. Reddy said the smell of the smoke helped his head and that he'd been craving cigarettes for six months, so every so often she handed him hers for him to take a puff. He handed it back to her, glazed in saliva. She threw it out the window.

He whined and hissed. Her eyes felt like BBs shooting down the highway ahead of them.

*

Just before noon the next day, Reddy lay in the backseat with the buckle jabbing him in the side, too nauseous to sit up. The fluid in his head dripped to one side and seeped into his ear. It was warm and thick. He begged for ice and she gave it to him in a cup. Then, he begged for ice cream. In Oklahoma, around sunset, she stopped at a 7-11. Reddy watched through the front window. The woman in the booth watched a little TV. Alex came out a few minutes later. She said she found a Ben and Jerry's in the back near the slushie machine, and she told him in a sleepy monotone voice that she'd taken a 44-ounce cup, dropped in the Cherry Garcia, filled the cup the rest of the way with ice and soda. At the counter, she paid a buck-twenty. They were low on money until her mom would deposit more cash into the account. Reddy drank the soda, which had turned into its own kind of slushie, and afterward, he opened the sticky ice cream and had that too. He couldn't get enough of the cold. All day, the sun burned black spots into his retinas. His headache migrated. At one point, it was stuck in his cheek, but the ice cream made it return to the back of his head, just above his neck and over his throat.

CHAPTER 8

*

Alex wouldn't sleep. She couldn't. She'd seen him there on the casino floor shaking like a fish on rocks. Below his clamped eyes, blood slipped from his mouth. Then, he stopped and was as malleable as a corpse. She was too afraid to scream. She hurried to the woman up front. A janitor came out from nowhere and, in seconds, hoisted Reddy from the floor and hauled him to the curb.

Reddy was awake again and saying, "Oh my God, oh my God." It was the most horrible thing she'd ever seen, and she'd seen *a lot* of horrible. She didn't know what to do.

The neck of his undershirt tore and showed his naked shoulder. For some reason, that's what stuck with her the most, his ripped shirt. The first thing she did before getting him into the passenger's seat was change it. Then, he turned to the sidewalk and puked. He'd been whining ever since then.

"Where've you been taking me?"

"I'll tell you later."

"Tell me now. I need a hospital."

"I'm trying to help you. Try to go to sleep."

"Don't take me home."

"I'm not."

"They'll lock me in that room."

"I swear I won't." There was no way she would take him home to that murderer.

Then, he started saying, "You should be my girlfriend and we'll get a place together," and talking about how he could get Social Security for them to live on.

By the time they passed Oklahoma City, they'd smoked four packs together. The only thing he wanted was ice and ice cream. At one stop, she lamely massaged his head.

The black road and black sky merged. There was little difference between the two, and she might as well have been guiding a boat along a current. She touched the wheel ever so slightly, searching for the horizon. After a while, his whines sounded like music. She tried to sleep and drive at the same time. The white-silver signs came in through her eyes and into her subconscious. She'd been awake for thirty hours. No longer did she think about how to drive. She did it. It was natural. She was a sea captain. She left her eyelids open, driving with some other part of her and took a nap. Her eyes hollowed out. The road drove into her, and she received it the way the ocean receives, and accepts, a sinking boat.

*

"Wanna play pinball?" she said. They were at a truck stop somewhere, and he seemed to be walking better. As long as he kept cold, as long as the pressure didn't change, as long as they didn't drive into higher elevation—or lower—maybe he could be okay. He didn't want to play. They placed their microwaved food on the flimsy table between two green Adirondack chairs that sat along the front windows. For the past four hours, Reddy's eyes leaked down his face.

He wished her a Merry Christmas, even though it was September—because a dancing mechanical Santa Claus waggled inside the window—but only heard the second half of his own voice, and he couldn't understand the urge to say this. Was it because at his core, he knew he would never see another holiday? If someone cared about him, they could throw him every holiday at once, circling in and out through a revolving door with platters: Easter ham, grilled hot dogs, bags of mini-Snickers, turkey, and red and green boxes of his favorite things.

The Big Bang smacked that night in the motel room. It

CHAPTER 8

opened and showed him off to the Milky Way. Up until the casino, his universe had been expanding, but now he swallowed it all up again like those clowns who swallow handkerchiefs, one tied to the next. She wished him a merry one, too. His hearing had a buzz in it.

They drove along later that night, smoking cigarettes, drinking coffee, stopping for gas and snacks, his eyes still burning. The wind rattled the seatbelt. It came in and out and aside from his pounding headache, all he could think about was how the quiet wasn't so bad when the buzzing turned into music.

"It's probably another tumor," he told her after practicing the sentence for half an hour in his mind. She tightened her grip on the wheel. He glanced away, but when he looked at her again, she had dimples, more dimples than he'd ever noticed her having. She smiled. Then, with her hands still on the wheel and her body forward, she craned her neck. She wasn't smiling. She was furiously crying.

He stared unmoving as she talked and yelled and cussed. She gestured with her left hand, making a motion as if she wanted to slap the windshield with the back of it. The metal handle of the door was in his back. He looked down the road to see where they were going and, as if God wanted to remind him of his headache, the road swished and shifted, and he reached out again and got nothing but air.

The car pinged off a guard rail and stopped.

She had her hands over her face, and he reached out his hand to hers, but his arm wasn't long enough to reach her a million miles away. He slipped back toward the door, ashamed that the psychological bruises of his sickness, his impending paralysis and death, and his unhappy family had turned into badges, as if every day he were awarded for waking up to the circumstances—even if only in his mind (and here the image of him split, again, to see himself in the anonymous eye of the public)—while someone like Aleksia had to start the feelings from the beginning.

She got back on the road, and he said he was sorry. She shook her head to indicate that he shouldn't be. They were closer now. Between the thumps in his head, he jumped from one broken thought to the next. He kept remembering how good it felt to be on her, to have pulled her pajama top up over her breasts—to have seen them bulging—so pure, so untouched, how she had begged him to touch her and the way he watched as sweat formed above her lip. He'd never been part of anything so complete, so clean in his life. He held onto her hip as he moved inside her.

"We could get a place together in this village in North Baltimore," he said, holding his head. She didn't say anything. His heartbeat picked up at the thought of it and he could hear the sound between his ears. She wore jeans, and their soft pack of Camel Lights stuck out between her thighs, her face still blushed from crying. He watched her pull one out gracelessly. He slid his hand across the vinyl seat and up the side of her thigh.

He saw her inhale.

He saw her inhale deeper, as if he'd dropped ice cubes down her shirt. She shook her head.

He waited for an appropriate time to say that they ought to get some sleep at a hotel. He believed a bed would fix his headache. His hair above his ears slipped with perspiration. He heated from the inside out and imagined wavy lines that sat with him. The white paint on the road snapped a jagged line. The signs smeared past, but when he looked at Alex, she moved so slowly, or not at all. The silence emphasized the strict stillness of her. He turned all of this into a poem, a quiet little poem, a soundless lullaby, an abandoned rowboat gliding up and down as waves rolled beneath it. Not even a whisper, not a soul around, no one watching, except maybe God or angels. The pain could be taken in, sucked in, given away in chunks. It could disintegrate. He let his muscles relax. She wasn't moving, except in the slightest way. It was too much. He would not try to explain himself any longer.

He was not a masterpiece—and no one would argue that—he was just a dead piece of meat thrown on paper, and he was born that way. He was born wrong. His muscles turned to jelly. Why wasn't she moving? On the side of the road, there was the plastic booth he sat in where he ate Fritos. On the other side was the Gorge. Ahead of him, the motel stairway. His parents were there around the bend, unknown to everyone in the world, in their simple clothing and unconscious lives, wanting, wanting, wanting, but they waved—each in a different way—his mother with an obvious white hand like a china dish, and his father with two fingers he released from his tightly folded arms. This is why his father never needed hugs; his arms hugged each other. He was built self-sufficient. Like a lit-up image on a screen, his parents faded out. An orange as tough and cool as a football passed by. When he poked it, he floated away. And there was Aleksia, naked as a tulip in the dark, rolling over in place like a rotisserie chicken followed by so many rolling green apples shining in the headlights, spread out evenly across the night as to suggest wallpaper. The white microscopic stars blinked, and the white microscopic stars hid. If he never got more than this, it would be enough.

He said, "Please, let's get a hotel," but from a cold cavity in his heart, he knew he would never get what he wanted again. She shook her head.

*

The car with its dusty, glassy headlights beaming through the dark in a yellowish glow pushed through the next night along I-40, where there were trees again, making the terrain less alien. Alex drove all night and into the sunrise with dry eyes. The cousins wore plastic sunglasses she daintily lifted from a revolving display in a convenience store. The sunlight made everything new. The pain moved through her like a warm river. They traversed a long bridge with the sun reflecting off a pyramid down below on land. It was Memphis. Her muscles turned to jelly. Alex gave in and put on the radio to help her stay up while Reddy's eyes pointed away with his cheeks hanging down. The radio station played Yes's "Roundabout," and she sang along, getting louder and louder.

They looked out separate windows but felt the same things.

Her apartment in New York City had a window that wouldn't open, a bed that squeaked when she sat on it, and a sink that wouldn't drain, but the price wasn't bad. In that room—no bigger than their car—she left herself when she went out, just hung herself up on the back of the door and went to the clubs. No one stopped her for identification, as if she were invisible.She came home drunk and, in the morning, tried her old self out again for an hour or so, long enough to hate it, and draped it over the bed post. Suicide was contagious. She washed her hands for twenty seconds. She looked for people and parties and good food. She tried not to think about the past. She tried not to think about what she saw at the Porters. It was a good time. But then one day, she was lying in

CHAPTER 8

bed with a hangover too heavy to lift and thoughts of Reddy crept in. There she was—so profoundly stuck to the mattress someone could've flipped it on its side and she wouldn't have shaken loose and there she was—thinking about *him*.

She pressed against the iron headboard. You get one chance to follow a finger-point to a constellation, one chance to love. She kicked the sheets off. The sperm and the egg bang you into existence. The springs squeaked. Three dimensions unfold like a vanity mirror. She lifted her legs with her hands. She tied the laces of her green sneakers. Some wake to believe it. Some wake to question it. She stole a car in Jersey and drove all night. Some —like she, like her parents, like everyone she cared about, woke to feel it— and loved every damned feeling it offered. Headlights blinded her. She drove 55. Especially the hard ones. Ate them up like meals ready to rot. The cuts. The insults. The burns.The tiniest thing could kill a person. A splinter in the bloodstream. A tumor the size of a pupil. This body belonged to her. She could use it to hit and steal, to break and fuck.

Her thoughts separated like fingers on a hand. She twisted the doorknob to the Porters. At the time, she expected the front door to be locked. It wasn't.She expected Reddy's bedroom to be unlocked but it was bolted shut. She slid the bolt from the latch. She expected to see an empty bed. That is to say—she thought he was dead like everyone else she loved. But he slept there without a thing in the room but the bed and the ceiling light fixture.

They drove from one town to the next, connecting the dots (Memphis, Nashville, and Knoxville) like the belt of Orion through Tennessee, and somewhere in southern Virginia they slept in the car for the night, Reddy in the back with his hands shoved between his thighs, and Alex, at one point lying on her back, but then, at another, squatting on the floorboard of the passenger side with her head resting on her folded arms. They kept the heat blasting because they were in the mountains, but when Reddy couldn't take the heat any longer, he reached over the seat and turned the car off.

Early in the morning, before the sun was up, a sheet of rain unrolled from the sky, which looked yellowish green from the parking lot sodium lights reflecting off it. By daylight, the sun burned the rain into a steam drifting and lifting around the car. Reddy wasn't awake yet, but she was ready to get back on the road. She slid into the driver seat, grabbed the keys, and turned them. The engine growled and kicked. She tried again. It growled more, and she let it go longer this time, knowing any second it would kick in, turn over, jump, and they'd be on their way. She shoved her foot into the gas, pumping it, and twisted the ignition again. It growled, growled, gurgled. The engine turned over with an explosion.

He slept through it. He was a rock statue with his neck bent, his chin pulled in, and his hands in fists between his legs. He stayed in the back most of the day, waking once to ask where they were. She made a V with her fingers, and after some time, he guessed Virginia. He said his whole body hurt, that he needed a hospital, to take him to Johns Hopkins. And after listing his pangs, he said, "When's it going to end?" But it was clear he didn't expect an answer. Exhausted, he pulled himself into the seat.

"I think I'm better," he said like a question, and then that he wished it would snow, but it wasn't even close to cold enough for that. Wayward gusts of sweaty wind battered the flanks of the car. Ahead, the traffic slowed down. A threesome of deer ran toward them through the grass. They were on Route 301.

"Nice Bridge," he said, pointing out a sign that read "Harry W. Nice Bridge."

Aleksia pretended to laugh, and that was good enough for him, so he opened the window, rolled up his sleeve and put his hand outside into the damp air. A flock of birds flapped above. A horse ran past along the road. "Oh, hi!" The sky was a gorgeous moss green.

"It's so beautiful," he said, and off to the right, he saw what looked like the backside of a llama stepping through the trees. He shook his head.

"When the movie was over," he had been talking about his first date with his high school girlfriend, but the story had drifted away from him somewhere in the Blue Ridge Mountains, "it was dark outside, and in the light at the end of the driveway, you could see it was snowing, and she got so excited. Maybe she was acting then too; I don't know, but I felt that kind of excitement you get at the movies, when the music's loud—that feeling you think can't happen in real life. That's what it was like." He groaned. "And she took my hand—I'd never touched a girl's hand in my life—and ran with me up the street, both of us laughing, until we hit this little wooded spot. And the snow lit up the ground, as if the trees and ground weren't there until the snow painted them in. Like something from *Alice in Wonderland*." He closed the window. Alex's shoulders softened. "You wouldn't believe it. On top of it all being the most beautiful thing I'd ever seen, it happened to also be a full moon, just like it's going to be tonight. I like talking. I've liked it so much lately, Alex." He sighed, out of things to say and self-conscious. "I love the snow," he said, but what he was trying to say was that he loved her.

After a little bit, he said, "We'd lie around naked all day."

"What was it you liked about her?"

"Why was I in love with her?"

"Yeah."

"I don't know! I can't figure it out!" He faced the window. "Maybe it was just that I had her or something." The bridge got closer. A huge body of water expanded in each direction. It was midday but getting dark. "It probably could've been anybody, but it was her, and she agreed to hang out with me, and I had her. I don't know. I'd never had anyone before." He turned back toward Aleksia. "When I told her what was wrong with me, she cried. She covered her face with her hands and burrowed her head into my armpit. Here was this girl, just crying at me, afraid I was going to die, her eyelashes sticking together. She was so warm, she melted me." He talked like it would be the last time in his life to talk. "Guess she's not worried about that now." Eventually, he said, "can I tell you something?"

Aleksia nodded. A line of hazard lights blinked into the darkness of the day ahead of them on the bridge.

"The other night—in the hotel room—I'd never done that before."

*

Aleksia banged her head against the horn in the traffic jam.

"Fuck. Fuck. Fuck." The Potomac River slept motionless below.

"What's wrong?" he shouted. She covered her ears. Wind smashed against their stopped car. "What's wrong? Why's everyone stopping?" The bridge trembled. She turned to him.

"We can't do this, you know."

CHAPTER 8

"I know," he said.

"We're cousins."

Reddy looked down at his hands.

"It's not right."

"I know."

"I don't want to hurt you."

"Yeah," he said.

"I want you to have all the best things life can give you. You're clever and passionate, and you're going to be a really great writer one day."

He couldn't respond.

"We have to walk away." She paused. "From each other."

"Yeah, but I don't really want to," he said.

"I believe that," she said. "I believe that. But do you understand?" she said. "I love you."

He thought for a moment, and said, "Yeah. I love you."

"We love each other."

"Yeah."

"Come on. We had a great time."

He didn't say anything.

"Well," she said, opening her door. "This is your chance to show me."

She got out. He pulled the lever on his door, but something prevented it from opening. The car rocked side to side. He could see her through the windshield, her hair throwing itself. Rain pelted the car. He crawled over the seat and got out on her side, following her. Other people were getting out of their cars, too, with their arms bent, shielding their eyes. "What's going on?"

She grabbed him by the arm. The static of her touch electrified him to his core. She smiled.

"Try it."

"Aleksia, seriously. I don't know how to do this."

She motioned in grand gestures, saying things he couldn't hear.

"I can't do what you think I can do." The volume of the wind cranked.

"I'm not giving up. You don't know what you can do because you haven't tried!"

"I don't know what you're talking about."

"You!" she shouted. "You are powerful!"

She came around to the front of him with wide strong eyes, her back to the ledge, the water far below.

Please stop, he said inside his mouth. *Please. I love you.*

I don't have anywhere to go, he thought she said.

She turned to the ledge, pulled herself up in her puffy green jacket. People were looking at them. She motioned more—a type of made-up sign language—and with every cell in his body he wanted to understand.

"Do it," she yelled.

"Alex. Stop! Get down. What are you doing? It's dangerous! Please!" Tears were popping out of his eyes. He reached for her little ankle. The wind pushed everything around. He was weak, and she was spinning and amped as a turbine. She communicated something above him. He heard bits.

"The car *something something something* . . . the place . . . trashed . . . *something* supernormal *something* of *something* . . ." She stopped. "Do something!" and that last *something*, he really did hear.

Across the water, a cloud formed like a smear and escaped the river like a crowd of ghosts. The spinning cloud was as thick as a cruise liner. She said a sentence repetitively, and his

CHAPTER 8

heart raced. He tried to hear her. Tried so hard.

"You can do it," she said. She pulled a small creature from her mouth and set it on the ledge. "If this doesn't work, don't forget me."

He thrust himself toward the edge, flung his hands to her.

In a flicker of a green flash, she disappeared.

He slid down the short wall to the cement screaming, screaming, screaming, screaming.

*

Ivan broke off at the Chesapeake Bay, turning the sky wet-cement gray and presenting as unassuming as a mist, floating droplets—though they went frigid in an instant, and the entire condition picked up its pace to twirl like plates atop plates atop plates. Nothing tried to stop it; no sirens sounded. It twisted along, sucking up water, plucking trees along the Potomac River—so slow, so fast all at once—and now tinting the air moss green and coming out of hell like a freight train.

When it passed Route 301, it erased the bridge and moved on, taking the curve of the river, and when it reached Baltimore, it was a mile-high wall of storm.

*

He had to get home. She left a voicemail, and it took him the entire thirty-minute bus ride to figure out how to listen to it. She was leaving, did it say? Could she have really said that? Could she have meant right now? Mark exited the bus, but now the bus stopped with its headlights on in the pouring rain—the rain that pounded sideways against his face and shoulder, the shoulder he'd only just learned to use—and the wind pushed at his pant legs, so he felt he was walking at the bottom of a river, and then it switched directions and he realized: he would have to outrun this.

"Freya," he said. "Freya," though he had so many more paces to go. His grocery bag rapped and smacked and pulled at his wrist. He let it go. It flung back so hard through space it broke a windshield. Turning toward the rowhouse, gripping that black railing, objects zipped toward him. A bicycle, a frog, an eel snaking through the air, and then—like a spray of BBs—small in the distance, but big in one second: crabs. He ducked, holding the railing with both hands, but one claw gashed his brow. "Freya," he said, but now he could barely breathe. The rain stung his skin. It was taking his breath, too. Taking it somewhere else. In the blurry, stained space, it looked as if the front door were open. A squeal behind him, and the bus scratched sideways down the street toward the light post. Sparks sprang out. He pulled his body up, electricity in the air, blood covering his eyelids.

He heard a shriek. Gripping the rail, he looked. A woman held the ankle of a child—the child flying like a kite. He had to reach her. Get to the woman. He started back down. The wind ripped the glasses right off his face. Risking opening his eyes, he saw the shape of the child fling from her grasp. She crawled to an iron railing, holding on, shoes peeling off. Another car slid sideways with its headlights on. Car alarms amped up. He couldn't get to her. He had to get in. Had to get to Freya. One foot and then the other.

What was that? Something caught him—a green jacket? With a burst of energy, he thrust himself up the rest of the steps. "Freya!" The mail stuck to walls. Everything was turned over. "Freya!" He checked each room as the rowhouse shook, let loose beneath him. The basement, he thought. But when he got there, she wasn't there. He ran back up to check the bathroom, with walls coming toward him. Wood splitting, the smell of sawdust in the air. The storm, it was so loud. He had no choice but to get back down there underground, where the water heater was, to curl up, to cover his ears with his hands, to push his bloody head into his knees.

It pounded. It ripped. It split. Cracked. Gift bags and bows swirled. The backyard came undone. An echo of screams and screams and screams.

And then, in two minutes, it was *all gone*.

*

Here we are, underwater together. We can breathe underwater. The minnows swim in and leave us as they please.

Bubbles escaped her nose. Her hair waved yellows, golds and greens. Her dimples peaked. This is what it's like to be in the Milky Way. Reddy took her wrists in his as they were freefalling, but this was gentle, being submerged. So dark, so quiet. Everything was good underwater. They could have a whole life in this place of no power lines, no poverty, no sickness, no light, no sound. Under the water, everything was soft. Their palms slid. Their fingers stretched. In this inner space, her eyes flashed supernovas, and they parted. She drifted to an untravellable place, lightyears away, dimensions away, on the other side of life, and he was plucked out by his chest.

When she'd jumped, one word slipped from under her feet.

The word was "no."

*

Mud caked the sliding doors. A mellow blue sky replaced the ceiling. A cloud pillow swept over.

In the kitchen, he picked up a chair and put it right side up. "Freya?" he said weakly.

The stove was gone. Looking off the ledge of the kitchen, there was the blurry cube-shape of it upside down in the grass. The blue-wallpapered wall with the toy boats knocked down the fence. The fridge next to him teetered on the edge.

"You okay?" he heard. The wall that separated him from his neighbor went somewhere with the roof.

"Yeah," he said. "You?"

"I'm all right," she said.

"You seen my wife?"

"She left," she said, and looking around, "My God. Everything is broken."

"Do you know where?"

"Everything is broken."

Neighbors spilled slowly into the street. The woman at the railing turned as dark as the dirt. She screamed and screamed and screamed from a tomato-red mouth. A helicopter chopped through the neighborhood. From up the street, came a woman carrying the flung toddler, its arms reaching.

From the other direction, an old man cried, "Over here!"

Mark ran.

"Someone's in here!"

"What can I do?" Mark said once he got there. "Where is she? Where is she?"

The guys shimmied a chunk of concrete from a pile of concrete. Mark lifted the fractured drywall.

A dog whimpered. He pulled it out gently by its limp, dry paws. Everyone cheered.

An ambulance zigzagged around the demolished vehicles and debris, lights spinning and a driver with his head halfway out of the vehicle, throwing his hand about. Inside his home, Mark found himself nailed to the carpet at the bedroom closet.

CHAPTER 8

Like a chimney after a house-fire, it stood unharmed. He rattled the brass handle until the door budged open. His clothes hung neatly on the left.

But aside from a few hangers and a hatbox, the right side was bare.

He made a dash through the trashed hall, putting to use his long legs, toward the front to see if the car stayed parked in the driveway, but barely able to focus without his glasses, fell. He damned it all, brushing himself off. With a jerk of his head in the direction of his shoulder, his eyes grabbed an ominous black hand posed like a tarantula reaching out of the back yard. The hand clawed higher into the sky than even the rowhouse, and in its black palm (as his eyes transitioned from blur to strained-focus he recognized it as the underside of the oak tree ripped from the earth) a bit of blue flapped like a flag and let loose in slow motion from its grasp.

He darted down the basement stairs. He yanked the sliding door through the muddy track with the fierce intention of a man who needed to come clean but, out of spite and fear, would choose to disrupt justice. Stepping through, he slammed the door on himself and dwelled briefly with his wrist to his eyebrow, shielding his eyes from the sunlight. And then he heard a creak so loud it may have been the heavens cracking apart. Instead, it was the uneasy refrigerator above him.

*

Water squished inside his socks. Reddy wrung his shirt out on the floor of a cold room, and someone peeled it from his skin. He didn't know what to do but to sit where they pushed him to sit and lie where they pressed him to lie. He stared vacantly into an imageless middle-space seeing only the green sparkle of her jacket, hearing only the word "no." They wheeled him on a gurney and the image stuck with him, unmovable, as if he'd been watching a home movie of his life and the tape got caught in the reels right where Aleksia jumps.

He fast forwarded himself to shake the image loose. He'd hit the riverbed with his wrist. Not knowing the way to the surface, he leapt from the bottom in another direction, swimming against gravity with a bit of air in his lungs.

He'd been pulled up onto a boat. He remembered that part. The pull of his pant leg, his cheek rubbing across slick fiberglass.

To keep his wet body warm, his heart raged a fire through to his fingertips.

*

Emma plunged a crutch into the mud, and then another, with one leg bent and shoeless, hopping along the drenched side yard of the Porter's rowhouse. She wore running shorts and a hoodie having burst out of a fitful nap to the furious sky, and pink lightning flashing one neighborhood at a time, and nothing on her mind but her friend -as if all this storm could reverse the truth and strike life into his body. She excelled in emergency situations as her life had been one long emergency. Even still, she'd shouted at her girlfriend, Kara, accidentally, and would have to apologize and explain, but she felt sick with urgency as they'd jumped curbs and cut the park in half with their tires to get there. Unphased by the interaction, Kara took the stairs up. Coming around the bend with crutches sinking, Emma flipped her blue hair from her face using the back of her arm and drew in a breath beside the monstrous void taking shape next to her. At first glance, it was a hole on its side, with gravity and all that, which could take her in to never be seen again. That big tree had been pulled from the ground like a

CHAPTER 8

tooth. At its base sat a folded body wrapped in blue. With her left crutch, she timidly tapped it. If she loved the person in there, why couldn't she bare to touch it? *He isn't in there,* she told herself. *That's his casing.* She jerked at the realization -Mr. Porter's eyes might be on her this minute. She felt seen from above, with a tickling whisper along her neck. But her attention was taken by the sound of electric vibration rattling through the refrigerator dropped to its side, partly cornered into the earth like a blunt spear. She crept upon it, easing the crutches into the bald yard, approaching the long denim legs bent in a hundred directions underneath it.

From the second floor, her girlfriend yelled into the neighborhood, "No one's here! The place is empty." Her voice opened, having popped her head out. She released a restrained squeak and wordlessly shoved things around in the rowhouse as Emma watched the cellphone vibrate, peaking its head from the pocket hem of Mr. Porter's pants.

Kara came around the corner behind her. She said *oh my god, oh my god, oh my god,* but her voice felt far away, as if under water.

"Is that Reddy?"

The phone went quiet. When it rang, again, Emma jumped.

"Don't answer it," Kara said at her shoulder which was all Emma needed to break her trance and thrust her into action. She handed her crutches to Kara who slung them over her shoulder. Emma bent down and edged the phone by the bottom with her thumb until it was released.She opened it, looking up to the sky that filled Reddy's old room.

"Hello?" she said.

"Hello. Is this the phone of Mark Porter?"

"It is."

"May I speak with Mr. Porter?"

"I don't think you can right now." Kara held onto her arm so she wouldn't fall over, being on just one foot. "He can't come to the phone." She paused. "But can I take a message?"

"Is this Freya Porter?"

"No. What's going on?"

"I'm sorry, well, we'd like to leave a message for one of them to call us back immediately at—"

"Just tell me what's happening."

"Mam," the voice hesitated. "Are you of relation to Reddy Porter?"

"Yes."

"This is the George Washington University Hospital. We have Reddy here—"

"Is he okay?" she interrupted.

Kara looked on with wide eyes.

"He's in stable condition."

"Can I pick him up? This is his best friend."

"The patient can only be released to a family member. I'm sorry."

"Okay. Thank you."

She closed up the phone.

"Did they say they have Reddy? How?"

Emma nodded. "My question then," she said, "is who's that?" and pointed her chin toward the body. She took back the crutches from Kara's shaking hands and opened the phone, again. "Was his mom up there?"

"No." Kara's lip trembled. "And the car's gone, too." Her voice quivered. "Want me to call the, uh, the cops?"

"Yeah." Now, Emma held Kara steady by the arm. "Don't look at the bodies. I want you to go to the other side of the

CHAPTER 8

house."

"What are you going to do?"

"Call his brother."

"Will you come with me, please?"

"Let's go." Emma followed her and watched as Kara did her best not to look in any direction but down. When they got to the side, they leaned against the torn-up vinyl siding. Emma found Timothy's number in the phone. "Here it is," she said. "This is going to be one of the hardest phone calls I'll ever have to make in my life."

"I know."

She dialed. As it rang, she whispered to Kara, "I'm sorry."

"For what?" she whispered back.

"This is what it means to be with me." Kara dismissed her apology with a shake of her head and kissed her on the shoulder. "I'll call the police. You call his brother," she said. "Let's bring your friend home -to our place."

The kindness offered broke everything inside Emma -in a good way, if things can be broken in a good way- so when Timothy answered *Oh, hey, Dad*, she could barely get the words to come. She breathed and sniffled into the phone while he made guesses.

*

It took three days for Timothy to get a flight in. Emma followed his blue pant legs down the hospital hallway. With every swoop on the crutches, her hair swung in her face. It didn't seem like he wanted to talk, and she understood. He'd lost too much too fast. As they approached the room, a nurse at the doorway said Reddy was almost done with his session.

"Session?" Emma said.

"With his speech therapist."

Then, in a quiet solemn tone, he asked Timothy questions.

"Was he speaking before the accident?"

"I think he was," Timothy said.

"I want to warn you," the nurse said, "he hasn't talked to anyone since he's been here."

The reverent mood was like that of a funeral, as if a line of people were to come down the hallway single file, shake their hands and mumble condolences.

Timothy stepped just inside the door. Emma followed. Reddy was sitting on the hospital bed facing the window. A woman had her knee bent on the bed as she wrote on his back with her finger and had his hand in hers. She folded his fingers into signs.

The speech therapist finally noticed them. She urged Timothy to get closer, to write something on his back.

"I don't know what to say," he said. He wiped his chin where the tears collected.

"Anything," the therapist said.

Timothy reached Reddy's back. He hesitated, his long finger shaking. Then, he started. He drew each letter out.

H-E-Y, he paused, B-U-G-L-E-T.

Reddy turned.

He threw himself into Timothy's lap, pushed his head into his armpit. "Timothy, Timothy," he said. "She's, she's gone. Aleksia. She's gone, Tim. She's jumped and she's gone. Tim, she's gone."

A therapist said, "It's okay."

Timothy hugged him back.

"She's gone. She's gone, Timothy. And I don't understand!" he screamed into Tim's chest, punching his head into him. "I don't understand!"

Timothy swaddled him with his long arms and pressed Reddy's hair behind his ear, looking at Emma. Emma looked away. She was falling apart. Finally, Reddy stopped screaming. He stared into nothing, breathing hard.

"I don't understand," he said, "I fought my whole life to stay alive."

The room remained quiet. Emma went to the window. Outside, two kids kicked a soccer ball down the sidewalk. A plane went over. How many people were looking out from the windows of this very hospital this very moment?

"What's your name?" the therapist said. Emma spun on her heel.

"Emma."

Reddy was sitting up now. On his back, the therapist wrote E-M-M-A, and Reddy softly repeated the letters.

Emma came to him and sat on his other side. She pushed her head into the crook of his neck and closed her eyes.

*

TELL YOUR FRIENDS YOU LOVE
THEM. TAKE THEM ON LATE NIGHT
ADVENTURES THROUGH DARK PARKS
AND SPRINKLERS. SIT IN THE CAR
FOR HOURS IN A PARKING LOT AND
TALK ABOUT DEATH. TALK ABOUT
DREAMS. MAKE PHOTOS OF YOU
PRIVATE TIMES TOGETHER. TAKE
PHOTOS WHEN YOU'RE SAD
TOGETHER AND LEAVE NOTES ON THEIR
CAR. IMAGINE IMPOSSIBLE THINGS
AND BE ABOUT YOUR SHARE
MUSIC. DANCE ON YOUR DRIVEWAY. A
HANDSTAND IN A GAS STATION AT 3AM. HOLD A
SEANCE, LIGHT CANDLES AND HOLD A
TRADE. WEAR EACH OTHERS CLOTHES
SEX IT WITH THEM. LOVE. TALK
ABOUT YOUR FAMILIES. TALK ABOUT
YOUR SECRETS. MAKE A MOVIE AND
HAVE THEM PLAY A ROLE. START A
BUSINESS TOGETHER. CHOOSE A
PLACE IN THEIR NEIGHBORHOOD
SMOKE CIGARETTES AND DRINK
COFFEE AND THROW THINGS OFF
THE NEAREST CLIFF. CANNONBALL
INTO A POOL. RACE THEM TO THE
OTHER SIDE. GO WITH THEM TO
EUROPE. NEW YEAR'S FIREWORKS.
FALL ASLEEP ON A TRAIN AND END
UP IN THE WRONG COUNTRY. GO
DOWN TO SONBORNE CANYON.
WHILE A WINDSTORM BEATS YOUR
TENT. WEAR EACH OTHERS CLOTHES.
MAKE HOT CHOCOLATE. WEAR
SHORTS AND MAKE MARGARITAS.
KNOW THEIR FAVORITE DRINK.
LISTEN TO THEM. THEY'RE TELLING
THE TRUTH WHEN THEY'RE TELLING
DO IT ALL AGAIN. IF THEY FALL OUT OF
THEIR SIGHT BRING THEM TO THE
HEADING IF THEY LOSE THEIR
TRIP HEADING IF THEY CAN NO
LONGER WALK. IF THEY PASS AWAY
BRING THEM ANYWAY.

Made in United States
Orlando, FL
22 January 2024